FATAL ACCUSATION

RACHEL DYLAN

FATAL
ACCUSATION

A Windy Ridge Legal Thriller

RACHEL DYLAN

Fatal Accusation
Copyright © 2016 by Rachel Dylan
ISBN-13: 978-1542547284
ISBN-10: 1542547288

NYLA Publishing
350 7th Avenue, Suite 2003, NY 10001, New York.
http://www.nyliterary.com

Be sober, be vigilant; because your adversary the devil, as a roaring lion, walketh about, seeking whom he may devour.

1 Peter 5:8

ACKNOWLEDGMENTS

Thank you to all the wonderful members of Rachel's Justice League. The writing journey is so much more special because of you. You are truly a joy!

I'd also like to thank Denise, Sue, and Gina for your help on this story. Many thanks to Leslie for her skillful and insightful editing.

As always, many thanks to my agent Sarah Younger and the Nancy Yost Literary Agency. Sarah, you understand how much these stories mean to me, and you always embrace my ideas even when they may not fit inside a neat and tidy box.

Windy Ridge holds a special place in my heart, and I hope that these stories will move you as much as they move me.

Finally, Mama, I know how much you wanted to read more about Pastor Dan and Windy Ridge. I hope that his journey will inspire you.

CHAPTER ONE

Pastor Dan Light sat in his office at Windy Ridge Community Church and prayed. A chill shot through him, but it wasn't from the Windy Ridge winter night. No, it was from knowing that there was a battle on the horizon.

Ever since the settlement a couple of months ago in the lawsuit between the New Age companies that plagued Windy Ridge, he'd had an uneasy feeling that the groups known as Astral Tech and Optimism were planning a direct attack on the church. And on all the believers in the community.

Lord, help me prepare the people in this church for what is to come.

He was broken out of his prayer by the loud sound of heels clicking down the church corridor toward his office. He looked up at his doorway and smiled. Finally, some good news.

"Olivia, it's so good to see you." He stood up to greet her.

While Olivia Murray was small in stature, she was strong in her faith. The petite brunette attorney greeted him warmly with a hug.

"I'm glad to be here," Olivia said.

"How was your vacation?"

"It was great. I went back to DC and visited my best friend Lizzie, along with taking care of some firm business." She took a seat on his couch. "And that's actually why I'm here. I have some news. Big news, actually."

"What is it?"

"The managing partner at my firm wants me to help start up the Chicago office of Brown, Carter, and Reed. Grant has already told me I can continue to stay at his rental condo for free, even though I'm going to still insist on paying him."

"That's great news," he said.

"So what have I missed while I was gone?" she asked. "You were really vague about things in our email exchanges."

That was for a reason. He hadn't wanted to bother her while she was taking a much needed break. But now that she was here, he would fill her in on what he knew. "While there haven't been any direct attacks that I know of from Astral Tech or Optimism, I can see the results of their efforts. Church attendance is at its lowest point since I started preaching here."

"Oh no." Her dark brown eyes widened.

"Yes. And I also hate to report that Stacey Malone hasn't stepped foot back in the church at all. I fear she may now be fully entrenched with Layton Alito and his people at Optimism."

Olivia stood up and walked over to where he sat behind his desk. "You don't have to shoulder all of this alone. I'm not going to walk away from here. You know that, right?"

"I do. But I also don't want you to underestimate how difficult this is going to be. We have to assume Layton and Nina Marie have fully joined forces."

"As two powerful CEOs of lucrative companies, they have a lot of resources at their disposal. We knew that the lawsuit was just the beginning. I've been praying a lot about this, and though it may seem like they have the upper hand, we're going to prevail. But we have to get organized and have a plan of our own. This isn't something that can be dealt with piecemeal."

He admired Olivia's staunch reliance on her faith. She was going to need it, as was he. They both had targets on their backs.

"Looks like I came to the office at the right time." Associate Pastor Chris Tanner walked through the door and made a beeline for Olivia. He gave her a hug before they both took a seat. "I didn't realize you were back," Chris said.

"Just got back from DC today. This was one of my first stops. I just told Dan the news that I've been asked to help start the Chicago office of BCR. I'll be here in the Chicago area indefinitely."

"That's wonderful, right?" Chris asked.

"I think so. I didn't want to leave Windy Ridge because I felt I had a lot of unfinished business to take care of, but I was concerned about how I could stay here given my job responsibilities in DC."

"The Lord really works in amazing ways, doesn't He?" Chris asked.

Olivia nodded. "I hear things are pretty tough right now."

"Yeah," Chris said. "Dan and I have been scratching our heads wondering how Layton and Nina Marie have been able to reach so many of our church members. We don't know their exact strategy, but I have a feeling they're responsible for our shrinking numbers."

Olivia frowned. "We have to find a way to stop them."

"I agree," Dan said. "And I'm open to any suggestions you may have."

"There is one thing I can do." Olivia paused and looked down.

"What?" Dan asked.

"Have a meeting with Nina Marie."

"Why?" Chris asked. "What good can come of that?"

"I've given it a lot of thought while I was away, and I still believe there is hope for her."

Dan thought Olivia was being a bit naïve and overly optimistic about Nina Marie. "I understand that you don't want anyone to be led astray, Olivia, but Nina Marie is really far gone."

"I realize that, but I can't help but feel like I have to make an effort with her."

"You know she's not going to want to hear any of that," Chris said. "She made it her mission to destroy all the believers in this community."

"I hear your reservations, both of you, I really do, but I'm not going to change my mind on this one. Please let me tackle this issue my way, at least for the time being. It's something I need to do."

"It's not that we don't want you to succeed. It's just that we're worried about your safety," Dan said. The last thing they needed was for something to happen to Olivia. She played a

3

central role in this struggle. Regardless of what Olivia thought, Dan was distrustful of Nina Marie.

"I'll be careful. I promise." She rose up from her seat. "I'm going to call it a day. I was up super early to catch my flight this morning. I'll be in touch with any relevant information I can gather."

"Please do," Dan said. "And we're very glad you're back."

"Me, too. Have a nice evening." She walked out of the office leaving him alone with Chris.

"I know you're struggling right now." Chris patted him on the shoulder. "Not only because you see the decline in the church, but also it was your first holiday season since losing Tina."

Dan felt his eyes get misty. Chris knew him all too well. The loss of his wife still weighed on him daily. He'd just experienced his first Christmas without her, and it was devastating.

"You don't have to say anything," Chris said. "Just know I'm here for you. Whatever you need. We'll get through all of this together as a church family."

"We're going to be tested," Dan said. He knew deep in his gut that it would probably be the biggest test of their lives.

"You're right, but we're not going to back down. We're going to fight this battle the Lord wants us to fight. We're going to rid our community of these occult forces."

Dan could only pray that Chris was right.

**

Nina Marie Crane tried to keep her facial expression neutral as she sat across the table from Optimism CEO Layton Alito. Her sworn enemy had now become her ally. At least for a season.

She would never forget that Layton had tried to kill her— and failed. Only after his inability to remove her did he want to join forces. And while she was definitely holding a grudge, she also wasn't stupid. They shared common goals as far as the evil one was concerned. So for now, she was forced to work with Layton instead of against him. She was CEO of Astral Tech, and she had to think about what was best for the company.

They were currently sitting at a large oak table in his study. The room was expansive and immaculately decorated, as was the rest of his mansion.

"Thanks for meeting with me," Layton said. He looked as handsome as ever. His striking blue eyes made direct contact with hers, but she knew better than to be influenced by his good looks and smooth ways. Underneath that exterior was a lethal man with a totally depraved heart.

"What do you want to talk about?" she asked.

"Our source on the inside at Windy Ridge Community Church."

"Yes, yes. How is Beverly doing?"

"Very well."

"I still can't believe you managed to turn her," she said. Beverly Jenkins was the financial administrator at Windy Ridge Community Church and a lifelong churchgoer.

"I can't take all the credit on this one. It helped that her and Louise started going to the same hair salon a few years ago. That changed everything. An unlikely friendship blossomed into something much more."

Nina Marie nodded, knowing full well that having Judge Louise Martinique on the side of Optimism was a huge advantage for them. She wanted Louise to be on her side, not Layton's. But that would require a lot of work, and she couldn't afford to divert her attention. "However it happened, it's a huge benefit to us now."

He smiled. "And the time has come, my dear."

"All right. So tell me about your plans."

"I can't tell you that part just yet."

She let out an exasperated sigh. "You're really starting to try me, Layton."

"Believe me. Once the news breaks, you'll understand and you'll thank me."

"But until then?"

"Hold tight and wait for the glorious news."

She took a sip of the expensive Merlot that Layton had provided her. Layton appreciated all the finer things in life. She wasn't quite as materialistic as him, but she loved nice things, too. Especially since she used to have nothing and be nothing—except a victim.

But that part of her life was over. She was in charge of her own destiny, and she'd never let a man control her again—hurt her again. And definitely not Layton Alito.

She'd placate him for now, but when the time was right, she'd destroy him. "Is that it?" she asked.

"Enjoy the wine, Nina Marie. Why are you in such a rush?"

"Since when do we actually enjoy spending time together?"

He raised an eyebrow. "If I remember correctly, we used to enjoy it a lot."

"There's no way I'm ever getting back in bed with you." If he thought that was a possibility, she was going to shut that down right now.

He waved his hand. "Don't be so uptight. Relax. I do have one more thing to discuss."

"And that is?"

"I heard a very interesting rumor this morning."

"And that is?"

"That the law firm of BCR is opening a Chicago office."

"Why do you care what Astral Tech's former law firm does in Chicago?"

He leaned in closer to her. "Because I heard that your favorite lawyer is going to move here to start the office."

"What?" Her hand shook and red wine splashed on the oak table.

He raised an eyebrow. "Ah, so I see this surprises you."

"I don't have to remind you how strong Olivia Murray is or what a threat she could be to our enterprise." Nina Marie stayed up at night remembering how Olivia had chosen to save her life. She still hadn't fully come to grips with someone acting as selflessly as Olivia did. But even though she was grateful, she couldn't have Olivia spoiling everything they were working toward.

Layton lifted his glass. "You should have a chat with her. Feel her out."

"How did you even find out about this?"

"Once again, Louise came through. She knows everything that goes on in the legal community, and the opening of a BCR office in Chicago is a big news item for law firms around here."

"Leave Olivia to me. I can take care of her."

Layton reached over and gripped her hand. Hard. "Make no mistake. If you don't deal with her, I will."

"Understood." She pulled away from his grip. "And don't put your hands on me." She'd had enough of this infuriating man. Throwing back the rest of her wine, she stood up. "I can see myself out. When you're ready to actually tell me the plan with Beverly, let me know. Until then, I don't think we have anything else to talk about."

**

Olivia walked into Grant Baxter's law firm the next day to take him to lunch. She had missed seeing him while she took her time in DC. Never could she have expected that her former opposing counsel would become such a good friend and a source of strength.

She had one more day before starting work at the Chicago office of BCR, so she wanted to spend some time with Grant. She walked up to the front desk and smiled at the receptionist.

"Grant's expecting you, Olivia. You can walk on back."

"Thank you." She strode down the long hallway passing Ryan Wilde's office along the way. Grant's office was at the end of the hall.

When Grant saw her, he smiled widely and his blue eyes sparkled. His thick dark hair looked as if it had been freshly cut.

"It's great to see you." He rose from his chair and hugged her tightly.

"It's good to see you, too. It's nice to be back in Windy Ridge, even though I did enjoy my time in DC."

"How's Lizzie?"

"Great. She's thinking about transitioning to a smaller litigation boutique to get more courtroom experience. It's a big decision for her."

"I can understand that. If she wants to talk to anyone about transitioning from a larger firm to a smaller one, I'd be happy to discuss with her."

"Thanks. I'll let her know." Grant had left a big law firm to start his own, and Olivia knew how much stress that had put on him. She had misjudged him when they'd first met, assuming he was just in it for the money, but there was a lot more at stake for him than that. She understood that now.

"You ready to go to lunch?" she asked.

"Yes, I'm starving."

They exited his office building and walked down the street to Grant's favorite pizza place near work.

Once they got settled in a booth and placed their orders— hers a slice of cheese and his two slices of supreme— she looked up at him. "Tell me what I've missed in Windy Ridge."

He looked her directly in the eyes. "I didn't want to bother you while you were away, but I think something is going on with Pastor Dan."

She thought Dan had looked tired yesterday, but she had been exhausted so she didn't think much of it. "How so?"

"He seems really depressed. I know the holidays had to be rough for him, but I can't help but think there's something else deeper going on. When I first met him, he was always so full of energy and passionate about everything. Now he seems tired and downtrodden all the time."

"Did you ask him?"

"Every time I ask how he's doing, he claims he's doing fine."

"Maybe it's just a cumulative effect. He's been through so much. First the death of his wife, and now this battle in his backyard. He's taking it all very personally—especially the decline in church attendance."

"Whatever it is, I hope he can snap out of it. The church needs him. The community needs him. He's the leader of the church, so he sets the tone for everyone."

She reached over and squeezed Grant's hand. "It's going to be okay. Pastor Dan shouldn't have to bear the burden for all of us. We'll get through this together."

"I've missed your optimism."

She laughed. "Please don't use that word."

The pizza arrived, and they ate in silence for a few minutes.

"How are you doing right now, Grant?" she asked.

"I've still got so much to learn and a lot of questions, but I haven't wanted to burden Dan with them so I've been talking a lot more to Chris."

"Your newfound faith is already strong. It's perfectly normal to have questions and want to talk things through. I'm glad I'm back now."

"I'm glad you're back, too. I really missed you, Olivia."

Her heart constricted at his kind words. "We've got a long fight ahead of us, but there's no one else I'd rather have by my side."

"Let's hope this is a new year filled with many good things to come."

She hoped that was the case, but she also felt like a storm was just around the corner.

**

As Othan exacted the punishment that was required, his fellow demon Kobal groaned in pain. They stood outside the L in Chicago as people bustled back and forth to get on and off the crowded train during the evening rush hour.

"You failed again," Othan said. "Your charges have gone back to their Christian faith. What do you have to say about that?"

The less powerful demon stared up at him. Othan enjoyed making him squirm. Kobal had great potential, but he needed more focus.

"I'm sorry, Othan," Kobal said. "I did everything I could, but the pastor was able to intervene. I wasn't able to convince them that our ways were for the best."

"Enough excuses." It was time to see what Kobal was really capable of. Put him to the test.

"I'll do whatever I can to make it up to you and to our master." Kobal stood proudly. His demonic form wasn't what most people would expect. Kobal presented himself in human form just like Othan. They could transform into various forms if necessary, but their ability to blend into the population gave them an edge.

"I'm glad you feel that way." Othan patted Kobal on the back. "Walk with me."

They walked down the subway platform as the snow started to fall more steadily. Othan adjusted his winter coat a little tighter. Not because he actually was impacted by the cold, but mainly out of habit.

"I'm anxious to start a new assignment," Kobal said.

"You've heard about our work in Windy Ridge."

"Yes, everyone knows about that."

"You're going to be working with me on expanding our reach in Windy Ridge Community Church."

Kobal gasped. "I won't let you down. This is a huge opportunity. I don't deserve it."

"Of course you don't deserve it." Othan couldn't help but smile. "If you fail, I will destroy you. Do you understand?"

Kobal nodded but straightened his shoulders. He was an arrogant demon who often acted too hastily without thinking of the consequences. Kobal reminded Othan of himself years ago. But to be successful, Othan would need someone like Kobal who could blend in with the humans and had a deep understanding of the mission.

"What do I need to do?" Kobal asked.

"First, I'm going to have you shadow Pastor Dan. There are going to be some events happening soon, and I'm going to need you to turn the screws where he is concerned. I've already had Zebar tailing him around the clock and that has had a great impact, but I need someone with even more power."

"I can do this, Othan. I promise you I can."

"This is going to be one of our greatest battles. With a victory in Windy Ridge, there will be no stopping us. The evil one will give us everything we ever wanted. Failure is not possible."

Kobal brushed the snow off his blue wool cap. "I'm ready to go to work."

"Perfect. Keep me updated." Once Othan achieved success in Windy Ridge, he would be handsomely rewarded.

CHAPTER TWO

S tacey Malone smoothed down her black designer skirt and adjusted her dark purple lace blouse—also designer, thanks to Layton splurging on her. Working with Optimism was by far the best decision she'd ever made in her life.

For far too many years she had allowed the church and her parents to dictate right and wrong. No more. Now she was officially an adult. Doing well at Windy Ridge Community College and thriving at her internship with Optimism. There wasn't anyone or anything that could stand in her way.

Once she stopped looking at every choice through a Christian tinted lens, she embraced her newfound freedom. Layton had given her an extensive budget to shop for new clothes and whatever else she wanted. Morena had been more than happy to help her shop and spend Layton's money. She'd finally found her people and her place in the world.

As she waited for Morena outside Indigo bookstore, she couldn't wait to hear Morena's ideas. Stacey had gone from dabbling in witchcraft and New Age techniques to becoming proficient in many areas over a short span of time. It helped she was fully dedicated. *No one has a hold on me. I'm free. Free to be the woman that I want to be. I set my own rules now.*

"There you are." Morena walked out of the bookstore. Her long blonde curly locks showing from under her bright pink winter hat. She didn't look anything like a stereotypical witch or gothic person, but Stacey understood how powerful this woman was and even more importantly, she had the ear of Layton Alito.

Layton was rich and powerful and interested in Stacey and her career. He also thought she was spiritually gifted. She'd never thought she was gifted in anyway before, and it made her feel special to hear his encouraging words.

"You wanted to talk?" she asked Morena.

"Yes. Walk with me. I need some hot tea. We can stop in at the coffee shop and catch up."

They made the short walk from the bookstore down two blocks to the coffee shop called Latte. Thankfully it was a short walk, because Stacey was freezing. There was about six inches of snow still on the ground, but she had chosen fashion over function and had only worn a light jacket. Now that she actually had nice clothes, she was putting a lot more time and effort into how she looked.

When they stepped into Latte the coffee smell awoke her senses, and she instantly started to warm up.

"I'm getting tea. What would you like?" Morena asked.

"Whatever you're having is good." Stacey found them a table and took a seat. She wondered what was going on. Morena was buzzing with energy.

A couple of minutes later, Morena returned with two big mugs of tea. She took off her wool coat and sat down. "So, I wanted to update you on some important news."

"What?" Her heartbeat sped up as she waited for Morena to speak.

"I can't give you all the details, but Layton has been working on something, Stace. And let me tell you, it's big. So big that I don't even know what it is. Just that we're told to be on alert and ready."

"Are you serious?"

Morena nodded and took a sip of tea. "I'm excited because this could be a huge shift in the balance of power in Windy Ridge. If it's as huge as I think it is, then we could be in for a radical shift."

Her mind raced trying to piece together what Layton could possibly have planned. "What should we do?"

"We're going to continue with your spiritual training." Morena took hold of her hands. "You have something special, Stace. Everyone can see it. The strategy will be to ramp up our sessions to get ready."

"You know I'm all in. Whatever you think I need to do." And she meant it. Yeah, when she'd first started down this path, she'd had a moment of weakness and had gone back to the church. But that was far behind her. Now she was one hundred percent committed to her spiritual powers.

"I'm glad, because there's so much left to do and more room to grow. The potential you have is limitless."

Stacey looked up and was surprised to see Layton walking toward them. If Stacey were honest with herself, she had a little crush on Layton. She also thought he felt something for her,, but he was hard to read. Was he interested in her as a woman or just as a member of Optimism?

"Layton," Morena said. "What're you doing here?"

"Well, you mentioned you were going to meet up with Stacey for a cup of tea, so I figured I'd find my two favorite ladies here." He flashed his perfect smile. "How're you doing?"

"Great," Morena said. "I was just telling Stacey that you were going to have big news we needed to prepare for, but you've been keeping your secret under wraps. So that just leads us to sit here and speculate."

He nodded. "I appreciate your patience."

"We can't help but want to know," Morena added.

"I understand. I'm also anxious with anticipation, but until the story breaks, I'm asking everyone to be vigilant, and then even more so after you hear what happens. Because that is when we're going to have our golden opportunity to strike at the heart of Windy Ridge Community Church."

Stacey couldn't help but be intrigued. She'd never seen Layton quite like this—filled with such excitement. Normally he presented himself in such a cool and calm way. But not today. There was fire in his eyes. "So this must be big?"

"Huge," Layton said. "I'll call a group meeting of Optimism and will be inviting Astral Tech members as well, as soon as the information is out in the public."

"Wait a minute." Morena put down her mug. "You still think it's a good idea to involve Astral Tech? I don't trust Nina Marie. They'll stab us in the back at the first opportunity. Why bother with them?"

Layton grinned. "That's the beauty of my plan. We don't have to trust her. She wields a lot of power, and right now, taking down the church has to be top priority. Make no mistake. I'm still in charge of this effort. Not her."

Stacey was still trying to understand everything that had gone down between the two companies, especially after the lawsuit was settled. It was clear she was missing some important pieces of the puzzle. She tried not to be too nosy and only ask critical questions, but she had put together the fact that there was some sort of truce between Layton and Nina Marie.

Stacey wanted to be able to be a major player in all of this and help the cause. "Is there anything I should be doing?"

"No," Layton said. "Just keep up the good work and wait to hear from me. Now if you'll excuse me, I have other business to attend to. You ladies enjoy your afternoon." He leaned down and kissed her on the cheek before doing the same to Morena.

Stacey took a deep breath and looked at Morena.

Morena reached across the table and grabbed onto her forearm. "Get ready, Stace. This is going to be epic."

**

That night Grant glanced over at Olivia as she sat next to him on his living room couch. He was so glad to have her back in Windy Ridge. They'd just finished a nice dinner of Thai food takeout and had settled down on the couch to watch the evening news.

His feelings for her grew each day, but he didn't want to mess things up by trying to take things too fast. She meant so much to him, and he planned to do everything in his power to build a real relationship with her.

"What's on your mind?" she asked him.

"Was just thinking about you, actually."

She smiled and warmth showed in her big brown eyes. "Anything you'd like to share?"

He took her hand and squeezed. "I was just thinking about how happy I am to have you back in town. I have to admit it was kinda lonely around here without you."

"I'm glad to be back, too."

"How do you feel about going back to work?"

"I'm ready. Taking a break was necessary after all that went on with the trial and the unexpected settlement. Not to mention the other spiritual battles we found ourselves in outside of the courtroom. I needed to take the time to get myself ready, not just for work, but for another fight. Layton isn't one to take defeat. He's going to come back at us. It's not over."

He'd been worried about the toll the trial had taken on her and the spiritual attacks she has sustained. But he'd never met a woman like Olivia before. Her strength was derived from her faith, and she didn't waver. Her faith was much stronger than he felt his would ever be. He'd only just come to know God, and he still had more questions than answers.

He glanced at the local news that had just come on the TV, and his heart dropped. "Olivia, look." He picked up the remote and turned up the volume.

A local news reporter stood outside the front of Windy Ridge Community Church. The blonde reporter looked squarely into the camera and spoke. "Breaking news tonight in Windy Ridge, a suburb of Chicago. This story is sure to rock this tight-knit community. Criminal charges are being brought against head Pastor Dan Light. I'm the first reporter on the scene, and events are rapidly unfolding. At this time, I don't have further details on the subject matter of the charges, but as soon as we have that information, we will get it to you."

"I have to call Pastor Dan." Olivia jumped up from the couch and walked over to where her cell phone sat on the kitchen counter.

He watched as she dialed Dan's number.

"He's not answering. We've got to do something."

"Okay. Let's take a minute and think." Grant's mind was going places he didn't want it to go. "We should try to reach Pastor Chris." He pulled out his phone and dialed Chris. Then he put it on speaker.

A few rings later and Chris answered. "Hello."

"Chris, it's Grant and Olivia. We just saw the news about Dan. What's going on?"

"I was just about to try to call you and Olivia. I'm trying to figure it out myself. The police came to the church, and they had a closed-door conversation with Dan. Then they took him into custody. They're taking him down to the station as we speak."

"Olivia and I will go down there now and try to figure out what's going on."

"Please do. There's no one else I can trust like the two of you. This is devastating. Especially since I don't even know why they arrested Dan."

"We're on it," Grant said. "We'll call you back when we know more." He ended the call and looked at Olivia. A frown pulled down at her lips, but she remained calm.

"We should get down to the station," she said.

He grabbed the keys to his Wrangler, and they walked out of his house in silence. Once on the road, she broke the silence.

"We need to figure out a game plan here. The only way we can see him is if we are representing him. I think I need to take the lead here. You're a plaintiff's lawyer."

"But you don't specialize in criminal law."

"I don't, but I have defended a couple of criminal cases before through our firm's pro bono program. And that's my plan for what to do here."

"And your boss is going to be okay with that?" While he wanted to help Dan, he also didn't want Olivia to jeopardize her career in the process.

"We have a very active pro bono program at the firm. I'm sure I can get it approved, and Chet will give me some leeway."

He knew Chet Carter was Olivia's boss, and she had a good relationship with him. "Olivia, we don't even know what he's being charged with. I think we need to prepare ourselves for the worst."

"You don't seriously think Dan could be guilty of a crime, do you?"

He didn't want to believe it. Dan had been a true friend and a spiritual beacon for him, but he couldn't help but have a shred of doubt creep in. He'd only known the man for a few months, and the skeptic in him had a lot of bad scenarios running through his mind. "Honestly, I'm not sure, Olivia."

She shook her head. "I'll take this on. I know that whatever they have accused him of, Dan is innocent."

One of the things Grant admired most about Olivia was her resolve. If only he could feel as certain.

**

Dan hadn't stopped praying since the police officers had arrived at his church office. He had assumed they were paying him a visit because of something one of the church members had done, but boy had he been wrong.

The words kept echoing in his head over and over again. Embezzlement, fraud, tax evasion. He couldn't even put his head around it. As he sat in the holding room at the police station, he tried to gather himself. *Think, Dan.*

They said they would let him make a couple of phone calls and that one of them should be to a lawyer. If he couldn't afford one, he'd get a court-appointed attorney.

Then there was something the officer said about an arraignment and bail hearing. Dan didn't have a lot of money. He had a modest pastor's salary. He had no idea how much bail would be set at. *Lord, I've been tested before. Losing my wife was the hardest thing I've ever dealt with, but I've never faced anything like this. Lord, I'm in the dark here. Please guide me through this situation.*

He was broken out of his prayer when the door to the holding room opened. Then he saw it was a police officer, but standing beside the officer was the literal answer to his prayers. Olivia. *Thank you, Lord.*

"Pastor Dan, I'm here as your attorney, assuming you'll have me." Olivia walked into the room.

"Of course." He was relieved to have Olivia on his side, so much so he almost broke down.

"Officer, I'd like a few minutes alone with my client," Olivia said.

The officer nodded. "I'll be right outside to escort you out when you're done."

She waited until the officer closed the door, and then she hugged him but he couldn't hug her back because he was in handcuffs. It startled him to have his movement so restricted. Standard procedure, the officer had said.

"What in the world is going on here?" she asked as she took a seat at the small table across from him.

"I have no idea, Olivia. I think I'm in shock."

"They're charging you with multiple counts of embezzlement, along with related charges for fraud and tax evasion."

He looked squarely into her eyes. "I didn't do anything wrong. I promise you. I've never stolen and certainly not from the church. Plus, I've always filed my taxes, and the taxes for the church are taken care of by our office. I don't know how this could have happened."

Olivia's dark eyes softened. "Dan, you know I believe you, but we do need to get to the bottom of the allegations here. There has to be some evidence for them to justify an arrest. The police don't just swoop in on a well-respected pastor if they don't have hard evidence. Do you play a big role in the church's finances?"

"No, I wouldn't call it a big role at all. I do help out Beverly from time to time if she asks for it, but Beverly is in charge of the day-to-day for church finances."

"Beverly Jenkins, she's on the church leadership committee, right?"

"Yes. And she walks the straight and narrow. The last thing I want to do is to start pointing fingers at other innocent people. It's bad enough for me, but I couldn't stand it if other church members were also implicated."

Olivia frowned. "I'm sorry to have to say this, but I think we must consider the possibility that she might have taken some improper actions with the church's books."

He shook his head. "No way. I've known Beverly for years. She wouldn't do anything like that."

"Is there anyone else with access to the church's accounts?"

"At the level of actually having any ability to touch the funds, just me, Beverly, and Chris. But like I said, the responsibility of handling our finances is out of my hands. Like most churches, I don't control the money, but at the end of the day I do have access

18

to the bank account. We're a large church, yes, but not a mega church that has a huge staff. We all pitch in where we have to."

"Pastor Dan, I don't like this. Something is terribly off here." Olivia said. "I'm going to push for your bail hearing to be tomorrow to get you out of here. It is absolutely crazy for you to be sitting in prison, especially considering the non-violent nature of the allegations. This is all white collar stuff." She paused. "Putting aside the fact you're innocent. These are the type of crimes we should be able to get bail for."

"Do you think you can do that? Also, I don't have much in the way of money to be able to pay the bail."

"Don't worry about any of that, Dan. Let me work on the details."

"Olivia, it means so much that you believe me in. I have no idea why this is happening to me. It all seems so strange."

"Think about it for a minute." She leaned forward in her chair. "Maybe we're dealing with some of Layton's games again. I wouldn't put anything past that evil man. He could be coming directly after you. By dragging your good name through the mud, he could definitely impact the church."

"But he would still have to have some sort of actual evidence, right?"

She nodded. "Yes. He couldn't just make it up and go the police with allegations. There has to be something concrete they think they have against you, and I'm going to find out exactly what that is. I'm sorry I won't be able to get you out right now. Given the time of day, you'll have to spend the night here."

"Don't worry about that. I'm tougher than I look. The Lord has a plan, even in the midst of all of this."

"Yes, He does. Grant is also here, but I thought it best to be the lead person representing you. I do have some experience in the criminal arena and quite a bit of white collar litigation background."

"There's no one in this world I'd want more as my attorney, but I'm afraid I may need to ask for a public defender. I don't think I can afford you."

She lifted up her hand. "Absolutely not. I am taking your case pro bono."

"And your firm will okay with that?"

"Yes. I'll figure that all out. I've done pro bono work before."

"Olivia, I don't want you to have trouble with your job because of me."

"Don't even say that. I'm an attorney and I can help you. And if it's like what I fear and Layton is somehow involved in this, then I need to be by your side."

He couldn't help the tears that welled up in his eyes. "Thank you, Olivia, and God bless you."

"Let's pray together."

And as they started to pray, Dan tried to turn it all over to the Lord.

**

Grant watched as Olivia walked toward him with misty eyes and made her way to the waiting area where he was sitting.

He stood up to greet her. "What are the charges?"

"Embezzlement is the primary charge, and they tacked on tax evasion and fraud."

Those were serious charges. If he recalled, the Illinois laws on embezzlement were quite stringent. "Wow. I can't believe this. What did he say about all of that?"

She ran her hand through her hair and looked up at him. "Unfortunately, he doesn't have any idea where this is coming from, but I have my own suspicions."

"What do you mean?"

"There are only three people who have access to the church's finances. Dan, Chris, and Beverly."

Grant blew out a breath. This was looking worse by the minute. "So you're saying one of them has to be guilty."

"Let's get out of here so we can speak more freely."

He could sense her mounting frustration. "Where do you want to go?"

"Back to your place so I can get my car. I need to go into the office this evening and get to work. I also have to call Chet and explain the situation to him. I plan to be in front of the judge tomorrow at a bail hearing."

They walked out of the police station in silence. When he started the car and pulled out of the lot, he wanted to resume the conversation now that they had privacy. "What can I do?" He cared so much for Olivia. He wanted to be able to help her in any way he could.

"First things first. Talk to Chris. We need to make sure we can trust him because he's going to be a key player in all of this."

"You have doubts?"

"I think he's clean, but the only person I have complete confidence in is Dan. And since he's my client, I have to do everything I can to protect him. You and I also need to talk about whether you want to come in as co-counsel."

He raised an eyebrow. "Is that what you want?"

"I wanted to talk to him by myself first, and now that I have some idea what we're up against including all the charges, I think it could make sense. Plus, if we're going to discuss this case, then it will be necessary because of the issues surrounding attorney- client privilege."

"You're right. I can't believe I wasn't even thinking about that. I guess my head isn't on straight right now." He knew they wouldn't be able to talk about the specifics of the case if he wasn't also one of Dan's lawyers.

"I want to make sure I can keep the privilege intact. So you need to decide now if you're in on this. And if you're not in on it, then we need to stop discussing this case."

"I think you could use the help. There will be a lot of work that needs to be done. You shouldn't have to take responsibility for all of this by yourself."

"True." She paused. "But I need to know that you believe in Pastor Dan's innocence."

That was a tricky question because he was in a state of confusion right now. "Lawyers don't have to believe their clients are innocent to vigorously represent them. We learned that on the first day of law school."

"You're right, but in this case, I can't take any chances."

He had to be open with her about his feelings. "Olivia, I can't lie to you. I want Dan to be innocent, but there's a tiny part of me that wonders if there could be anything to these allegations. I want to be by your side helping prove that he's been wrongly accused. The man I know wouldn't do anything like this."

"All right. Grant, I trust you to do the right thing here. There's also something else I wanted to bring up."

"Go ahead." He was curious to know what was on her mind.

"I think Layton has to be involved in this somehow."

Whoa. He hadn't seen that coming. "What? We don't have any evidence of that. How would it even be possible?"

"I'm not willing to believe this is all a coincidental setup. Think about it. Layton has resources everywhere and a huge bank account. He can make things happen."

"Still, that would be a pretty elaborate scheme for Layton to pull off." He knew better than to underestimate Layton. His moral compass was turned around backward. "But knowing him like I do, I can't say I would be shocked. He's dirty down to the core."

"I know Dan didn't do this. Which means someone wanted him to take the fall. Layton has the biggest motive for that. And, for that matter, I guess Nina Marie could also be involved as well. I'm not sure what the state of relations is right now between the two of them personally or what the status is between the two companies."

There were too many variables in play. Especially when you added in the spiritual elements which, for Grant, was still very new. "Yeah, I guess when you put it that way…"

"We always knew the lawsuit between Optimism and Astral Tech was only the first part of a larger spiritual battle. Unfortunately, this could be the next phase. Even the worst case scenarios I came up with didn't look anything like this."

Keeping his left hand on the wheel, he reached over and squeezed her hand. "You've faced down the threats before. You're a fighter, Olivia. I have faith that you can handle this. God won't abandon you."

"He won't abandon *us*," she said.

Grant could only pray that was true.

CHAPTER THREE

Deputy Assistant District Attorney Tony Sampson reviewed the files in front of him as he sat in the corner of the deli preparing for the arraignment where bail would be set. The last thing he had expected to do in his career was to bring criminal charges against a well-liked pastor in the community, but here he was doing exactly that. The evidence had been striking—thanks to a whistleblower from inside the church.

He had big goals. Right now he was sitting as the number two in the prosecutor's office, and he wanted to run the office one day. He only attended church to keep up the appearances that he actually adhered to the Christian faith because it was somewhat expected in his job. But in his experiences, the hypocrisy that came out of churches was enough to make him reject religion. He was perfectly okay living by his own standards. He tried to do the right thing—most of the time, anyway.

He almost choked on his sesame seed bagel when Layton Alito walked in and headed straight toward him. With his head held high, Layton took a seat across from him.

"Hello, Layton. What brings you here?" Tony asked. He clenched his sweaty hands together.

"I just wanted to say hello." Layton smiled, but it didn't put Tony at ease. Just the opposite. Something about Layton gave Tony the creeps, and that was saying a lot considering the type of people he was exposed to each day in his line of work.

"You saw the news, I assume?" he asked Layton.

"Yes, I did. I've told you before Pastor Dan and I don't see eye to eye. If he's guilty of the charges they're reporting in the media, then he deserves to be held accountable just like any other citizen. Isn't that right?"

"As a prosecutor, I go where the evidence takes me. No matter who the defendant is. That's an oath I took to uphold the law." Tony hadn't figured out Layton's exact angle. He'd met him multiple times in various social circles, but when Layton had contacted him the other day, Tony had been surprised. But what had shocked him even more was the business proposal Layton had offered him. A seat on Layton's non-profit board. In Tony's mind, there had to be some sort of strings attached.

"Have you given any more thought to my philanthropic proposal?" Layton asked, his blue eyes never breaking eye contact.

Actually, Tony had been thinking about Layton's proposal nonstop since he had made it. There was a part of him that desperately wanted to take the offer, but he was already working around the clock. Adding a non-profit board seat to his resume would be impressive, but to add more responsibility on his plate seemed like a recipe for disaster. "While I appreciate your proposal, my schedule is simply outrageous right now. And if I do something, I like to do it full on."

Layton raised an eyebrow and didn't immediately respond. "If you change your mind about the opportunities my non-profit or my company can provide, then you know where to find me. I'll let you think about the opportunity, and I surely hope that justice is served through your prosecution."

"I'm committed to finding out the truth, so I don't know if this is the right time for me to take on any additional responsibilities like a board seat, but let me think about it a little bit." He didn't want to totally lose an opportunity if it would advance his career. Layton was known to be a mover and shaker in the community. Could he find a way to balance the demands of it all?

"Think about it. We could use someone like you on the board. It's going to be an exciting time to be involved. And we have one sitting judge on the board. Louise Martinique. Do you know her?"

Of course he knew her. She had a stellar reputation. "Yes, I do."

"Well, then. Take the time you need to make a decision. I know things are hectic right now. I'll let you prepare for court." Layton stood up and walked out of the deli.

A deeper wave of unease washed over Tony. He couldn't put his finger on why Layton unsettled him so much. He didn't really have any specific interest in his New Age company. He didn't even fully understand what New Age was, but Layton had insisted the non-profit wing of the organization was more focused on community-building projects. That's probably why someone like the esteemed Judge Martinique would be serving as a board member.

But he needed to stop worrying about Layton Alito and start focusing on the impending arraignment for the pastor of Windy Ridge Community Church. He had to determine what his strategy was going to be at the hearing. Should he push for a high bail? If the allegations were true, Dan Light might claim to be a man of God, but he was crooked. Tony had no issues with pushing for a high bail, but he wanted to make sure he stayed on the good side of the judge who might be more sympathetic to the pastor.

Tony finished up the last sip of his coffee and made the short walk a few blocks down to the courthouse. He was right on time. The hearing was set for eleven a.m., thanks to the petition filed by the pastor's attorney. He wasn't quite sure how a pastor would be able to afford a world-class law firm like BCR to represent him, unless of course, he had money hidden away from his shady practices at the church. That was certainly a possibility.

He walked into the courtroom ready to go, but as he entered the room, he stopped short when he saw his opposing counsel. Olivia Murray didn't look anything like what he had expected. The short brunette attorney made direct eye contact with him—her large brown eyes sizing him up. She looked to be in her thirties. So they hadn't sent a senior partner—nor had they sent a rookie either.

"Are you Tony Sampson?" she asked him.

"I am. And you must be Olivia Murray." He outstretched his hand to be polite. She gave him a firm handshake.

"I hope that you're going to be reasonable about bail."

Ah, she was already posturing. Two could play at that game. "That's going to be for the judge to determine."

"Of course the judge is going to make the ultimate decision, but as the prosecutor on the case you're surely going to put forward an amount for the judge's consideration."

"True. I try my best to be fair after taking in all of the facts of the case. The pastor can't be doing too poorly to hire you."

She crossed her arms in front of her. "Actually, I'm taking on this case pro bono. So, no, Pastor Dan wouldn't be able to afford my normal hourly rate. Not even close."

"Really?" Now wasn't that interesting. Why would she have taken this case? He knew big firm lawyers took on pro bono cases, but she seemed to be particularly invested. Was she trying to get her time in the media spotlight to further her career at the firm? That was probably the most likely option.

She didn't say anything else and walked over to the defense table to wait for her client to be brought in by the deputy. He opened up his briefcase and pulled out his normal essentials and put them on the table. Once the charges were presented and Dan entered his plea, then they'd discuss bail. He'd just make a few points about why the bail should be set at a higher rate than the defense would request and then have a back and forth.

He watched as the uniformed officer led Pastor Dan Light in handcuffs to the defense table. Taking a moment, he looked at the man. Lean, probably standing about five ten, with dark hair slightly graying on the temples. Dan certainly didn't look like a hardened criminal, but he'd been a prosecutor long enough to know that you couldn't judge someone based on their appearance. That was even truer when dealing with white collar crime. When you were in a position of power like a pastor, you had a fiduciary duty to the people giving money to your church.

The judge presiding over the hearing today was Judge Randy Matthews, and Tony was quite familiar with him. Matthews wasn't exactly known as being tough on crime, but he wasn't a lightweight either.

As a prosecutor, it was Tony's job to know everything about every judge. Because even though most of his big cases ultimately went before a jury, the judge still had ultimate control over the courtroom.

"All rise," the tall bailiff said with a loud voice.

Judge Matthews walked into the courtroom. He was known to be a fitness guru and looked closer to forty, even though he was in his fifties.

"Everyone can be seated." Judge Matthews looked at Olivia first and then at him. His big dark eyes were serious. "Today we have an arraignment and bail hearing for Dan Light."

"Your Honor." Olivia stood up. "I'm Olivia Murray from the law firm of Brown, Carter, and Reed. I'm here representing Mr. Light, and I filed the motion for an expedited hearing today. I'd like to officially enter my notice of appearance on the defendant's behalf."

"Very well, Ms. Murray. You've discussed the criminal charges with your client, correct?"

"I have, Your Honor."

"Then let's get started. Mr. Light, the charges against you are embezzlement, fraud, and tax evasion. Mr. Light, do you understand the charges against you?"

"Yes, Your Honor."

"And how do you plead?"

"Not guilty, Your Honor."

"Let the record show that the Defendant has entered a plea of not guilty. Now let's turn to the issue of setting bail. Mr. Sampson, the floor is all yours."

Tony took a deep breath and stood up tall. He'd done hundreds of bail hearings before, but for some reason this one felt different—more important. He knew how much media coverage was going to be on this case. And while he wanted to be fair, he also wanted to be seen as tough on crime—whether it was gangs or white collar. "Your Honor, given the serious nature of these crimes, including that this is a Class X felony under Illinois law, with the special circumstances of embezzlement from a place of worship, the state would argue that the bail be set at a million dollars."

27

"Your Honor, that's absurd." Olivia shot up out of her seat as soon as the word million had come out of his mouth.

He knew he was taking a risk, but it was time to play hardball. See how she reacted to his first big move in this game of chess.

"One at a time," the judge said. "Mr. Sampson, that number is quite high. Could you please elaborate on your justification for the state seeking that amount?"

Tony nodded. This was the part he would particularly enjoy. "These crimes are disturbing given that Mr. Light is the head pastor at Windy Ridge Community Church. He had a fiduciary duty to his congregation, those that entrusted him and his church with their money. He violated that duty."

"I perfectly understand that fiduciary duty is an element to proving your embezzlement claim, but today isn't about proving your case. It's about setting bail. So explain to me how does that go to the bail amount?" the judge asked.

"Since the allegations here are so serious, and Pastor Light has been a fixture in this community, I would argue that he is a flight risk. He has connections and the ability to evade this prosecution. And I'm sure there are those powerful few around him that would want to help him in that endeavor."

"Your Honor, I'm sorry, but I can't stay silent given these slanderous statements against my client. There isn't even a shred of evidence that any of the words coming out of Mr. Sampson's mouth are true. Just the opposite. Pastor Dan Light is a man of modest means and, contrary to what you heard from the prosecutor, he doesn't have rich and powerful friends waiting in the wings. I'm not going to get into the merits of the case here, because I know that isn't appropriate, but a million dollars for bail is outrageous. We would have no problem surrendering Mr. Light's passport to quell any of these irrational fears put forward by the prosecution, but beyond that, I would ask that the bail be set at an amount nowhere near that."

"What would the defense suggest?" Judge Matthews asked.

"Fifty thousand, Your Honor," Olivia said.

"Now Ms. Murray is the one being outrageous," Tony said. He hoped that he hadn't overplayed his hand.

"I've heard enough. I'm setting bail at one hundred thousand dollars and taking Ms. Murray up on her offer to surrender Mr. Light's passport."

He knew better than to try to pick a fight now with the judge over this. There would be plenty more opportunities ahead, but he couldn't help feeling like he'd obtained the first victory.

**

"We'll get the money for your bail," Olivia said. She wasn't exactly sure yet how, but she had a few ideas.

"A hundred thousand dollars is a lot of money, Olivia. Definitely more than I have."

"There are other options. People from the church and the community who will want to help you."

He shook his head. "Olivia, as a minister, once you're accused of things like this … there's no one who is going to stand up for you. There's only one thing worse that they could've accused me of." He paused. "But besides that, I don't think I'm going to have a lot of friends lining up to help me."

Olivia refused to believe that. "I think you're wrong. I think most of the church will rise up to help."

"You don't understand. Something has been terribly off with the church for the past month or so. I knew it in my gut. This is all part of something larger, Olivia. And I'm willing to do my part in fighting it. If that means sitting in prison, well, Paul also sat in prison for a long time and he was innocent."

She refused to just let him sit in prison without a fight but, his invocation of Paul only made her more proud to be representing a man of his character. "No, I think you can be much more effective if you're free. I believe you're right about one thing, though. This isn't coincidental. The false allegations against you are part of a grand plan to take down the church in Windy Ridge. We're going to fight this. Not only because your reputation is on the line and the fact that you've been wrongfully accused, but because we knew this was coming and we made a commitment to fight it. Are you with me?" She looked into his eyes, and for the first time since she'd returned to Windy Ridge, she saw the old Pastor Dan.

He nodded. "Yes, try to make the bail. If we can't get the money from those who want to help, then it's not meant to be. I will do everything in my power from behind bars. There's not many things more powerful than a man imprisoned who has all the time in the world to pray."

Her heart warmed seeing Dan's faith come back strong, and she choked up. "We are going to fight this, and we are going to win. Not just the lawsuit, but the war against the evil one here in our community."

"Olivia, I don't know what I or the church would do without you."

**

Nina Marie sat inside Latte waiting for Olivia to arrive. Much to her surprise, Olivia had seemed very open to a meeting.

The woman had been on her mind constantly after the events of last fall. Normally, she would've been able to move on from something like that, but Olivia's actions had greatly impacted her. Even though she wouldn't want to admit it to anyone.

She had hoped that maybe there would be an outside chance she could talk some sense into Olivia. Get her to leave the area and go back to DC. Or, at the very least, get her to focus her energy on something else.

But that idea had been hatched before she'd heard the news about Pastor Dan's arrest. That was a game changer, especially since it appeared Olivia was going to be representing him.

When Olivia walked into the coffee shop and headed toward her, Nina Marie took a deep breath. This woman was always so full of life. It made her sick to her stomach. Nina Marie had never met anyone else like Olivia, and Olivia always treated her like she mattered. It boggled her mind how a devout believer would want anything to do with a person like her. Someone who had sold out to darkness and willingly so.

Today Olivia wasn't smiling, her expression serious as she took a seat at the table.

"Hello," Olivia said.

"Thanks for meeting with me."

"I'd actually planned on reaching out to you, but then I got sidetracked by the events of the past couple of days. I don't suppose you'd have anything to do with that?"

Right for the jugular. It made Olivia a good lawyer. A great one, actually. And she did the whole thing with a calm demeanor. You never saw her coming. "Listen, I know you have to be devastated about what happened to your pastor, but I can guarantee you that this one was not me."

"Layton then," Olivia said flatly.

"I didn't ask you here to talk about Layton or the pastor."

"All right. I'm listening."

She took a deep breath. What she was about to say was difficult. Speaking the truth wasn't something that came easy to her these days. "Olivia, you represent everything that I work against, but you also put yourself in danger to help me in my time of need, and for that I will be forever grateful. You saved my life and that's not something I take lightly. Especially because you jumped into harm's way when you had the opportunity to cut and run to safety, and I know you did that to protect me without regard to what would happen to you."

"And I would do it again a heartbeat." She paused. "But let me guess, even given all of that, you still want me to leave you and this town alone?"

"You're a smart woman. And for some reason that I can't explain, I actually like you despite all of our differences of opinion, but you shouldn't be in Windy Ridge right now. You're too big of a threat to everything I'm working on. You and that church and those people are my enemies."

"It doesn't have to be that way, Nina Marie." Olivia reached out and touched her hand.

It took everything she had not to move away, but she didn't want to show weakness. Olivia's touch made her nervous. This was a woman of God, and that freaked her out. "It has to be, Olivia, and even if I wanted to give you some reprieve, I can guarantee you that Layton has no such soft spot. If anything, he'd relish the opportunity to take you out once and for all."

"So let me get this straight. You invited me here to tell me this to try to protect me?"

"Yes, exactly!"

Olivia shook her head. "That's the thing you don't fully understand. My God is bigger than any threat that you or Layton or anyone else can ever pose. And I'm not afraid of a fight."

She took the opportunity to break contact with Olivia and put her hands in her lap. This woman was stubborn, and in the end, Nina Marie feared it would be her downfall. "You saw firsthand what Layton is capable of. He's a monster. He's more driven than anyone I've ever witnessed to succeed at his mission, and if you're a target, there's no stopping him. You're not listening to reason. You rely too much on your faith."

Olivia smiled. "I'll take that as a compliment, not an insult."

Olivia was maddening. It seemed there wasn't any way to get her out of town. "I've done all I can to help you. I can't guarantee your safety for what happens from here, but I had to warn you."

"I understand, Nina Marie. As far as I'm concerned, you can have a clear conscience. The fact that you even care about what happens to me shows you aren't completely a lost cause."

Nina Marie couldn't help but laugh. "Dear, if you start trying to preach to me again, then you're wasting your breath. Nothing has changed on that front. You know exactly where I stand."

"But you don't have to keep standing there. You can move. You can change, and I'm willing to help you in any way that I can. All you have to do is say the word, and I'll be right there by your side."

"That's never going to happen. Ever. So you should stop and put that out of your mind. Why would I ever follow a God that has allowed such atrocities to occur? That has followers who brag about their Christian values and then hurt the ones they claim to love." She stopped. She'd already said way too much and could tell that by the look of curiosity on Olivia's face.

"The person that hurt you may have claimed they were a believer, but I can promise you that they weren't carrying out the will of *my* God."

"You have absolutely no idea what you're talking about."

"I think I'm much closer to the truth than you want me to think."

"Even if you were, it doesn't change anything."

"It does because you're acting out of hurt. Out of fear. Out of feeling betrayed. I can see that's what led you to the darkness. To a path that might feel better now but will eventually destroy you. I may not know exactly what you endured, but since I've gotten to know you, I have come to understand that this person from your past has left you wounded. I'm offering you a way out, Nina Marie. Right now."

"No. No." Her stomach started to churn. She couldn't handle this anymore. Not with that look of concern on Olivia's face. "I've said everything I came to say. Whether you choose to listen to my warning is up to you." She stood up from the table and started to leave. Olivia grabbed onto her arm.

"I'm not giving up on you, Nina Marie."

"Then you're a fool." She shrugged off Olivia's grasp and walked away, knowing this wasn't going to be her last encounter with Olivia.

CHAPTER FOUR

Olivia knocked on Associate Pastor Chris Tanner's door. She looked over at Grant, who stood beside her. "Chris sounded distressed on the phone," she said.

"This is hard on everyone," Grant said.

Chris opened the door. "Thanks for coming over so quickly. Let's go sit in the living room and talk."

"What did you find out?" Olivia asked. She'd never seen Chris so disheveled. His shirt was untucked and his eyes bloodshot—almost like he'd been crying. Which was difficult for Olivia to imagine given the former Army Ranger's toughness.

Chris took a seat in one of the living room chairs across from the sofa where she and Grant sat. "I don't even know how to say this."

"Whatever it is, we can handle it," Grant said.

Chris looked at her, then at Grant. "I went to visit Beverly, and what she told me blew my mind." He paused. "In doing the church's finances, Beverly noticed some discrepancies, and after looking into it, she found that money was being siphoned off into an account. The account is in Dan's name."

"No way," Olivia said. "That's ridiculous."

Chris shook his head. "I don't know how we can completely ignore evidence like this. Don't you understand the implication of what I'm telling you?"

"I wouldn't have expected you to turn your back on Dan so fast." Olivia couldn't help but say what she was feeling. Would

Chris really flip on his friend and mentor so quickly? Nothing about this situation felt right. "What if there's a big mistake? Or if Layton is involved in this? Have you even considered all of that?"

Chris held up his hand. "Wait, I didn't say anything about turning my back on him. I'm just so confused. I also have a duty to the congregation, too. We have to figure out what's going on. My phone won't stop ringing. People are demanding answers, and I have no idea what to tell them. They call and ask if their money has been stolen. If Dan's a criminal. If the church is going to take immediate action to remove him. It never ends."

"Take a deep breath," she told him. She glanced over at Grant looking for support, but he didn't say anything. She feared he might be questioning Dan, too, and she needed a united front. In her heart, she knew the type of man Dan was, and he wasn't a thief. She wasn't going to let him down when he needed her. "Listen to me. Both of you. Dan *has not* and *is not* stealing money from the church. There is zero possibility he is the one who did this. So we need to figure out how he was setup and who is involved."

"I want to believe that, too," Chris said. "Believe me, I do. But good men do bad things sometimes. I know how stress and pain can get to people. Maybe his wife's illness sent him over the edge and caused him to act in ways he never would've before."

She couldn't believe Chris was even entertaining something so crazy. "Where's your faith here, Chris?"

"Olivia, I do have faith. That faith is ultimately in God— not in men. And like I said, I have a responsibility to God first and foremost. Then to the church. Then to Dan. In that order. So when presented with this type of factual evidence, I have to examine it and try to figure out a plausible explanation. I can't just say, well, I don't like what I see, and I'm going to pretend like it doesn't exist. You're going to have to face the same exact things since you're his lawyer. We all need to be able to examine the facts and make rational conclusions."

She had to hold back her frustration and try to get through to him. "Don't you see? This has to be part of Layton's bigger strategy."

"The problem is we can't imagine how Layton could've pulled this off," Grant said. "And before you get into Layton's spiritual powers, which I'm not going to deny, there still had to be someone physically coordinating this scheme for your theory to hold true."

"I'm not suggesting there is a purely spiritual explanation for this, but I am suggesting that Layton is both evil and powerful. He has the financial and human resources to make things happen." She took a breath. "And Chris, how well do you know Beverly? We can't throw Dan under the bus while blindly accepting everything Beverly is saying as the truth."

Neither man said a word for a minute, and she knew that she had made a good point. Everyone was just assuming Beverly was innocent in all of this, but given those who had access to the church finances, Olivia's job was to question each person's credibility. And that even meant the man sitting in front of her. Chris also had access to the financials, but she was smart enough to realize her approach with Chris was going to have to be more nuanced.

"All right," Chris said. "I'm anxious to get Dan's name cleared. So anything I can do to help, count me in."

"Tell me everything you know about Beverly Jenkins."

"She's been a member of Windy Ridge Community Church since she was a child. Long before Dan or I came into town. She's trained as a CPA but took the job as the church financial administrator about ten years ago."

"And as I understand it, the only three people with authorization to touch the church funds are Dan, Beverly, and you?" She put it out there and looked him squarely in the eyes to see how he'd respond.

"Yes," he responded without hesitation.

It was like he didn't even realize the implication of her question. Which actually weighed in favor of his innocence. "And why do you trust Beverly so completely here?"

"What possible motivation could she have to lie about this? These types of allegations rip churches and communities apart. If anything, her motivation would've been to explain it away."

"What if she was the one who embezzled the money?" Grant finally piped up.

"Now that's a stretch," Chris said.

"More of a stretch than Pastor Dan stealing it?" Olivia asked. "I don't think so. If she did find something suspicious, why not confront Dan about it first before going to the police? Why automatically go to the authorities without hearing his side of the story?"

"Look, Olivia," Chris said. "I get that you're Dan's attorney, and I know you have to ask questions, but I think you're so biased about this that you're not being objective."

"What do you mean?" she asked.

"It's clear from the time you showed up in Windy Ridge that you and Dan developed a really deep bond. You don't want to think someone you cared about and trusted would betray you, but unfortunately, I know all too well that it is possible."

"And all this time I thought that you and Dan also had a special bond."

"This isn't easy for me. I am tormented about all of this."

She looked over at Grant. "What do you think?"

"You both have valid points, but I agree with Olivia that no one should place their unquestioned faith in Beverly."

Chris nodded. "I understand. This has totally turned my life upside down, and you all know we're facing some serious spiritual opposition right now."

There was no doubt in her mind that forces of darkness were attacking Chris. "What we need to do right now before we discuss anything else is pray. We can't win this battle on our own."

**

Micah hovered over Chris's living room as he watched the scene unfold. The angel Ben was right beside him.

"This is even worse than we could have imagined," Ben said.

"I know. The demonic forces are attacking Chris and putting all kinds of doubts into his mind. I'm glad Olivia finally suggested that they pray. Sometimes they all want to solve problems on their own without realizing they aren't only fighting against flesh and blood. They need to remember how much power they have in prayer."

Ben nodded. "The power of prayer and the faith of true believers is the only thing that can help. Othan and his demon cohorts are building up a strong force in Windy Ridge. I haven't seen anything like it in years. They've staked out Windy Ridge as the place they want to do battle, and they're not going to let up anytime soon."

"We can't forget though that even in this dark time, we know how it all ends. The victory has already been secured in Christ."

A loud laughing noise had Micah turning around. There was Othan and another demon that he didn't recognize standing beside him.

"You two are pathetic." Othan sneered. "And you're completely delusional if you think you're winning this war. Look around! The preacher is locked up in prison. The church will be destroyed in this community. Your own associate pastor is ready to convict Dan. I'd say that it's looking pretty good from our side."

"You're getting way ahead of yourself," Ben said. "And I see that you felt the need to bring reinforcements this time. What, were you worried about facing us by yourself?" Ben eyed the other demon.

Othan chuckled. "Not reinforcements. This is my apprentice, Kobal, and he's excited about this new assignment. Stacey and him are becoming good friends, too."

It was like Othan had shot an arrow through Micah's heart. It bothered him greatly that they had lost Stacey to the darkness.

"Why are you here?" Ben asked. "You have absolutely no place in this house."

"That's where you're wrong," Othan said. "Chris's doubts and fears are the perfect breeding ground for us. Can't you see? He's not only doubting his boss, he's doubting everything. And that's where we come in and just help him see what lies beyond because he's already opened the door."

Micah had heard enough of this. "In the name of Jesus Christ, I command you to leave this place."

Kobal shrieked. He wasn't as battle hardened as Othan, but Othan knew that it was time for them to go. Even given

Othan's tough talk, they were still taking a risk by showing up at Chris's house, especially with Olivia and Grant there, too.

"You won't be getting rid of us that easily," Othan said. "We're stronger than you are and have more soldiers ready to fight."

And just like that, Ben and Micah were alone. The demons had fled.

"This is war," Micah said. "And they're partially right. The evil forces in Windy Ridge are outnumbering those who believe in the Lord. It's like we're going into battle with one hand tied behind our backs, and this church scandal will only make that worse."

Ben looked over at Micah. "Once again, we're placing so much on the shoulders of one woman. Olivia is called to defend Dan and, in doing so, defend the church in this community."

"She's proven to be a strong woman of unrelenting faith. If we do our part, I know she'll do hers, but we're going to have our hands full dealing with the fallout. Especially given how fragile Chris and Grant seem at this point in their belief in Dan's innocence."

"Othan and his demons are going to go right after them because they can sense their weakness. Grant is a new believer, so he is an easy and prime target. He doesn't have the years of faith as a foundation, but I'm not sure what is going on with Chris. This is not like him."

"I think he believes he is doing the best thing for the church, but his doubts are leading to a ripple effect. And unfortunately, just like Othan said, it's providing the enemy with an opportunity to prey upon him."

"We must continue to help him and pray for them all."

**

Grant watched as Olivia struggled with phone calls trying to gather up the money to make Dan's bail. It was obvious to him that the church members were not rallying around the pastor, but Grant hated to push the point because Olivia already had enough on her plate.

He hated to see her struggle, so he tried to talk to her when she got off the phone. "If only this weren't Illinois, you could go to a bail bondsmen. But we're one of the only states where that isn't allowed."

She shook her head. "He wouldn't have wanted me to do that anyway. If we couldn't raise the money from supporters, he was content with staying put."

"That's crazy. Better than him sitting in prison."

"That's the thing. Dan doesn't see sitting in prison for a crime he didn't commit as a huge problem. Not like the way we do. I think it would be better for all of us if he were out, but our options are limited right now. I'm disappointed in the congregation."

"How're you holding up?"

"I can't believe how quickly people have turned on him. Frankly, I'm shocked." She looked up at him. "We have to figure out a more effective way to combat whatever Layton has unleashed on this town. Tomorrow is Sunday. I wonder how many people will show up to church."

"Maybe a good number just because they will want to talk about what has happened and get the latest information."

"I don't know if Chris is the right person to be speaking to the congregation about all of this right now. He seems shaky at best, and our meeting with him did nothing to assuage any of my fears. If the associate pastor thinks the senior pastor is guilty, then, of course, the members of the church are going to follow suit. That would be disastrous for Dan and the church's future."

"Did you really think Chris came across that way? I thought he was just being cautious. Taking his duty to the church seriously."

"If it were only that, then maybe I could understand. But I felt like there was an undercurrent that was much more sinister. I think Chris is a prime target of Layton's right now." She paused. "I have to say this, Grant. I know you won't like it, but you have to consider you're also in the crosshairs."

"Don't add me to your list of problems. Yeah, I realize that I'm still very new to all of this. But the last thing I'm going to do is turn my back on you—or this fight. I'm in it for the long haul."

"Not just standing by me, but also by Dan?"

"Like I said before, I can't tell you that I won't ask questions, but the fact you feel so strongly about this counts for a whole lot in my book." He didn't want to make her promises that he couldn't keep. But no matter what, he had her back. That much he was certain of.

"I'd like to see how things go at church tomorrow. You'll be there, right?"

"Of course." Although he had to admit to himself that the draw of being with Olivia right now was stronger than the draw to be at church. He knew that as a new believer he wasn't going to just get everything immediately. But lately, he'd felt a little off. He couldn't help but wonder if Olivia was right. Were Layton and his coven of evildoers trying to sabotage him along with other members of the church? "Your strength never ceases to amaze me."

She walked over to him and grabbed onto his shoulders. "Faith doesn't just pop up overnight. I've had many years of ups and downs to get to where I am now, and I have to say that what I experienced last fall during the litigation changed me forever. To be in the midst of a battle so much larger than me and to feel the effects of it all firsthand only made me rely even more on the Lord. And I believe with all of my heart that the Lord has great plans for you in this struggle as well, Grant."

"What if I don't?" he asked before he even could stop himself.

"You can and you will. We can't let demonic forces destroy us or this town. Our God is bigger and stronger than anything they can throw at us. Don't ever forget that."

He moved a step closer to her, as he felt his feelings only deepen for her. But the last thing he wanted to do was to push things too quickly. "If Dan is innocent, then we still need to determine how this happened."

"I know. Depending on how church goes tomorrow, we can figure out our next move."

He hoped that this wasn't all going to blow up in their faces.

**

Tonight's Optimism meeting at Layton's house was like most—half meeting, half party. And they certainly had a lot of things to celebrate. Pastor Dan was behind bars, Chris Tanner was

41

ready to turn on him, and Windy Ridge Community Church was in total disarray.

What a perfect way to spend a Saturday evening. The wine and champagne were flowing, the appetizers were perfect, and there was absolutely nothing that could spoil his amazing mood.

He looked over at the front door as Stacey Malone walked in. She continued to impress him. She was magically gifted, and he thought if she stuck with it, she might even rival Nina Marie one day. It was his job to make sure she was happy and continued to work for the cause—and *his* cause, more specifically.

With that in mind, he made a beeline for her. When she saw him approach, her eyes lit up—always a good sign.

"Layton, how are you?" she asked.

"Wonderful, my dear. You look stunning this evening."

She looked down at her dress and her cheeks turned pink. "Morena helped me pick this out. I appreciate your generosity. I never had anything appropriate to wear to your functions before. I feel like I fit in so much better now."

"I would accept you in jeans and a T-shirt, but you do look beautiful. The color suits you." Her dark blue flowing dress made her look like a princess out of a movie. He'd been very careful to contain himself around her, because having her in his organization was more important than any romantic inclination he had. Besides that, he could pretty much have any other woman he wanted. He didn't want to ruin things with this special woman. He'd learned his lesson with Nina Marie. Better to not get involved with women skilled in the dark arts.

"Layton, you said you had something big coming, but I had no idea it would be something like this." She took a step closer to him. "I would've never thought Pastor Dan would've stolen money from the church," she said in a low voice.

Of course Dan hadn't stolen anything, but it was better for him not to be open about that with Stacey. Not when she wasn't that far removed from the church and still in a fragile state where all of that was concerned. No, he'd play it differently.

He put his hand on her shoulder, drawing her closer to him. "I know. It's mind blowing, but I've never trusted that man. He hides behind his supposed God, but in the end it's all about him. He's really no different than many of the men I've dealt with all of my life."

She looked up at him with those innocent doe eyes, but he didn't feel any guilt about lying to her. He had her best interests at heart.

"I'm still floored about the whole thing."

"I guess you just can't really tell what goes on inside someone. He fooled a lot of people, Stacey. Don't be so hard on yourself."

"It's just difficult to comprehend. Even given my feelings about the church and wanting to leave it, I never thought Dan was a bad person. He always seemed honest. Maybe a bit too delusional about his own faith, but not a criminal."

"Don't let yourself get consumed by his misdeeds. And besides, look at this as an opportunity for Optimism. It provides us with a mechanism by which to spread the news of our beliefs and the power that we all can have as individuals. Our message will resonate loudly now, and I'm going to be looking to you to be one of our main advocates."

She put her hand on her neck and fiddled with her necklace. "Me? No. I'm so new to the group, Layton. You need people with more years of experience. I'm literally just starting out in all of this."

"But you're extremely gifted. Your natural gifts put you ahead of people who have been practicing New Age techniques for years."

"Layton, you are too good to me, and you have far more confidence in me than I have in myself. That's for sure."

"You are destined for greatness, Stacey. You could be running this business someday."

She sucked in a breath. "I don't even know what to say."

He'd pushed her enough for one night, but she needed to gain confidence. "You don't have to say anything right now. Why don't you go get yourself a drink and start mingling? I want us to all have a good time for a bit. Then I'll make some business announcements."

"Sounds good." Stacey looked across the room. "I see Morena just got here. I'll go say hello."

43

"Great, we'll catch up later this evening." He needed to build Stacey's ambition. She was the next generation.

**

Stacey took a deep breath as she approached Morena. She was still shocked by Layton's comments. She realized that she may have some special gifts, but his compliments made her wonder if she had been underestimating herself. She'd never been told by anyone that she was a superstar—just the opposite—that she was just one in the middle of the pack. Maybe that was all about to change.

Morena made eye contact with her and smiled. Morena looked beautiful tonight, as always. She wore a black, short cocktail dress that was elegant and probably more expensive than most of Stacey's old wardrobe put together. Thankfully, Layton had given Morena his credit card to go shopping with her to get clothes to fit into the crowd at events like this.

Morena pulled her into a tight hug before releasing her. "Can you believe the news?"

"I was just telling Layton that I was shocked by the whole thing."

"You know what this means, don't you?" Morena asked.

"I'm guessing it could mean a lot of things."

"Yes, but as far as our work goes, now is the perfect time to recruit new members to our group. Their confidence in the church will be shattered. So while tonight is a time for celebration, you and I need to get to work tomorrow. I just got in an order of new supplies, too."

"Including the crystals?"

"Yes. We'll have all the tools we need to continue."

Stacey smiled at her friend and mentor. She'd fully embraced the New Age mysticism, including working with crystals and other various items. "The work we're doing is very important. That much I know."

"Oh, wow, Stace." Morena nudged her shoulder. "It looks like the Astral Tech VIPs are starting to arrive. That's Nina Marie."

Stacey couldn't help herself as she craned her neck to get a glimpse of the infamous Nina Marie. She didn't know what to expect, but the auburn haired woman had definitely gotten the attention of the room. She wore a sparkling, long ivory beaded gown that accentuated her thin frame. She'd heard so much about this woman it was odd now seeing her in person. Layton's enemy that was now his friend. She didn't know for sure all the details on how the two of them had come together, but reading between the lines, it seemed like a marriage of convenience.

Nina Marie started walking their way, and Stacey watched in anticipation. The last thing she wanted to do was act like a fool in front of this woman. Nina Marie was the CEO of Optimism's chief competitor. But, for now, she was a part of their alliance to take down the church in Windy Ridge.

Nina Marie walked past her, chatting with the man next to her as they made their way to the bar, but then Nina Marie stopped suddenly and turned around. Nina Marie's dark brown eyes focused in on hers.

Nina Marie said something to the man beside her and then walked by herself over to where she and Morena stood. Stacey assumed that Nina Marie was coming over to talk to Morena. But instead, Nina Marie looked directly at her.

Uh oh.

"I don't think we've met before. I'm Nina Marie Crane."

"I'm Stacey Malone." She outstretched her hand to Nina Marie, and when she made contact, a feeling unlike anything she'd ever felt shot through her. A combination of power and pain.

"Ah, Nina Marie. I see you've met one of our up-and-coming members." Layton popped up right beside her.

"Where have you been keeping this one, Layton?" Nina Marie asked as if she wasn't standing right there.

"Stacey's a college student who has been interning for us, and I hope to have her on full time once she graduates."

Nina Marie reached out again and touched her arm. She couldn't help her reaction, which was to take a step back.

"You don't have anything to fear from me," Nina Marie said softly.

But Stacey didn't believe this woman, and she was immediately afraid of what could happen to her. She'd heard Nina Marie was very powerful, but she had no idea that someone could wield this type of spiritual energy.

45

Thankfully, Layton pulled her over to him, wrapping his protective arm around her shoulder. "Why don't you run and grab a drink, Stacey, while I discuss a few business items with Nina Marie?"

She didn't waste any time and walked quickly to the other side of the room, looking for a restroom to regroup. Morena was right behind her.

"What in the world happened back there?" Morena asked her.

"That woman." She paused sucking in a big breath. "She frightens me."

**

Nina Marie watched as Stacey hightailed it away from her. Then she turned her attention to Layton.

"Nina Marie, whatever you're thinking, just stop it right now," Layton said.

"I have no idea what you're talking about."

"Stacey is a member of Optimism. She's not up for discussion. If you try to mess with her, you'll have to deal with me."

"Ah, you like this one, huh? Maybe she and I really do need to have a chat then."

He clutched hard onto her upper arm and squeezed, but she broke away from him.

"What did I tell you about putting your hands on me?"

"I just want to make myself abundantly clear."

"I have no interest in your plaything, Layton, but you better watch out for that one. Her strength was unlike anything I've felt in a long time."

"She's young and still has much to learn. That's why I've taken her under my wing."

"You don't understand what it's like to be a woman. She needs a female in her life."

"She has Morena."

Nina Marie laughed. "Morena is good at parlor tricks, but she is not an equal to either of us. This Stacey girl could be the real deal."

"If you try to poke your nose into this, you'll regret it."

She sighed. Layton was up to his old games again. "I thought we were supposed to be working together right now for the greater goal we have."

He nodded. "You're right. Stacey's just come from a fragile situation. She used to be a member of Windy Ridge Community Church. So all of this has come as a shock to her. I'm probably being a bit overprotective right now."

"When are you going to speak to the group?"

"Soon. Grab yourself a drink and some hors d'oeuvres." He looked down at his watch. "I'll speak within the hour."

He walked away to talk to other guests. Yeah, there was no chance she was going to leave Stacey alone. This girl had some serious potential, and she'd much rather have someone like that on her side than on Layton's.

CHAPTER FIVE

Layton looked out into the living room that connected to the parlor. It was time to conduct some business before dinner was served. Tonight he had a large group because the crowd included not only his Optimism members, but also a solid contingency from Astral Tech.

He didn't trust Nina Marie, but teaming up on a temporary basis was a guaranteed recipe for success. The believers in the town simply wouldn't be strong enough to withstand the onslaught of both groups working together. Especially since their beloved pastor was currently sitting in prison. He couldn't hold back the large grin spreading across his face at the thought of Dan rotting behind bars.

But he had a different game to play here tonight in front of a large audience, and it was time to do it.

"Thanks to everyone for coming this evening. I hope you're having a wonderful time enjoying some great food and wine and meeting new friends." He paused for a moment. "Before we sit down to our dinner, which I've been promised by the chef is going to be utterly amazing, I want to talk about some issues affecting our community and our two organizations."

He surveyed the room and had the full attention of the group. "I'm sure everyone has heard by now that the police have arrested Pastor Dan Light of Windy Ridge Community Church. The primary charge against him is embezzlement—he was stealing from the church coffers. As members of Optimism, we've known for a while that Dan wasn't to be trusted, but these charges reinforce the opinion we've had, but we should use this as an opportunity. Everyone knows our agenda includes removing the influence of the church in our town. With their pastor in prison, many church members will be questioning whether they should continue going to that church. Our job is to be friends to them in this very difficult time, and then show them there is another way. A way that doesn't include being blind followers of church doctrine."

"Do we have any more information on how this all came about with the pastor?" one of the Optimism members asked.

Layton smiled, but he had to play this carefully. "My sources actually tell me it was someone who works for the church that went to the police."

A few gasps came out from the crowd.

"Yes, I know everyone is very interested to see how this whole thing will play out."

"Is he still in prison?" another person asked.

"Yes. I'm not sure what his bail situation is. But last I heard, he was still in prison."

"We have to be careful," Nina Marie stood up. "If he stays in prison, he'll try to play the martyr card."

"That would be assuming his church was behind him, but from all I've heard, that isn't the case. Even his associate pastor is doubting him."

Nina Marie strode up to where Layton stood. He figured she'd want to assert some authority tonight, and at this point, he wasn't even bothered by it.

"We need to figure out the best way to use all of our collective resources and talents," she said. "Each one of our respective groups has particular strengths, and beyond that, we have many members with specialized skills."

"And I completely agree with you," he said. "But I want tonight to be one of celebration and getting to know each other. We can certainly have a business meeting to focus on the details of our action plan. In the meantime, though, we can talk about a couple of key strategic ideas. Nina Marie has a great point. Think about what you bring to the table and how it can be used in our effort to rid this community of the Christian faith."

"Remember," Nina Marie said. "A lot of these church members are going to be upset. They're going to feel betrayed, and that's where we can come in. Providing an alternative to their faith. A path that focuses on their own personal power."

"Yes," he said. "Our fresh approach will be interesting to those who have felt duped by the church."

"And the Astral Tech app can be used to help those who are not as familiar with the New Age lifestyle become acquainted quickly."

Of course Nina Marie would have to push the app. As part of the settlement agreement between the two companies, Astral Tech had to pay Optimism a small royalty, but Astral Tech got to keep selling their app. That was all well and good. Nina Marie was better at marketing technology than him. He preferred the more old-school ways of influencing, but he realized that for the younger generation, it was important to have the technological edge. "Remember, everyone, we're on the same team here. I know it still may be odd for some of you because we were in such a hard-fought lawsuit against each other not that long ago. But if Nina Marie and I can put that aside, then we expect all our members to be able to do the same. We can't afford to lose this golden opportunity to change this town forever."

"Layton is right. So why don't we use this time to really get to know each other? Learn what we can do together."

"I couldn't have said it better myself, and on that note, let's have dinner." What an amazing evening. Everything was falling into place beautifully.

                                    **

Olivia walked into church the next morning with Grant by her side. This was going to be one of the most difficult services to get through. The congregation was in total disarray.

When she stepped into the chapel, a wave of cool air rushed over her. She looked around. There were a lot of people there, but they were upset. Some of them were even in small groups huddled together and crying.

"This is bad," Grant whispered.

"We knew it was going to be tough." She looked up and saw Chris walking toward them.

She reached out and gave him a tight hug. "Are you ready for today?" she asked.

"I didn't sleep at all last night. I feel such a huge weight of responsibility on my shoulders today, and I'm not even sure what I'm going to say. A normal sermon seems dreadfully inappropriate right now."

"Chris, just speak from the heart. Whatever God lays on you." She was about to make a big request of him, but it was something she had to do. "I'd also like to ask you if I could speak to the congregation as well. Once you're done, of course."

"Do you really think that's a good idea? You're Dan's lawyer. I don't want to be seen as having some sort of agenda here."

She blew out a frustrated breath. Chris's words let her know which way he was leaning in all of this, and she was still troubled by the fact Chris had seemed to give up on Dan so easily. Something didn't add up. As she looked into Chris's bloodshot eyes, she saw a man who was tormented.

"I should go get ready to start the service," Chris said. His eyes softened. "And yes, Olivia, of course you should speak if you feel led to. It's what Dan would want."

"Thank you, Chris."

He nodded and walked up to the front of the church.

"Let's get to our seats," she told Grant.

"What can I do to help you?" he asked.

"Just having you here to support me makes all the difference in the world. I can only pray that the hearts of the people haven't been totally hardened against Dan."

He placed his hand gently on her back, and they found their seats. "Are you worried about what Chris is going to say?"

"Yes, but there's nothing I can do except try to advocate for Dan after Chris is done."

The worship started, and it was evident to her by the sound of weak voices that people were not fully engaged. Even the worship team on stage wasn't their normal selves. It broke her heart to see the church turned upside down like this, and it also made her angry. She refused to let Satan take down this church.

So while those around her may not have lifted up their voices, she sang, not caring what people thought about her.

When they finished the worship, they took their seats and she glanced over at Grant. She wondered what he was thinking. As a new Christian, this all had to be very difficult for him to digest and understand. She could only pray that these setbacks wouldn't cause him to turn away from his new faith.

Lord, this church is under attack, but I know that You are greater than anything that can come against us. Please give Your believers in this building strength to face the enemy.

Grant reached over and placed his hand on top of hers. She knew in her heart that she was starting to have real feelings for this man. Feelings that went beyond friendship.

Chris stood at center stage and looked out into the congregation. It was so quiet in the chapel she could hear her own breathing. "I know everyone here today is hurt and has a lot questions. There's confusion, anger, and sadness. Unfortunately, I can't stand up here and tell you that I have all the answers—or really any of them at this point."

He paced back and forth on the stage not saying anything else for a couple of minutes. The silence was deafening. She had no idea what he was going to say next.

He turned and faced the people again. "I can't stand here and proclaim Pastor Dan's innocence. I wish I could. I prayed I could. That I could come up here today and tell you this was all a big mistake and that Dan would be freed any day now."

She watched as tears filled Chris's eyes, matched by the ones that were already falling down her face.

"All I can tell you is that I'm praying for guidance, and that even though I know it's hard, now is not the time to leave the church. Just the opposite. We are stronger as a family in Christ than we are as a fragmented group of individuals. I'd also urge you not to feed into the gossip mill of the community. Under our criminal justice system, Dan will get his day in court, and under the law, he is innocent until proven guilty. But as the current acting pastor of this church, all I can do is ask you to stay, to pray, and to know that God's love is stronger and more powerful than any of these challenges."

He continued on with a very short sermon and when Chris's eyes met her own, she knew it was time. "Olivia Murray has asked that she be able to say a few words today. You should know she is acting as Pastor Dan's defense attorney. Olivia, please come on up."

Her heartbeat raced as she stood up from her seat and walked down the aisle and then up the steps to the stage. One of the tech support people handed her a microphone. Taking a deep breath, she prepared to speak, not knowing exactly what to say. It was imperative she fiercely advocated for Dan. Not as his lawyer, but as his friend.

"Thank you, Chris, for allowing me the opportunity to speak today. As Chris just told you, I am Dan's attorney, but today I want to talk to you as a fellow member of this church. Last year I met Dan Light when I came to town for the trial between the two New Age groups this church knows all too well. Even though I walked into this church as a stranger and was entangled in a legal mess with members of the occult, Pastor Dan welcomed me with open arms. He and his faith were instrumental in me being able to face down those challenges from powerful and sinister groups. I chose to take Dan's case because I have absolutely no doubts about his innocence. Chris wants to gather all the facts, and that he feels a duty to this congregation to get it right. But I implore you today to pray on all of this and to believe that the man who has been standing up here and preaching for the past decade is a man of honor. He's been there for each of you time after time. He's performed marriages and funerals. He's taken those calls in the middle of the night when you most needed him. He's sat at the bedside of a dying loved one. He's visited you in the hospital. And now, when he needs you to stand by him and believe that he is a man of God, I ask that you don't turn your back on him. Because I know one thing for certain. He's never turned his back on you."

She watched the faces of those in the audience. Some seemed sympathetic, while others skeptical. But all she could do was speak from the heart. She was about to ask the congregation to pray with her when a woman stood up. It wasn't someone she was familiar with.

"I've been watching the news. I read all about this, and the evidence seems very damaging against the pastor. I, for one, came today to hear what the church had to say about all of this. But I can't attend a place like this with a black mark over the pastor. So for me and my family, this will be our last day here."

Her heart sank listening to this woman's words, and then things went from bad to worse. A man stood up from his seat. "I agree with her. My family is also leaving this church."

"Me, too." Another voice rang out.

And just like that, multiple people were gathering their things and walking out. What could she do?

"Please, wait," she said.

But most people ignored her and kept making their way out of the chapel. There were still some people in their seats, though, and she had to focus on them. "For those of you still seated, I'd ask that you realize how important it is we stay as a strong body of Christ—united against the schemes of the devil."

Chris walked over to her, and she knew her time was up.

"I appreciate everyone coming out today," Chris said.

He clenched his left fist, and she could tell that he was stressed about this turn of events. She'd never been at a church service where multiple people walked out.

"I know this wasn't a traditional service. We're all doing the best we can under the circumstances. I also understand that you have to do what you feel God is leading you to do, but I hope you would still give this church a chance. We need you here, and for many of you this has been your church home for years."

Chris closed in prayer, and when Olivia opened her eyes, she noticed a few more empty seats. A churning sickness filled her stomach. They had not won the battle today. That was for sure.

**

Dan sat in his prison cell, deep in prayer. It was the strangest thing because he'd found more peace since he'd been in prison than he had in months. The thing about being in prison was that there were very few activities to occupy his time. So he'd been spending his days and nights talking to God.

Maybe the Lord put him there for a larger purpose, and on his mind right now was the inmate he'd been talking to who was in the cell directly across from his.

"Pastor," Jim Dunn said.

"Yes," he answered.

"You've been quiet so far today."

"It's Sunday, Jim. The first Sunday I haven't been preaching in quite a while." As he said the words, the reality of the situation really hit him.

"Well, Pastor, you don't even want to know how long it's been since I stepped foot inside a church."

"That's the thing about Jesus. He is willing to take us exactly where we are right now, even if we have tremendous sins in our past."

"Even sins like mine?" Jim asked.

"I don't know what your sins are, but if you repent of those things, you can find forgiveness in the Lord."

"Robbery and assault," Jim said. "That's why I'm in here. You've been nice enough not to ask the past couple of days, but I feel like you should know. I broke into a home and had an altercation with the man of the house. I stole some things. Got caught a couple of days later."

"Are you sorry that you did that?"

He was met by silence.

"That's the first step. You have to actually have some contrition for what you've done."

"I was stupid and that got me locked up."

"I'm not talking about getting caught. I'm talking about what you did in the first place."

He paused, taking a deep breath as the silence stretched. "The look of fear in the woman's eyes as she screamed when she saw me before her husband came rushing into the room. I'll have to live with that guilt forever. It doesn't feel good."

"That's the thing, Jim. You're here, receiving punishment for your action, but the Lord is willing to forgive you if you meet him here. You said it's been years since you went to church, but since you did go at one time, I'm assuming you know about the Lord."

Jim nodded. "I know the basics, but I haven't followed all of the commandments…"

"It's not really all about the Ten Commandments. Yes, those are good concepts to follow, but the redemptive power of Christ through the ultimate sacrifice for us as sinners is what's really important." He didn't intend to start preaching, but he couldn't help himself. "Christ died on the cross for the sins of the world. Then he arose on the third day so that we may all have everlasting life if we repent and believe in him."

"It's hard for me to believe why God would love someone like me. I've lied, cheated, and stolen most of my life. Started when I was a teenager."

"God does love you. More than you could even know."

The inmate who was next to Jim started laughing. "Jim, you're taking religious advice from a pastor who stole money from his church. Do you realize that? That's why he's in here with us. He's not man of God. He's just a common criminal. You need to get your head checked by the prison shrink."

Jim looked at him. "I've heard those rumors about you, Pastor, but I didn't know what to believe. You don't seem like the stealing type."

Dan nodded. "Those are the charges against me, but I'm innocent. I did not steal from the church."

"I believe you," Jim said.

The other inmate laughed loudly. "Well, don't be trying to fill my head with your nonsense about God and religion. I've got better things to do than listen to that kind of stuff."

"You're not even part of this conversation, Billy." Jim's blue eyes narrowed.

"Don't say I didn't warn you." Billy crept back deeper in his cell.

"I wouldn't let him bother you," Jim said. "But I have to ask, do you have a good lawyer? If you didn't do it, then you need a good attorney to help you. Public defenders are worthless."

"The public defenders aren't worthless. They're just overworked and underpaid, but thanks to the Lord, I do have an amazing attorney, and she is really smart and dedicated. At the end of the day, though, my faith is in God, not in the legal system."

"How can you say that?"

56

"I've been through a lot in my life, Jim. I lost my wife not long ago. So being in this cell doesn't begin to compare with the pain I went through. I'm not worried about myself, but I do worry about my church and those people who believed in me. I don't want them to think that I would've betrayed their trust, because I would've never done anything like that."

Jim shook his head. "Man, I don't know that I could ever have your type of faith. Don't you ever get angry at God for all of this? For putting you here? For your wife's death?"

"I'm not going to lie to you, Jim. There have been some really dark days. Days when I didn't even want to get up and out of bed to go into the church. Days I questioned everything. But even through all of that, I knew God was working. There is a Bible verse that says all things work together for good for those who love the Lord and are called according to His purpose. It's one of my favorites, and I have to remind myself of it often—especially through trying times when everything seems to be falling apart. But having faith is all about believing, even when it's hard to do so. Even when it seems like there is no hope. When you can't see the hand of God at all. I know in my heart that God is near. The Holy Spirit provides comfort through the valleys and the darkness of night."

"Now you're getting really deep on me, Pastor."

He chuckled. "Honestly, I don't know if I'm talking more for your benefit or mine right now. Sometimes I even need to be reminded of these things, particularly at a time like this."

"Are you going to get out on bail?"

"I told my lawyer if she could get donations for the funds, then I would accept them, but I don't know if that's going to happen. The Lord has a plan for all of this though."

"Well, I know this sounds far-fetched, but what if God wants you here? If you believe like you said that he's working behind the scenes and all, what if you have a reason to be right here in this prison?"

"You know, Jim, I think you may have hit the nail on the head. Before I was arrested, I was having a really rough time. Nothing seemed right at the church or in my life. It was like a dark cloud was hanging over my head. I felt disconnected and depressed. But since I've been in here, I've had so much time to pray and talk to God. To not just ask God for things, but to listen."

"You really think that God talks to you?"

"He will talk to you, too, but you have to be still and listen. You have to be open to His presence and His will."

"I'm not saying I get everything you're talking about here, but I have to say that it has made me start to think." Jim paused. "And you know what else?"

"What?"

"Looks like you still got to preach that Sunday sermon after all."

**

Grant looked into Olivia's dark eyes filled with hurt, and to see her in pain made him upset as well. He hadn't known what to expect at the church service today, but it was worse than he could've ever imagined. From his count, three-fourths of the church had gotten up and left by the time it was all said and done.

And even some of those who remained had probably only done so out of a sense of respect for church itself. If Olivia's fundraising efforts for bail were any indication, there were only a few people in the church who actually wanted to stand by Dan.

"You've barely eaten your pizza," he said. They sat in his favorite pizza place and their now standard post-church lunch spot.

"I don't really have much of an appetite," she said quietly.

This wasn't the Olivia he'd come to know. The woman in front of him seemed defeated. "Olivia, since when have you let obstacles stand in your way?"

"What do you mean?"

"You're upset right now, and I get that. It was a tough thing to witness, but feeling sorry for yourself isn't going to help you, Dan, or the church."

Her eyes narrowed. "What, do you think I'm having a pity party or something? You weren't the one up on that stage, Grant. Seeing people literally walk out of church after you've poured your heart out trying to advocate for an innocent man. You have no idea what that was like."

"You're right. I don't, but I know you and you're stronger than all of this. Olivia, your faith is more rock solid than anyone I know. If anyone can navigate through all of this, it is you, but you need to keep your head up and push forward." He hoped he wasn't pushing her too hard, but he felt like she needed some tough love right now.

"You're not exactly very sympathetic to what I'm going through."

"I'm speaking honestly and openly to you, and I hope you value that much more than me trying to just pat you on the head and say it's all going to be okay."

"I don't really appreciate your attitude right now. I'm hurting and I need a friend."

The last thing he wanted to do was to hurt her even more. "I am trying to be your friend, and because I care so much about you, I don't want to see you upset or defeated. You've already done so much for this community. The battles you've waged have been something I can't even begin to comprehend. All I'm saying is you're the person God has chosen here, so you can't waste time nursing wounds. You've got to get right back out there."

She leaned forward in her seat and put her hand on top of his and met his eyes, this time more determined. "You're absolutely right. I'm not a quitter."

"No, it's the last thing in this world that you are."

"But I'm not sure what the best next steps are."

"You don't have to have it all figured out. All you have to do is be willing to take the next step." He placed his other hand on top of hers. "Olivia, I hope you realize that you're not alone. I'm right here."

Her eyes misted up. "Everything is so out of whack right now. I can only keep praying for strength and guidance. I appreciate you doing what you can to remind me of the bigger picture."

"We can work through this together. It seems like the bail fundraising effort is not going to work. So Dan stays in prison for now unless there's something we haven't thought of."

"I'm meeting with him tomorrow and will see what he says now that he's been in prison for a few days about how it's going. I've been praying for his safety while he's in there."

"I have been, too. It's been such a whirlwind, but we should start working on the investigation and developing his defense. Do you think your firm would hire an investigator?"

"Yes. Since we're taking it pro bono, that's all part of the deal."

"I never got to talk to you about how Chet took the whole thing about you wanting to do this case?"

"He's good with it. I'm already doing a lot by moving out here to help start up the Chicago office. BCR is committed to being a leader in pro bono. They expect all their attorneys to bill a minimum number of hours each year to pro bono. It's even part of the evaluation process, and the firm always likes to take on the cases that are high profile. The more BCR is in the news, the better, and they want to ensure the best likelihood of success, so getting an investigator shouldn't be a problem. What're your thoughts on what they would do?"

"We need someone who can dig into all the financials plus work the human side of things."

"Do you have any recommendations?"

"I have a couple of people in mind. Plus, I can ask Ryan, too. Between the two of us, we should be able to get together a short list to interview."

"Great," she said. "And I've started doing the legal research on all the elements under Illinois law that the prosecution will have to prove for each charge."

"We should also think about timing. I don't know whether the prosecutor wants to put this on the fast track or slow walk it."

"Maybe it depends on how strong he thinks the case is. That's one more thing we need to add to our list. Perhaps even the investigator could do it. We need to know everything we can about Deputy Assistant District Attorney Tony Sampson."

"Yeah, given that most of my work is civil litigation, I haven't had any exposure to him," Grant said. Olivia made a good point. "If this guy has an angle, we need to know what it is." He gathered his thoughts and then decided to raise an issue she might be sensitive about. "Olivia, I think it's our job as Dan's attorneys to do everything we can to investigate and vigorously defend this case. I know you believe that there are spiritual aspects at play here, and I'm not discounting that."

"But?"

"There is a big human element to all of this. Choices and responsibility that go beyond the spiritual realm. If Dan is innocent, then someone else framed him. They are the guilty party here. I just want both of us to keep that in mind."

"I realize this is a legal fight just as much as a spiritual one, but I can't just act like it's completely business as usual. We both know that Layton and Nina Marie have plans for Windy Ridge to spread their New Age message and to ridicule believers."

"Which gets back to the question of whether they would've gone to such lengths to do that. Why fight within the legal system? Why not just focus on the spiritual strategy?"

"Because this kind of allegation against a pastor is exactly the type of thing that brings down a church, and if today's service is any indication, then they're winning. We need to turn the tide."

"Let me try to set up that investigator meeting ASAP." He paused. "Make no mistake though, Olivia. I'm here for you. I know we're not going to see eye to eye on everything all the time, but I think that's one of the reasons we became friends. We do challenge each other. At the end of the day, though, I want you to know how much you mean to me."

"I know that," she said softly. "I value our friendship so much."

But he realized that she didn't have a clue how much he cared for her. Because in his heart, she was so much more than just a friend.

CHAPTER SIX

Olivia sat across the table in the small holding cell. As Dan's attorney she was able to meet with him face to face. The guard stood right outside the door.

"First, how're you doing?" She looked into his eyes and held her breath waiting for his response.

He smiled but didn't immediately respond.

"You're smiling?"

"Because I'm doing better right now than I've been in a long time."

Immediately her pulse kicked up. Was Dan delusional? Had he fallen ill? "Dan, are you sick? Is it the food? Or the conditions?"

He shook his head. "No, Olivia. You have it all wrong. I actually feel great. I know everyone thinks of prison as being an awful place, but since I've been here, amazing things have happened."

"Like what?"

"Well, for one, there's another inmate who is in the cell across from mine, and I've been able to talk to him about Christ. We've developed a fast friendship."

"That's great, Dan, and once again I see that you are putting others ahead of yourself, but we still have to worry about the charges against you. I really don't want you sitting in prison."

"Don't you see, though? The Lord is using me here. I've felt more useful here this week than I have in months at the church. The feelings of despair and doubt that have been surrounding me have no hold on me here. I know it may seem crazy to you, but in prison I have found freedom and a burning desire to witness again and preach that I haven't felt. What if I can touch more lives of the men here?"

A mixture of emotions flowed through her. The lawyer in her wanted to reach out and shake Dan and tell him to get a grip. That they needed to develop a plan to raise the funds and get him out of prison as soon as possible. But an even larger part of her looked at Dan and could feel the Holy Spirit moving through this situation. She hadn't seen Dan this happy since she first met him last year. Maybe the Lord was working something miraculous through all of this. "I can see God is at work here and using you, but I have to tell you I'm going to fight as hard as I can to clear your name. You can come back and visit the prison as much as you want to minister to inmates, but you'll do it with a badge of innocence stamped on you."

"And I want that, too. I'm not saying I want to give up on the case and stay in prison forever. All I'm saying is, for this moment, I feel like I am in the right place. But I do want you to defend me and clear my name. Have you found out any more about what happened?"

"It's crazy. Beverly is the one who referred this matter to the police."

"Really? Are you certain?"

"Yes, and I have to tell you I have some strong suspicions about her."

"You can't just condemn her for this. Maybe she thought she was doing the right thing."

"Maybe. Or maybe she has a hidden agenda and set you up."

"But why would she do that?"

"That's one of the things we plan to find out."

"And how is Chris doing?"

She'd expected him to ask, but she hadn't been really sure how she was going to answer if he did. But now in the moment, she knew she couldn't mislead him. He deserved to know the truth. "Honestly, he's having a really hard time."

"Does he think I did it?"

"He is conflicted. Due to the nature of the allegations, Chris has a duty to the church to fully look into things and not blindly accept your innocence."

"I don't fault him for that, Olivia. He's a good man, and trying to protect the congregation."

"It's not just that. In the interest of telling you everything, I feel like he's really down and questioning everything and everyone. He's usually so strong. It's almost like I've been dealing with a different man."

"These are tough times, and they can rattle even the strongest of men."

"I guess so."

"I need you to do something for me."

"Of course. You name it."

"I need you to be there for Chris. I can sense you're upset with him, and I appreciate your loyalty. But he's going to need people in his corner right now. It's actually easier for me in here than it is for him out there. So anything you can do to help him, I'd really appreciate it."

"I'll do my best."

"Should I even ask how church went yesterday?"

She thought it better not to say that it was an unmitigated disaster. "It didn't go well."

"I figured as much. We were already in a fragile position, and these charges really tipped the scales against us. I can't blame people for being hurt and confused. In the end, though, I believe it's all going to work out."

"All right. I'll keep you posted, and keep up the good work here, Dan."

"I plan on it."

**

Grant sat in his law office and waited for Olivia. He'd been able to schedule a meeting with a private investigator. A few screening interviews had been conducted, and none of the others had the skill set he was hoping for. So he went back to one he had used.

He'd worked with Abe Perez on a case a couple of years ago. Because of Abe's background, Grant thought he'd be a good fit for this. Abe had worked on the police force right out of college for ten years before becoming a PI.

His intercom beeped. "Grant, Abe Perez is here to see you."

"I'll be right down. Please take him to conference room two."

He finished up the email that he was drafting and then picked up his notepad and a pen and headed down to the conference room.

When he walked in, he saw Abe and walked over to shake his hand. "Abe, good to see you again."

"It's been a while. How've you been?"

"Good. Staying busy."

"And you like being out on your own?"

"Love it. It's hard work, but it's totally worth it. I'm glad I took the risk. I don't know if you've met my partner Ryan Wilde. He's out in a deposition today, but we worked together at my old firm. He's been a big asset here."

"Yeah, I don't think I know him. You also mentioned something on the phone about another lawyer."

"Yes, Olivia Murray. She should be here any minute. She's really taking the lead here. I'm just assisting."

"Great. Can't wait to meet her. From what you've told me so far, this seems like an interesting case."

They made a few minutes of small talk while they waited on Olivia to arrive. When she walked into the room, he took a deep breath. She looked even more beautiful today than normal. He had to be careful or he was going to get hurt. He realized that.

"Hi." She walked over to Abe and offered her hand. "I'm Olivia Murray."

He smiled. "Abe Perez. Nice to meet you."

As Grant watched them shake hands, a jolt of jealousy hit him. He had absolutely no reason to feel that way, but he couldn't help it. It also made things worse because he got the distinct impression that he had stronger feelings for Olivia than she did for him.

"Let's have a seat and get started," Grant said.

They sat down at the table, and the mood shifted to considerably more serious.

"I'm ready when you guys are," Abe said. He had his laptop open and a notebook in front of him.

Olivia proceeded to fill him in on the background facts and getting him up to speed on where things stood with a lot more detailed information than he'd been able to give Abe over the phone.

"So, if I'm hearing you right, you believe the pastor was set up to take the fall here?" Abe asked.

"I definitely believe that," Olivia said. "Grant, on the other hand, I think is still a bit on the fence."

"It sounds to me like I need to do a deep dive on the pastor and on Beverly Jenkins. If she is involved in some way, I'll find out how. People like to think they're crafty and can cover their tracks, but in my experience, there's always some evidence left behind."

"I agree," she said.

"But there's one thing I have to warn you about." Abe looked directly at Olivia.

"What?" she asked.

"You would be hiring me as an investigator. I don't have an agenda. I look for the truth, wherever it leads. So it could be, and I'm just putting this out there, that I find evidence implicating your client. I will bring that evidence to you in the same way I'd bring any other evidence. I believe a lawyer needs to know what's out there on all sides so you can do your job, but I want to be able to do my job as well. Will that be okay with you?"

"I understand," she said.

"I don't want there to be any misconceptions if you decide to hire me for this case."

"I know from talking to Grant that you have a substantial background in law enforcement. That's one of the main reasons I wanted to speak to you, because you understand the system."

"My history on the police force has helped me become a much better investigator. I'd bring my full skill set to a case like this."

"All of this sounds good, but before we officially move forward, I also have to say something from my side in the interest of full disclosure."

Grant knew exactly where Olivia was going, and he didn't have any idea how Abe would react.

"Sure, what is it? Better to get it all out into the open now," Abe said.

"You have to realize, given that my client is a pastor, there are some religious issues that would naturally flow from this case."

"Of course. That doesn't bother me at all."

"But I wanted to let you know it may be a lot more than you expected, and I wanted to explain that to you up front."

"How so?" Abe asked.

Olivia looked over at him and then back at Abe. "There are two New Age companies that are players here. One is called Optimism and the other is Astral Tech. They are run by Layton Alito and Nina Marie Crane."

"And why are they involved?" Abe asked.

"These groups hate the church. Their New Age beliefs cross strongly over into the occult, and they've made it their mission to try to wipe out Windy Ridge Community Church."

Abe raised an eyebrow. "So you're trying to tell me that these New Age groups have a beef against the pastor."

"Exactly, and that these people are truly evil and will stop at nothing to pursue their agenda."

Was Olivia going to bring up the whole angels and demons thing? Based on Abe's initial reaction, he hoped she'd keep that to herself, at least for now.

"So I'm telling you all of this because I want you to be aware that this may not be a cut and dry situation. I don't know what your religious beliefs are, but I didn't want to hide anything."

Abe leaned back in his chair and crossed his arms. "I'm not deterred by any of this. I appreciate that you told me what you think is going on."

Grant worried for a second that Olivia was going to push this issue given Abe's skepticism.

"Thank you," she said. "If you're on board, I've got a retainer agreement from my firm for your services. The billing rate is in the agreement. If you have any issues with that, we can negotiate it."

He nodded. "Thanks. I'd like to review it and then we should be good to go."

"Thanks. As you can imagine, we're anxious to get started." She pulled a document out of her bag and walked it over to Abe. "Why don't we give you a few minutes to look it over."

"That'd be great."

Grant stood up and walked out of the conference room with Olivia by his side.

"So you think you're going to like working with him?" he asked.

"I think he has the background we need on something like this."

"I was worried there for a minute that you were attempting to scare him off." He laughed.

"No. I just didn't want to hide what I feel like is an important aspect to this investigation."

"How did it go with Dan?" Grant hadn't wanted to get into those details in front of Abe at this point.

She looked up into his eyes and smiled. "You wouldn't believe it, but Dan is thriving in prison. He's sharing his faith with the inmates, and he says he feels better than he has in months."

Grant thought that was odd. "I have to say something."

"I don't think I'm going to like this."

"What if he feels like he's somehow making amends for his wrongdoing? And that's why he wants to be there?"

"You have so little faith," she shot back.

He hadn't expected her to have such a strong reaction. "It's not my faith we're talking about here, Olivia. The situation with Dan is strange. We knew he was feeling off lately."

She shook her head. "I told you this at the beginning. I really don't need you second guessing his innocence. It's not productive."

"I'm just being completely honest with you."

"And you don't think it's possible that God is using this situation for a larger purpose? That Dan is actually making an impact at that prison?"

"I guess it's possible." But Grant had a nagging bad feeling about the entire thing.

"Can I ask you something?"

"Of course."

"I'm having some concerns about where you are in all of this. I know that you jumped in headfirst last year into this spiritual stuff. Given that you lived your whole life being a skeptic, I wonder if you have some of those thoughts creeping back in."

"You think I don't believe anymore?"

"That's not what I said. I asked whether you were having doubts."

It frightened him how well Olivia understood him. Because if he was being honest, he was having doubts. Not necessarily about God specifically, but how all of this fit together and what his role was. "It's complicated."

She nodded and took her hand in his. "I told you months ago that this road could be challenging and that there would be many questions. I don't expect you to have unrelenting strength or faith at this point in your life. I do appreciate your honesty and that you trust me enough to tell me how you're feeling."

"Olivia." He took a step closer to her. He wanted to wrap his arms around her, but he wasn't sure how she'd react. And besides that, Abe might walk out of the conference room any minute.

"Yes?"

"Maybe we should continue this conversation later in private."

"That's a good idea. I'll go check to see if Abe is done reviewing the retainer agreement."

He watched as she walked back down the hall. He hoped the Abe could get down to the truth and, even more so, that Olivia would be able to handle it.

**

Stacey sat in Latte reading a new book Morena had given her about witchcraft. She'd been a little hesitant at first to embrace the full-blown aspects of witchcraft, but the more she learned, especially about the history in America, the more riveted she was.

In fact, she'd devoured a few books on the Salem witch trials over the past few weeks.

And because she knew what she'd seen with her own eyes last year, or at least had dreamt in a vivid way, she believed she could have contact with the spiritual realm. The idea of that happening again on her own terms excited her and drove her to push further.

Every once in a while, there were whispers of doubt in her mind, but she kept reminding herself she wasn't hurting anyone. That all of her efforts were used for what she believed were the greater good. More independence, openness of thought, a culture where everyone could take their own path. That was what she was focused on, and her path right now was a bright one. This internship and the subsequent offer for full employment after college had changed everything for her.

There was also a part of her that thrived on the power she felt when she was practicing witchcraft. It wasn't like she was sitting around with voodoo dolls and pins trying to get revenge on the mean girls from her high school. No, she was calling upon guidance and spirit strength from another realm, and it was unlike anything she'd ever known. A world of different sense and experiences was wide open to her like she was staring out at the ocean, and there was literally no end to where she could go.

Her whole life she'd been a wallflower. She didn't have a big circle of friends. Her family didn't have money, and often she was content to blend in with the crowd.

For the first time in her life, she wanted to stand out. She had a fabulous new wardrobe and, even more importantly, a huge dose of confidence, thanks to Layton and Morena. Definitely not the church.

Her thoughts drifted to Pastor Dan. It was difficult for her to imagine him being a criminal and a thief, but stranger things had happened. She'd learned a long time ago that people in life let you down, and it was dangerous to put blind faith in anyone.

"Stacey," a female voice said from behind her.

She turned around and saw Nina Marie standing there with a smile on her face. Immediately, a sense of apprehension washed over her. "Hello," she said, trying to be polite.

"I love this place, don't you?" Nina Marie held a brightly colored coffee cup in her hand.

"Yes. I come here all the time."

"Do you mind if I have a seat?"

She couldn't say no. That would be entirely rude, and besides, they were supposed to be working together now. "Sure. Go right ahead."

Nina Marie grinned and sat down across from her. Today she wore a simple, yet elegant blank pantsuit. She got the impression Nina Marie was always put together. She could only hope to be that refined one day.

"What're you reading?" Nina Marie looked toward the book on the table.

There was no point in trying to hide it. Nina Marie understood this New Age world much better than she did. "It's a book on advanced witchcraft told from a New Age perspective."

"May I?" Nina Marie pointed to the book.

"Of course."

Nina Marie picked it up and silently flipped through it for a few minutes. At first she thought it was all for show, but then she realized that Nina Marie was actually reading parts of it.

She thought it best to just let her do her thing, so she sat quietly enjoying her vanilla chai latte. Nina Marie's tortoiseshell glasses framed her face perfectly. She figured Nina Marie was probably in her forties, just like Layton. She watched as Nina Marie started to frown. Then she finally put the book down and looked back at her.

"Stacey, this book is rubbish."

"What?" She wasn't expecting her to say that. "It's a top seller in its category."

Nina Marie leaned forward. "Is it trendy? Yes. But it's a bunch of bull. They're trying to get you to buy into their way of thinking so you will start purchasing all their products. Take it from someone who knows a great deal about marketing and promotion, especially in this area."

"So you think the author doesn't know what she's talking about?"

"I don't. It's fluff, Stacey. Pure and simple. I can't imagine that Layton recommended this book to you."

"No. I found it on my own." She felt her cheeks burn with embarrassment.

"Oh, I'm sorry. I didn't mean for it to come out like that."

"It's okay. No offense taken."

"Can I tell you something?"

"Sure." She had no idea what Nina Marie was going to say.

"I don't want you to take this the wrong way, but I have a feeling that you'll understand once I explain."

"All right."

"From the very instant I met you, I knew that you were unique. I mentioned it to Layton, and he got all territorial on me."

"He's a strong-willed man."

"Exactly. He's a man, and I want to share something with you. I was foolish for a bit a while back and fell for his charms. He's handsome, smart, powerful, and rich. What more could a girl want?"

Did Nina Marie think she was dating Layton? "I think that you're mistaken. There's nothing going on between me and Layton."

"There may not be now, but I would be remiss if I didn't tell you, woman to woman, that I think Layton wouldn't be good for you."

"Like I said, nothing is going on there, and I have no intention of starting anything. I'm completely focused on school and work right now. Not any guy. Even if he is a man like Layton."

"Good. Then let me take it a step further. I think you're special, but I also think Layton has certain limitations."

"What do you mean?"

"As a woman, you have a different set of abilities in the spiritual realm than a man does. Layton can help you, that's for sure, but he can only take you so far. There are things that he will never be able to tap into because he's a man."

"But I have Morena helping me out, too."

"Morena is fairly sophisticated, but she doesn't have my level of experience."

"What are you suggesting?"

72

"I'd like to work with you. I believe with my help there is truly no limit to what you can achieve."

Her offer was tempting, but what in the world would Layton say about it? "I'm flattered, but I'm still not sure how this would all work. And … Layton is pretty particular about my training."

"Don't give Layton another thought. You need to be looking out for you. Layton knows how powerful you are, and he doesn't want to be challenged by a woman. Believe me. I've lived through that and it wasn't pretty."

"But you can't seriously be suggesting that I work with you behind Layton's back."

"That's exactly what I'm suggesting."

"I need to think about this."

Nina Marie grasped onto her hand, and immediately she knew this woman was the real deal. And it frightened her even more.

"Take all the time you need." She squeezed her hand. "But I know you can feel this is the right thing for you. I don't have an agenda like Layton does. I truly want to help you."

"Thank you."

"Make no mistake about it, Stacey. Layton Alito is a dangerous man. He'll have no hesitation about taking you out if you become too powerful. You need to watch your back."

She watched as Nina Marie stood and walked away. A chill shot down her arm at Nina Marie's warning. Did she really have anything to fear from Layton?

CHAPTER SEVEN

Tony Sampson sat at his desk in the prosecutor's office and ended the phone call. He had just double-checked and found out that Dan Light was still behind bars. Why in the world hadn't he made bail? There could only be one plausible response. His church family hadn't come forward with the money. That had to be a devastating blow to a man like him and to his attorney.

Nothing about this situation seemed right to him, but he was planning on working this case just like any other. Even though it had a lot of media attention, he needed to build a rock solid case to put before a jury. If he weren't able to construct that type of case, then he'd need to start thinking about a plea deal. The worst scenario for him and his career right now would be to suffer a loss.

It had been a while since he'd taken an embezzlement case to trial, so he wanted to brush up on the required elements under state law. He did a quick search in his legal research database of choice and pulled out his legal pad to draft a quick checklist.

Element one, fiduciary relationship. Check. As the church's pastor, there was no doubt on element one.

But as he reacquainted himself with the rest of the three statutory requirements, that's where the facts and evidence building would come in.

Element two, acquisition of property through the relationship. Dan had access to the church's bank account given his role as pastor, and it helped his case that only three people had access, that he knew of.

Element three, taking ownership of the property for their own personal gain. He'd need to be able to show Dan used the money for his own personal use and not something for the church. He was still trying to track down what Dan did with the money.

Element four, actions are intentional. He felt this element was pretty easy. There was no way that type of financial transfer happened multiple times by accident. No, it was certainly intentional.

So, in short, he had to be able to prove that Dan took the money from the church's accounts and funneled the money into his own personal accounts, and that he did so intentionally.

As he examined the file of bank transfers in front of him, it seemed fairly cut and dry. But one thing that was bothering him was what had Dan actually done with the money? It had been put into his account, but that's where the trail ended because he hit a dead end at the transfer to an unidentifiable offshore account. Given the strict privacy and banking laws outside the United States, it was likely they'd never know for certain who controlled that offshore account.

In his experience, embezzlers used the money to make purchases of things—like boats, beach houses, or fancy cars. And so far he hadn't been able to track down a single tangible asset. Which led him to wonder if Dan had a gambling problem. That would explain the need for large amounts of cash. He jotted down some notes to remind himself to explore that avenue.

He leaned back in his chair and thought about timing. He wanted to move this case along quickly but not at the expense of having all his ducks in a row. He'd have one of the younger attorneys help him with connecting all the dots and doing the required research.

His phone rang and he answered it, welcoming the distraction from his current train of thoughts.

"This is Anne from the visitor's desk. There's someone named Layton Alito here asking to see you. I didn't have him on your visitor's list for the day. Do you want me to send him up or turn him away?"

He knew Layton was going to follow up, but he hadn't realized it would be so soon. "Send him up, Anne. Thank you."

He took in a deep breath and tried to quickly gather his thoughts. Did he even have a final answer about joining the Optimism non-profit board? He hadn't had the time yet to do the deep dive on the organization, but if Judge Louise Martinique was involved, then that spoke volumes.

A couple of minutes later, Layton was standing at his door. As usual, he looked completely professional wearing a dark suit and gray tie.

"Come on in, Layton." He rose to shake his hand.

"How're you doing today?" Layton asked.

"Great, and yourself?"

"I'm doing wonderful. Nothing like a bitter winter day to make you enjoy being indoors."

"Please have a seat. I know you probably didn't drop by for small talk. So what can I do for you today?"

"I wanted to check in with you to see if you had given my offer of taking a seat on the Optimism non-profit board more thought."

"I haven't had a lot of time to focus on it. Our workload in this office is very heavy. Given state budget cuts, we're all expected to do more with less."

Layton leaned in a bit toward him. "I completely appreciate that, and if you're too busy, I have another very interested candidate who would also be a great fit for our organization. But, of course, I wanted to discuss it with you before I extended the offer to someone else."

Well, this wasn't ideal. He didn't want to pass up a great opportunity, even if he hadn't done all of his due diligence. What was the worst that could happen? If he took the board seat and it didn't work out, he'd just resign and someone else could take his seat. "I didn't say I wasn't interested. I'm very interested. So much so that I'm willing to accept the position."

Layton smiled. "You are a very smart man. This will only open up more doors for you and your career, and it just so happens that our next meeting is tomorrow. That's why I wanted to go ahead and fill this seat, so we'd have a full board again."

"When and where?"

"We meet at various locations. For this meeting it will be at my house, tomorrow at seven p.m. I can send you the address so you'll have it. Also, since most of the board members work long hours, I'll have dinner prepared. So you don't have to worry about that either. Just show up and we'll be good to go."

"I must admit that I haven't had the time to fully educate myself on the non-profit or the core business."

Layton waved his hand. "No worries. You'll catch on quickly. Your legal background will be a bonus for us. Of course we have Louise, but having your viewpoint will be important. It should be a win-win. You'll get to beef up your experience by having a seat on a well-established non-profit board, and we'll get the benefit of your skill set."

"I look forward to doing something new and benefiting the community. As a prosecutor, working within the community is important."

"I think you'll really enjoy the work."

Since Layton was right there in front of him, he figured it best to try to get some additional information from him about the Optimism non-profit. "Do you have a minute to give me some more background on the company and specifically the non-profit arm that I'll be working with?"

"Absolutely. I'll just start at ground zero since it seems like you're not very familiar. Optimism is one of the nation's leading New Age companies. We provide a range of products for consumers, ranging from books to jewelry to technology. Our chief competitor, Astral Tech, focuses even more on the technology side. You might have been aware of the lawsuit last year that ended up settling. The bottom line there is that Astral Tech is focusing on their app. Optimism has made the strategic decision to focus more on tangible products for the consumer."

"And how do you sell your products?"

"Through the website mainly, but many of our books and other publications can be found in specialty bookstores. Like the bookstore we have in town called Indigo."

"And just a basic question—how does Optimism define New Age?"

"New Age is the way most people understand a more holistic way of life connected to spirituality and meditation. Optimism takes that a step forward and really focuses on individuals and the power that people have to shape their own futures. And that's actually a perfect way to help you understand the connection we have to the non-profit side of our work."

"How so?" Layton's description so far had him interested. He didn't care anything about yoga or meditation, but he was a strong proponent of an individual being in control of his or her own destiny.

"We run several programs in the community that focus on equipping people with the skills they need to succeed. We have a job skills program where people come in and meet with an advisor to help them on their interviewing skills and resume. It is especially beneficial for those who feel left behind in the current workforce. We also run a soup kitchen once a week. In addition, we've started a clothing donation program that has been entirely successful and we hope to expand. Louise has actually been instrumental in that effort. If a person looks good, it gives them so much confidence. So we have our hands in multiple altruistic efforts, and the board is always interested to get fresh ideas as to how we could positively impact the community. If you have any ideas, then we'd be completely open to that."

"That sounds great. Thanks for taking the time to help get me up to speed."

"It's my pleasure. I look forward to our board meeting tomorrow night." Layton stood up and offered his hand again. "I'm glad that we're going to be working together."

"Me, too."

"See you tomorrow then." Layton walked out of his office.

Tony sat back down at his desk. Everything Layton said made him feel better about this partnership. He wondered if this was going to be a golden opportunity for him.

**

Nina Marie decided to treat herself to a shopping trip to take her mind off of all the craziness that was going on and just do something fun. Sometimes she did get a bit lonely. She didn't have any close friends but had many more acquaintances than she could count. To the outside world she was the life of the party, a socialite with never a hair out of place. But on the inside, it would just be nice to have someone to do simple things with. Like go shopping or get her nails done.

Yeah, she could ask one of the Astral Tech members, but they all looked at her as a leader. Not an equal. And that persona was too important for her. The power she had over Astral Tech was everything. It was definitely more important than her bouts of loneliness or pity parties.

After she had bought three new dresses and two pair of shoes, her spirits were decidedly higher. As she walked out of the shoe store, someone bumped into her, making her drop a couple of her bags.

"Hey, watch where you're going," she said. She immediately bent down to pick up her bags without even looking at the culprit.

"Please let me," the deep voice said.

She looked up into the big, dark eyes of a strikingly handsome man.

"I'm so sorry. This was completely my fault. I was looking down at my phone and didn't even see you. Are you okay?"

"Yes, I'm fine." She was immediately drawn to this man, but she didn't know why.

"Here you go." He lifted the bags up off the floor and handed them over to her. When his hand touched hers, she instantly felt a spark.

"Thank you." She didn't want this man to just walk away.

"Any chance I could buy you a cup of coffee to apologize?"

She hesitated only for a moment, but then realized that's exactly what she wanted. "Sure. That would be nice."

"We can walk down to the food court where there's a coffee shop."

"Perfect." She paused. "I'm Nina Marie Crane."

"Abe Smith. I'm sorry I ran into you, but I'm not sorry to have met you."

She couldn't help but laugh. "That's a pretty bad pickup line."

He grinned, showing a dimple in his left check. "I know."

They chit chatted on the walk down to the food court. Nina Marie assumed he'd buy her coffee and then they'd go on about their business, but he asked her to sit down while they enjoyed their drinks.

"So what do you do, Nina Marie?" he asked.

"I'm the CEO of a New Age tech company."

"Really? Like incense and meditation stuff?"

All the generic stereotypes always amazed her. New Age was so much more than that, and Astral Tech was so much more than New Age, but making an outsider understand what she did was always difficult. "That's a piece of it for sure and what popular culture thinks of, but it's not just that. It's a complete way of life that brings out one's own personal spiritual journey and taps into the power that an individual has in their own life."

He took a sip of his coffee as he made direct eye contact with her. This guy didn't crack any jokes or make fun of the concept. He just sat and intently watched and listened to what she had to say.

"How did you get into that?"

"It's a long story maybe for another time, but the short answer is that I was not satisfied with the way my life was going. I was looking for more and needed to take control of my life instead of it being in someone else's hands."

"Believe me, I get that."

"But that's enough about me. What about you?"

"Nothing nearly as exciting as being CEO of a big tech company. I work construction and odd jobs. So it appears that you're way out of my league." He laughed.

"That's ridiculous. I don't judge someone by their career choice." Looking only at the outside is what had gotten her in deep trouble before. She had moved beyond that.

"Really? That's not something I hear every day."

"Your career is only part of you. It doesn't define you. I care more about getting to know what makes a person tick."

He leaned forward. "I really like that approach. I'd like to know more about you. I know we've only just met, but I can't help but feel like I've known you for much longer." He picked up his cup and took another sip of his black coffee. "And yes, I guess that sounds like another awful pickup line."

She laughed again. "Maybe just a little bit."

"So what brings a powerful CEO out to the mall in the middle of the day?"

"I just needed some 'me time'. I know that probably sounds very shallow."

He shook his head. "Not at all. I imagine your job is very stressful."

"You don't know the half of it," she said.

"I'm a good listener, if there's anything you'd like to get off your chest. And since I don't know your business or any of the people involved, I can be completely objective if you need any advice."

She carefully considered Abe's offer. "I am in a high-stress position. Made even more so because of the rocky relationship I have with our chief competitor in this town."

"Wait," he said. "There's not one, but two New Age companies in this town? Isn't that weird?"

She imagined it would seem very odd to an outsider. To someone who didn't understand that Windy Ridge was the current epicenter of New Age thought ... and even more of those who followed the evil one. "Windy Ridge is a unique town. There is a special interest here in New Age ideology. My competitor, Optimism, started first. My company, Astral Tech, was formed to provide an alternative to their company."

"Well, by the brand names on your shopping bags, it looks like you're doing well, right?"

He was perceptive. "Yes, very well, but the CEO of Optimism is always trying to get one step ahead of me. You know how it is with competitors. And I, being the competitive person I am, want my company to be at the top. We got sued by them last year and ended up settling for a variety of reasons, but I still haven't let that go, you know?"

"Totally. I'm also very competitive. I hate losing. Can I ask you a weird question?"

"Sure."

"Is this New Age stuff like a religion to you?"

"Religion has so many connotations."

"Tell me about it."

"Ah, not a religious man yourself?"

"No. Religion is messy."

This man was getting better and better every minute. "Well, then, it seems like we are on the same page."

"I think there's a big hypocrisy problem with the church. Just look at that guy—that pastor who just got arrested. Did you see that? It's all over the news."

She nodded but was careful to keep her expression fixed. She couldn't give away all she knew about this. "Yes, you're right. It was a big story. I know people who have gone to that church, too."

"It's awful, those innocent people being taken advantage of. If that's what it looks like to believe in the Christian faith, then I want no part of it, that's for sure."

"What about innocent until proven guilty?" She wanted to see how he responded to that.

"Come on. I mean, I still think he should have a fair trial, and if I were on the jury, I'd try my best. But sitting here with you today, if everything I hear about in the reports are true, then he's a crooked man who deserves to go to prison for robbing those innocent people."

"I totally agree with you, and he'll get his day in court. He'll end up getting the punishment that he deserves. It has been my experience that those who most loudly proclaim the faith are those who have the most to hide."

"Sounds like you've been burned before."

All right. Now they were starting to tread in dangerous territory. She wanted to deflect the conversation, but before she could say something else her phone started ringing. "Sorry about that. It's work." She looked down and saw some messages from her assistant.

"You probably need to get back to the office, huh?"

"Unfortunately."

"I've really enjoyed this, though. Is there any way I could maybe see you again? Take you dinner?"

"I'd love that." She pulled her business card out of her purse. "My office and cell are on there."

"Great. I'll call you."

Nina Marie walked away feeling like her luck was about to change. Maybe she'd just found a good solution to her loneliness.

**

"Abe made contact with Nina Marie yesterday." Grant sat across from Olivia in her new office at BCR. "He's going to meet us here in a little bit to give us all the details, but I have some insight from our call."

She cocked her head to the side. "How did that go?"

"Abe almost thought it was too easy. His impression is that Nina Marie was really interested in him and will accept a dinner invitation."

"The more information he can get from her the better. Although, the subterfuge approach is a little troubling."

"That's how PI's have to work sometimes, Olivia. We aren't in a perfect world here. We have to take the battle to the enemy to be able to help Dan. Just keep that front and center in your mind." He didn't want her to get caught up in PI tactics. There was a larger battle waging.

"Believe me. I haven't forgotten what's at stake here—for Dan and the entire community."

He had to shift gears for a minute. "Can we just take a step back for a second? Your new office is amazing. BCR really went all out with the opening of this office."

"Yeah. The commute from Windy Ridge isn't even that bad. Since they decided not to go into the heart of downtown Chicago, they were willing to be further out and that's how we got such beautiful and spacious office space."

Grant looked out the huge window and could see the Chicago skyline. The BCR office made his look simple by comparison. But BCR was a top global law firm, and he was basically a two-man plaintiff's firm operation. They weren't even in the same league.

From the fancy artwork hanging on the walls to the plush furniture, everything about the BCR office screamed money. He'd specifically taken a different path. Although right now, his and

Olivia's worlds intersected, he wasn't under any delusion that their firms were on par.

"What's even better than the cushy office are all the resources we have at our disposal. I spoke with Chet again and briefed him on the current state of the case. He's all in as far as getting me whatever we need to defend this thing. So we should spare no expense."

"Got it. I know we're still in the process of trying to develop the defense—and get evidence to substantiate that Dan was framed, but can we also start thinking about themes?"

"Yes, but I have to say, that will depend somewhat on what the investigation turns up. I have to keep reminding myself, though, that this is a criminal case not a civil one. As the defense, we don't have to prove Dan's innocence. The burden of proof is on the prosecution to prove beyond a reasonable doubt all the elements to the embezzlement claim."

"Right, because our system in America is innocent until proven guilty, but what about the tax fraud allegations?"

"We have to start with embezzlement. If we win on that claim, then there's no tax fraud because he wouldn't have had the money and withheld it from his tax returns."

"True. We need to be able to present a plausible alternate explanation for all of this."

"I think we have to be more direct with the jury than that. We have to push for it being a frame job from the start. There is no innocent reason for that money being taken out of the church account and put into Dan's accounts. We need to be able to show that he didn't move the money. Someone else moved that money and subsequently spent the money."

"If this was a civil case, then you'd depose Beverly, but the criminal rules are different. I think the only way you'd be able to depose her is if you could demonstrate that the deposition would be needed to preserve testimony, but I don't think you have that ground here. She's going to be around for trial."

"Yeah, I agree with you. She's my prime suspect. I plan to try to break her. If I can't do that in a deposition, then it will just have to be when she takes the stand."

He smiled. This was the Olivia he knew.

"Why're you smiling?"

"Because the old bulldog trial lawyer is back. I like seeing you in your zone."

"Much better than the woe is me look, huh? I guess we all have moments of weakness, but right now I'm one hundred percent focused on proving Dan's innocence. I've been doing a lot of thinking after our talk the other day, and you were really right. About everything. The spiritual battle is taking place all around us, but my job, first and foremost, is to advocate for Dan in the criminal case against him."

"I think that's the best course of action."

"But I still can't turn a blind eye to everything that is going on at church. I want to try to get through to Chris. Dan was much more sympathetic to Chris's position than I am."

"Once again, though, you win the case, you clear Dan's name, then people will return to the church."

"And what if there has been too much damage in the meantime?"

"I'm not saying to stick your head in the sand but to realize there are some things that are out of your control."

"But they are not out of God's control."

"I honestly don't know how you do it, Olivia. Always so steadfast, regardless of the circumstances."

"If I lose my faith, Grant, then I lose everything."

And in those words, he realized how much of a gulf there still was between the two of them. He didn't know if he'd ever have that kind of unrelenting faith.

"You look like you're deep in thought."

"Just thinking that I'm a long way from you in the faith department."

"We've had this discussion before. You'll come to grow into your faith, Grant. Just give it time and put in the effort."

"I'm trying. This whole thing feels like it has set me back a bit though."

"Setbacks are normal. That's no need to question everything or beat yourself up over it. Talk to me, Grant. Tell me what's really bothering you."

He ran his hand through his hair and wondered how he could try to explain himself to her. To a woman that never questioned her beliefs, but then he realized that she had understood him from the start and listened to him when he was a total skeptic. "My mind is all jumbled up. Right when I felt like I started to gain my footing, I feel like the rug has been pulled out from under me."

"Is it the fact that Dan was accused of this or that you have doubts about his innocence?"

"I don't even know. At first I was just caught completely off guard by the allegations. I've looked up to Dan since I got to know him. So it was a real kick to the gut to have this happen."

She stood up and walked around the desk. Then she took his hand and pulled him up out of his seat. "You're stronger than your realize, Grant. Don't let doubt and fears overtake you at this point. That's how the devil works. His schemes are intricate and well-played, but you have truth and the power of God on your side. I know this has all been so much to take in, but the biggest travesty of all would be if you step away from God because of it. That would destroy Dan. And even more than that…"

"What?" He waited a few seconds for her to respond.

"It would destroy me."

It felt like something wrapped its hands around his heart and squeezed as he processed her words. She did care about him—he knew that, but did it go beyond her desire to bring him to God? "Olivia, don't say things like that. I would never want to hurt you." He grabbed onto her waist and pulled her closer to him.

She looked up at him with her beautiful brown eyes, and he could no longer think of anything else to do but the one thing he'd wanted to do since the moment he first met her.

He leaned down and pressed his lips firmly against hers. This wasn't a simple peck. No, if he was going to make this leap, he wanted her to know that he had real feelings for her that went beyond the strong friendship they'd forged.

There was fear streaking through him—a fear of rejection, that she would push him back and say that she cared for him, but only as a friend. But it never happened.

She kissed him back just as fervently, her lips warm and soft against his. She wrapped her arms around his neck, and then he understood just how far he had fallen. He was invested like he'd never been with another woman before.

When he ended the kiss and pulled back from her, she was smiling.

"I'm glad you're smiling and not hauling off to punch me in the face for overstepping."

She laughed. "I just have one question."

"Okay." He held his breath waiting for her to ask.

"What took you so long?"

CHAPTER EIGHT

S he looked into Grant's blue eyes and smiled. Her heart fluttered and she waited for him to speak.

"Believe me, Olivia. I've wanted to kiss you for a very long time, but I've been worried about how you would react. Or whether it will ever be the right time for us given all the obstacles that keep popping up."

She took his hands in hers. "You're right. It's never going to seem like the right time, and we could always make excuses, but I think there's something special between us. Something that I couldn't deny even if I wanted to."

"But it sounds like you don't want to deny it?"

"No, but we still need to take it slow. I'm probably different from most of the women you've dated."

He smiled. "You are completely different, but in the best possible ways."

"Thanks, but I'm not so naïve as to realize that you probably have a different set of expectations for a relationship."

He shook his head. "Olivia, I know where you're going with this, and you should know I'm committed to taking things at whatever speed you want. Even if that means there's no speed at all."

Her heart opened up to this man. They'd already experienced things together that most people never would, but there was so much more to go on their journey together. "Thank you for that," she said with a brief hug. However, before he could reply, she pulled away slightly leaving her hands in his while looking up and saying, "But we also can't let what is happening between us affect our work."

"I agree one hundred percent." He squeezed her hands.

Her office phone rang, and she reached over to pick it up. Her assistant told her that Abe had arrived. "Please bring him back to my office." She placed the phone back down.

She looked at Grant. "Abe is here."

"I can't wait to hear all about his meeting with Nina Marie."

A couple of minutes later, Abe was escorted into her office by her assistant. He greeted them both with pleasantries and handshakes.

"Good to see you again, Abe," she said. "Please have a seat and make yourself at home."

"This is an impressive office," he said.

"Thanks. It's all brand new. My firm is very excited about starting a branch in Chicago." She sized up the man sitting in front of her. He was undoubtedly handsome—jet black hair, dark eyes, a hint of stubble. But she didn't have an ounce of attraction to him. Her heart was held by the man beside him. She had to wonder, though, what Nina Marie would think of Abe Perez. Maybe she was about to find out.

"So we're anxious to hear how everything went with Nina Marie," Grant said.

"Well, I tracked her from her office to the mall where she went on quite the midday shopping spree. I ran into her and managed to talk her into having coffee with me."

Ah-ha. Her initial instinct was right. Nina Marie would've never had coffee with the guy unless she had some level of interest. "What did you learn?"

"I tried to ask as many questions as possible without tipping her off. She clearly believes in her company and the work that they do. She has a big hang-up about Christianity. She didn't go into details, but someone who was a Christian hurt her before. I think she is using her current work as a way to combat those old feelings."

"Did you bring up Dan?" she asked.

"Yeah, and she was quite happy about his arrest. Like I said, I couldn't pry too much, but I think I laid the groundwork to be able to find out more. I'm going to call and ask her to dinner."

"And if she says no?" she asked.

Abe smiled. "I don't think that's going to happen."

"So you laid on the Perez charm?" Grant asked.

Abe laughed. "I tried my best. Told her I was in the construction business. I didn't want her to think I was a corporate guy. I've got a cover built up if she decides to try to track me down and do some research."

"Your cover is all part of your PI business?" she asked, intrigued by it all.

"Yeah. I have a couple of different aliases and businesses set up in case I need them. I use the same first name but different last names. So she thinks I'm Abe Smith."

"She didn't try to convince you to get exposed to her New Age beliefs, did she?" Grant asked.

"No. She wasn't pushing it at all, but I'm sure she'd tell me more if I seemed interested. I tried to set that up by telling her that I was skeptical of Christianity. I opened the door, and she walked right through it."

Olivia didn't want to freak out Abe, but she also needed to go a little deeper into the situation than she'd done at their first meeting. It wasn't fair to keep him in the dark if he was going down this road. "Abe, given that you're going to be spending more time with Nina Marie, I think I need to tell you something else."

"What?" Abe asked.

She looked over at Grant, but he didn't say a word. "Nina Marie believes she has spirituals powers."

"Like a witch?"

"Something like that, yeah."

"You don't really believe in all of this New Age stuff, do you?"

"These groups use New Age as a cover for even more sinister activities," Grant said.

"You don't think it's all a gimmick to try to get people to buy all of their products?" Abe asked.

"Grant is right, Abe. It's a lot more than some of the trendy New Age beliefs that are in pop culture. These groups go way beyond that. I'm a believer in the word of God. So I do believe there are forces of evil at work in this world. I also have seen Nina Marie in her element, and it's not pretty. So I couldn't let you go in without being prepared for that."

Abe turned his attention to Grant. "And what's your take on all of this?"

"I used to be a skeptic—a complete atheist. But I lived through some really scary experiences last year during the trial I told you about between the two companies, and I found God through that process."

"Wow," Abe said. "The two of you are really deep into all of this." He rubbed his chin and looked at her and then back at Grant.

"We aren't trying to push any of this on you," Olivia said. "I just wanted you to know all that is at work here—especially from Nina Marie's side, and not knowing what your beliefs are, I wanted to put it all out there."

"I grew up in the church. My family is from Venezuela, so religion was a big part of my upbringing. My grandmother spoke of spiritual warfare, but I never took any of that too literally. I thought it was all just cultural traditions passed down in my family."

Relief flooded through her. At least Abe would have some frame of reference for all of this.

"Well, my friend," Grant said. "You may just get to experience it firsthand now, depending on how this case goes. Are you okay with that?"

"Like I told you both before, I will be fine, and I can definitely handle a delusional woman."

"We didn't want you to be caught off guard," Grant said.

"And I do believe in God, don't get me wrong. Although for the past few years, I haven't been an active churchgoer for a variety of reasons."

That had her antenna going up. What was Abe's role going to be in all of this? Maybe his involvement was going to serve a greater purpose.

"But all of this New Age stuff is far out there for me," Abe said.

She could sense he was still skeptical about Nina Marie's abilities, but now he would at least have be prepared in case something does happen. She did think it interesting that he was able to put on a front for Nina Marie. Usually she was quite good at ferreting out someone's beliefs. "I get that you may not buy into all of this, but I urge you to keep your guard up. Stay in character with her. Because she's very attuned to where people's religious feelings lie, and that could put you in jeopardy."

"I've got this, you two. Don't worry about me. Focus on developing your legal case. In addition to the angle with Nina Marie, I've started digging into the electronic paper trail on the financial side."

Her heartbeat sped up at the mention of that. "And?"

"So far everything looks like a clean transfer from the church account to a savings account in Dan's name. Then the trail gets dicey because the money is transferred to an offshore bank account. I'm having a hard time getting information on that account given all the privacy and international issues, but there's no evidence that Dan is tied to it. It still looks bad though."

"Dan says he didn't even monitor that savings account. He set it up years ago, but it wasn't his primary account so he didn't check it."

"It's true the account in question isn't his primary one, but as it stands now, the evidence shows the transfers being made from the church to him and then large sums being transferred offshore. I'm going to try to find out where the money went, because that is the key question. Although I have to tell you, the whole 'I never monitored my account' thing may not be too convincing to a jury. So just putting that thought out there for you to chew on."

"I'll try to get more details from Dan on why that was exactly," she said. There had to be a good reason, but Abe brought up a great point. They needed to be able to present a logical story to the jury. One that would make sense to the average person. She wrote herself a note to discuss these details with Dan at their next meeting.

"I'm also looking into Beverly Jenkins as you requested. So far the initial background check came up entirely boring," Abe said. "Not a single red flag of any type. But I'll keep working."

"Thanks for all your work on this," she said.

"You're more than welcome. Guess I'll hit the road, unless you need anything else?"

"I think I'm good. Grant, anything from you?"

"Nope. Just keep us posted on how it goes with Nina Marie."

"Of course. I'll try to get the dinner set up as soon as possible. I didn't want to come on too strong, but I realize time is of the essence here." He walked out of the office, leaving her alone with Grant.

"What do you think?" she asked him.

"I don't think he really has any idea just what Nina Marie is capable of. But at this point we have the element of surprise. She's interested in him romantically and doesn't see him as a threat."

"Let's hope he's good enough to keep her thinking that way."

**

As Tony's GPS spouted out the notice that he had arrived at his destination, he looked over and blew out a breath. "Wow," he said out loud as he looked at the house.

As he turned into the long driveway, he couldn't believe it. There was a valet service. He knew Layton had money, but he had no idea it was at this level. Making these types of connections could be vital to his career, so he was glad he hadn't blown off this opportunity.

He pulled up to where the valet stood and provided him with the key. His grey Durango was out of place amongst the luxury brands, but he had to remind himself that he was a prosecutor. No one expected him to be riding around in a Maserati.

He walked up to the door and rang the bell. A moment later, he was greeted by a smiling Layton.

"Come on in, my friend. Welcome to my home."

"Layton, I'm left speechless by your home." He stepped into the foyer and had to make sure his jaw didn't drop. Huge chandeliers hung overhead and fine art adorned the walls.

"Thank you. I take a lot of pride in this place. Come with me and I'll introduce you to everyone."

He wanted to make the best first impression possible, so he followed Layton down the hall and into a big room where people were sitting on the large couch or other chairs. Many of them had drinks in their hands. The mood seemed jovial as laughter filled the air.

"Everyone," Layton said. "I'd like to introduce you to Deputy Assistant District Attorney Tony Sampson—our newest Board member."

Tony didn't recognize anyone else in the room except Judge Louise Martinique. He greeted each person and tried to commit their names and faces to memory.

When he came to Louise, he smiled. "So nice to see you again, Judge Martinique."

"The feeling is likewise, and, please, call me Louise. We're not in court here. I'm going to love having another lawyer on the board with me."

He met a couple other men, including a doctor and a marketing executive.

Then he turned his attention to the final person. A gorgeous blonde with long curly hair.

"I'm Morena Isley." Her bright blue eyes locked onto his.

"Very nice to meet you, Morena. What a unique name."

"Thank you. I work on the business side at Optimism and also at the Indigo bookstore. Are you familiar with it?"

"I've seen it, but I don't think I've ever visited it."

"You should come in sometime and see what we have to offer."

"I'll have to do that." If it meant seeing Morena again, then he'd certainly be making a trip to the bookstore.

"Since we're all here, why don't we move into the den and get started with the business on our agenda," Layton said. "Then we can enjoy dinner afterwards."

Tony followed the group down the hall and into another room that had a large circular oak table. He also noticed the high-tech audiovisual equipment. It was like Layton's house had everything you could ever need. Maybe one day he'd be able to afford something like this, but that would require a lot of moving pieces falling into place.

There were documents placed out at each seat around the table. He took a seat in between Louise and the marketing exec. Even though he wanted to sit by Morena, he needed to play it cool. This wasn't about a romantic entanglement. He had a job to do here and planned to take this position seriously.

"Okay, everyone," Layton said. "The first item of business. The final preparation for our annual charity ball."

Tony listened carefully and took copious notes as they worked their way through the agenda. After watching the meeting unfold, it was clear to him who the power players were. Layton was at the top of the food chain and no one else was close, but Layton did seem to rely on Morena a lot for most of the details and logistics.

"There's one final item that isn't on the agenda, but I did want to discuss," Layton said. "We're currently seeing an upswing, a renewed interest in our organization, and what we're finding is when we ask these new members about why they sought us out, there is a common theme. A high dissatisfaction rate with their current place of worship."

Uh, oh. That got his attention.

"There's even more to it than that," Morena said. "We seem to be getting a chunk of new members from Windy Ridge Community Church. We need to make sure these people are especially made to feel welcome after all they've been through lately."

"I may need to excuse myself from this part of the conversation," Tony said. The fact a sitting judge was watching his every move made him even more cautious. He didn't want to give the appearance of any sort of conflict of interest.

Layton held up his hand. "Tony's right. We don't want to put him in any awkward position given he is the prosecutor on the Dan Light case. So why don't we just stop this direction of the conversation and simply point out that we are getting new members, and we want to form a welcoming committee to

95

introduce them into our organization." Layton looked over at him. "And Tony, I hope that you'll also consider joining our organization. Being on the board is one thing, but we'd also like to invite you into the group. That's probably a discussion for another time, but I'd love for you to learn more about our spiritual side. I'm sure Morena would be happy to talk to you one-on-one about that."

Now that was an idea he could get behind. "That would be great, and I appreciate your sensitivity to my current position."

"On that note, why don't we adjourn and go enjoy dinner? It's going to be out of this world."

Tony got up out of his chair, and Morena headed his way. She pulled out her card and gave it to him.

"Call me and we can set up a time to meet and talk about the organization some more."

"Perfect." He still wasn't sold on this whole New Age thing, but if it meant spending more time with the beautiful blonde, he was all in.

**

Nina Marie had changed clothes about five times. Since when was she so nervous about going on a date? Ever since she had met Abe Smith she couldn't stop thinking about him. And when he'd called and asked her to dinner she tried to act nonchalant but, on the inside, her stomach was doing cartwheels.

She needed to keep herself in check, though. She could go out with this man and enjoy his company, but what she absolutely couldn't do is actually develop any sort of true feelings for him.

As she threw off the dress and pulled on another one, she finally was settled on her outfit. Now all she needed was some jewelry to finish off the look.

Abe had suggested dinner at a nice restaurant called Vine. She'd done her research after they'd met at the mall. He'd been a little modest in his description of his work. He'd made it seem like he was a construction worker, when really it appeared like he had his own construction company. But all of that was a bonus in her book. It was refreshing that he wasn't full of himself. She'd dealt with enough egotistical men in her life.

Abe seemed pretty traditional and had asked if he could pick her up from her house. She'd been a bit unsure about that, but in the end, she'd decided to say yes. She looked down at her favorite watch and saw that he should be arriving any minute.

Taking one more look at herself in the mirror, she was satisfied with her decision—the simple, yet elegant, black dress seemed like the perfect choice. She smoothed down her hair and adjusted her glasses. Then she applied some coral lipstick she knew went well with her hair and skin tone.

The doorbell rang, and she was impressed that he was right on time. That was already a point in his favor.

She opened the door, and her breath caught when she saw him on the other side. He wore khakis and a navy blue dress shirt. He still sported the stubble on his chin, which fit him perfectly.

"You look amazing," he said. Then he handed her over a bouquet of colorful pink, purple, and yellow tulips and carnations. "These are for you."

"Thank you so much." This man was a real gentleman, and she loved that he didn't bring roses. The mixed bouquet was much more to her liking.

"You have a nice place here."

"Thanks. I did all the interior design myself. Let me put these in some water, and then we can get going."

"No rush."

"Feel free to look around. I'll be right back." She walked toward the kitchen to get a vase and some water.

She pulled out her favorite pink crystal vase from the cabinet and arranged the flowers. As she looked at them, she realized that she was smiling widely. The night was off to a wonderful start.

"Abe, I'm ready." She walked out of the kitchen and found him in her living room staring at one of her paintings.

"Do you like it?" she asked.

"Yes. It's so unusual."

"You're looking at the painter."

"You did this?" he asked.

"I did."

"You really have a special talent. I can't ever imagine being able to create something so beautiful."

"You build things though. It's a different type of beauty, and speaking of that, why didn't you tell me you actually owned your own construction company?"

He grinned. "I see you've been checking up on me."

"Well, I did just randomly meet you in the mall. I don't normally take people at face value."

"That's actually good. There are a lot of psychos out there."

She nodded. "I know it."

By the time they were having dessert two hours later, Nina Marie couldn't remember laughing so much in one night. Abe was not only incredibly handsome, but he had a killer sense of humor.

"So tell me more about this whole New Age thing."

"You really want to know more? Or are you just being polite?" She thought that maybe he was trying to act interested because he could tell how much of a big part of her life it was.

"I'm being serious. I did some research on the Internet after we talked."

"You did?" She was impressed he would take the time to do that.

"Yeah. But there was so much out there, I couldn't really make heads or tails of it, and then I started to wonder what distinguishes your company from your competitor."

"That's a good question. We're definitely more on the cutting edge on the tech side. I don't want you to take this the wrong way, but the man who runs Optimism is pure evil."

"Evil?"

"Yes. He actively seeks out the dark side."

"Are you talking about the devil and demons?"

"Exactly."

He leaned in. "Do you believe in all of that?"

She thought about how honest she should be. She liked him. It would be easier to tell him she didn't believe. But she didn't plan on having a one-night stand with this guy. She wanted something a bit more, so she decided to put her cards on the table and see how he reacted. "I actually do believe in the entire spiritual realm. The realm of the unseen."

His eyes widened. "I see."

"Have I completely scared you off now?"

He shook his head. "Not even close. But I'd like to understand your role in all of this. I already know how you feel about Christianity, but I also can't imagine that you're into the dark side either. You're much too nice for that."

If only he knew. "I guess that's a compliment."

"Of course. You don't seem to have an evil bone in your body."

She sucked in a breath and tried to compose herself. How was this man seeing a completely different person than who she thought she was? "I'm a lot more complicated than you might think." *If only you knew the truth.*

"I'm used to dealing with complicated. I'm sorry if I shouldn't have brought that up."

"You have no reason to apologize. I've had a wonderful time tonight." Maybe it was best to try to short circuit this before things got too strange.

"A nice enough time to do it again sometime?"

"Yes. I'd like that." Before she had a chance to overthink it, she decided to ask him. "Also, I have this charity event. It's actually an event hosted by the CEO of Optimism. It's a black tie type thing—you'd probably hate it, but…"

"I'd love to go with you."

"Really?"

"Yes. When is it?"

"This weekend."

"Sounds perfect."

As he smiled back at her, she hoped that she wouldn't regret inviting him to the charity gala—and into her life.

CHAPTER NINE

"Thanks for taking the time to meet with me, Beverly," Olivia said. She sat on the small beige couch in Beverly Jenkins's living room with a cup of tea in her hand.

The church bookkeeper had a small but cozy home that was only minutes from the church. Beverly didn't have to meet with her, especially since Beverly knew she was defending Dan. But the fact she'd agreed to the meeting made Olivia feel a little better.

"Of course, of course. Anything I can do to help, I'll do it. I already feel so upset about this whole thing. It's been really difficult for me, as I'm assuming you could imagine."

Olivia looked at the fifty-plus-year-old woman. She knew that Beverly used to be a CPA but retired early to work at the church. Besides that, she didn't know much else about her.

"You've probably figured out by now that you're going to have to be a witness in Dan's trial."

She watched as Beverly clenched her fist around the floral coffee cup. "I have figured it, but that doesn't mean I like it. I don't think anyone wants to be put on the witness stand and questioned, and certainly not given the situation here. If there was another way, I'd love to know about it."

"Unfortunately, I think you're stuck as far as being a witness. As Dan's defense attorney it's my job to figure out whether you'll be part of our defense—or alternatively whether you're actually going to be someone the prosecution will rely on. So having this discussion will help me make that decision. All I ask that is that you're honest. I can take the truth, but I need to know what you believe happened."

Beverly nodded. "That makes sense."

Olivia had decided to have this informal and hopefully friendly meeting before things got much more contentious at trial. She wanted to get a read on Beverly and what all it is she would say.

"I knew you'd want to talk. It's just a difficult thing to discuss, but I guess that it has to happen." She set down her cup.

"Let's take it slow. Why don't you start out by telling me why you went to the police instead of going to Dan first?"

"I'm so sorry, Olivia. This is all my fault."

"Why do you say that?"

"I found some discrepancies in the accounting. Once I noticed something was off, I started digging. Then I kept digging deeper and deeper. Until..." A big tear fell down her cheek.

Olivia couldn't help herself and reached out to pat Beverly's hand. This woman seemed to be really hurting over all of this. "What is it, Beverly? You can tell me. Remember, honesty is all I'm asking for. I'm not going to judge you or your actions. I'm just trying to get to down to the bottom of all of this."

"There was an account money was being funneled into, and when I found that out, I was going to go to Pastor Dan. But once I was able to get details on the account, then I realized that he was somehow involved. I had to go to the police."

As the last words came out of her mouth, the single tear turned into full out bawling.

"Beverly, just take a deep breath. A few of them actually."

Beverly did as instructed. Olivia was patient with her and even pulled out some tissues from her purse and offered them to Beverly, who dried her eyes, trying to compose herself.

"Okay, Beverly. How're you feeling? Can we go on?"

"Yes. I'm sorry about that. It just comes flooding back to me when I talk about it like this."

"No problem. It's a tough situation we're all in right now, but I have to ask you this. Is there any way you could've been mistaken? Could the money have accidentally been transferred to one of Dan's accounts?"

She shook her head. "Maybe if it was a one-time error, but I am very careful. Olivia, this paper trail is over a year long. You can't replicate mistakes like that, and I gave the information I had to the police. I'm not privy to the details of their investigation."

"So you didn't go to Dan because you thought he was guilty?" She needed to hear Beverly's answer to this.

Her eyes welled up again. "I was so afraid that he was. With his wife's awful illness, I thought maybe he just broke down and thought he needed the money to pay the bills. I didn't think he was out buying sports cars or anything like that, but sometimes in desperate times, people do bad things—even if they're God-fearing people. That's what I believe happened here. If you want my honest answer, that's what it is. So, yes, I do think Dan is guilty, but I still think the man deserves a fair trial. If I'm on the stand though, and I raise my hand and swear on the Bible to tell the truth, then I'll tell it just like I'm telling you now. As his defense attorney, I'd imagine you'd not want me to speak like that, but I hope you understand that I have to do what's right. I know you can appreciate the predicament I'm in right now."

"I do appreciate it, and I am glad that we got to have this talk. I can't imagine how hard it was for you to go through all of this, but I have to tell you that I'm going to do everything in my power to try to prove that Dan is innocent."

"Olivia, if you can do that, then God really would've worked a miracle."

As she looked into Beverly's eyes, she wondered if there was any way that this woman was lying. That she was actually guilty. But even if she thought that before, it would be really difficult to make a jury think this woman was somehow involved. Olivia's job had just gotten a lot harder.

**

Dan looked forward to his meeting with Olivia. He had so much to tell her about the work he'd been doing in prison. Yes, he

102

still dealt with a couple of inmates who gave him a hard time, but he'd been able to lead a few others to Christ just by talking and sharing his testimony.

The guard led him to the small holding room where Olivia was. Dan smiled when he saw her.

"It's good to see you again," he said.

"How're you doing?"

"Better than I ever expected I would be. My ministry is spreading throughout this prison. I have guys coming up to me during rec time. I never in my wildest thoughts could have imagined that God would use this experience in this way."

"I'm so glad."

"And how are you doing?" he asked. She seemed tense, and he had to think that something more was going on.

"I'm all right, but I do have some additional questions for you."

"Whatever you need. I've got nothing to hide."

"I want to talk about this bank account of yours where the money was funneled into. One of the big questions that keeps coming up is how could you have not known what was going on in this account? And why wouldn't you have been using it?"

This was actually a painful spot for him, but Olivia deserved to know the truth.

"Whatever it is, Dan, you can confide in me. Remember we have attorney-client privilege."

His stomach sank. She actually was thinking that what he was about to tell her was going to implicate him. "It's not what you're thinking. I opened that bank account years ago. It was supposed to be our child's college fund and savings account."

"Your child?"

"We were having trouble conceiving. When my wife finally was able to get pregnant, we were so excited." Even talking about it years later made his heart ache. "She miscarried, and we were never able to conceive again."

Olivia's eyes were full of fresh tears. "I'm so sorry, Dan. I had no idea."

"We were very private about the whole thing."

"So the bank account?"

"I didn't have the heart to close it, but I also didn't ever mess with it after that. So I had no reason to be looking at the account activity because, in my mind, there was none. I've been doing a lot of thinking, and all I can come up with is that someone accessed the account and made the transfers."

"They not only put the money into your account, but then moved the money to an offshore account that we haven't been able to associate with a person yet."

"It's not me."

"We don't have any proof linking you to the offshore account, but the fact that the initial transfer was to an account in your name is the controlling fact for them to prove embezzlement. I spoke with Beverly yesterday."

"I already told you that she's innocent."

"Why do you have such unquestioning faith in her?"

"She's been a faithful member of the church since she was a child. There's no way she's a criminal."

"I know you don't want to go down that road, but it's my job to examine everything, and to provide reasonable doubt. She had the access and the ability, which means I have to consider her. Given her background in accounting, she makes a more likely suspect. But I also have to look into Chris as well."

"I hate that you're investigating my people."

"Dan, the most likely scenario is that one of them is guilty. That they framed you and smeared your good name. I need to ferret out the criminal and make sure they are the one who is punished for their crimes—not you."

Deep in his gut, he knew Olivia was right. "It just breaks my heart to think of one of them doing that to me, to the church, you know?"

She nodded. "I do. Which is why I'm going to work as hard as I can to find out the truth."

"Have you heard anything from Layton or Nina Marie?"

"No. But I still have suspicions that they had to play some role in all of this. We're working with a private investigator. I'm hoping that he can connect some of these dots."

"What if Layton or one his people hacked into the systems to set me up? And neither Beverly or Chris had anything to do with it?"

"I guess that's theoretically possible, although that would be pretty difficult. But with those guys, you can't rule anything out. I'll have our investigator work that angle, too."

"Regardless, there had to be some tampering happen because someone got into my account."

"True. We'll have to see how good they were at covering their electronic tracks." She reached out and touched his arm. "I told you before and I'll tell you again. I'm going to clear your name, Dan."

"And I appreciate all you're doing for me. Is Grant doing any better?"

"I think so. It's been a whirlwind for him ever since he met me." She laughed. "Seriously, though, I just tell him to take it one step at a time. He keeps wondering why he doesn't have unwavering faith, and I explain that it has to be built and cultivated over time."

"He's fortunate to have you in his life. We're all very fortunate. You're such a blessing, Olivia. God continues to use you in amazing ways."

"And you are being used for God's glory even in this prison."

"Yes. Thank the Lord for what he's doing here."

"I'll be in touch."

"Let's pray before you leave." As he led the two of them in prayer, he knew the battle was raging all around them, but the Lord was providing them with much needed protection.

**

Micah and Ben looked down on Olivia and Dan as they prayed.

"You know Layton thought he'd prevail by putting Dan in prison, but what he didn't realize was that this is only making Dan stronger," Ben said.

"I agree with you, and it's strengthening Olivia, too, and whether Grant realizes it, he is growing stronger through all of this, even with the questions that plague him."

"Do you think Olivia will realize that Beverly is behind this and working with Layton?"

"I do. Especially now that Abe is on the case. We have to stick close to Abe, though. If Nina Marie realizes that she is being played, it could get really ugly."

"This is an opportunity for Abe to reconnect with his faith," Micah said. "He's been withdrawn for years."

"And he's going to stay that way," a deep voice said.

Micah turned and saw they had unwelcome visitors. Othan and Kobal faced off against them.

"Why are you here, Othan? Be gone from this place," Ben said.

Othan laughed. "This is a prison. Do you realize what type of stronghold this is for us? You're the ones who need to leave."

"Well, you haven't been paying attention then, because Dan is transforming lives."

Othan slapped Kobal hard and he let out a scream. "You were supposed to be monitoring this situation closely, you fool."

Kobal stood in silence and let Othan continue to berate him. This was demon infighting that Ben and Micah had no interest in taking part in.

Micah looked over at Ben who nodded. They'd leave for now and let the two demons take their losses out on each other. Tomorrow was another day in fighting the good fight.

**

Stacey sat in her office at Optimism with the crystals laid out in front of her and her new book that classified all the spiritual elements to each type of crystal. Her first order of business was to categorize all of the crystals and learn about each one.

Morena had told her this was going to be an important part of her training in New Age spirituality. Before she opened the book though her thoughts went back to Nina Marie's warning words. She'd largely tried not to think about their awkward conversation at Latte, but there was still something nagging at her about what Nina Marie said.

Nina Marie was more powerful than Morena, but Morena was still playing a critical role in her training and providing her with a strong female role model. Layton had been so good to her, and it was hard for her to imagine being disloyal and asking for Nina Marie to mentor her.

She'd just go on with business as usual and try to forget that Nina Marie ever brought up the topic. She was doing perfectly well with what she had, and she knew that she had even more potential to unmask.

As she surveyed the chart of crystals, she saw that each crystal listed had a picture and a corresponding description. She was immediately drawn to the clear quartz stone. The description said that this stone had psychic and mediumship qualities. That piqued her interest because one area she wanted to learn and grow in was psychic connection.

She was also intrigued by the bright blue color of the lapis lazuli. She picked up the stone and immediately felt a connection to it. Reading the description it said this stone had a lot of different functions, including healing and increased spiritual enlightenment.

"Hey there."

She looked up and saw Morena standing at her office door.

"I see you've started your work on the stones," Morena said.

"Yes, and I'm already fascinated." She held up the lapis lazuli. "Isn't this striking?"

"Yes. Lapis lazuli is one of my favorites, as well. You'll get to know each type of stone and what they can be used for. Adding this skill set to your repertoire is going to open you up to a whole new level of spirituality."

"I'm going to jump in. No holding back. You've taught me enough to know that."

"That's my girl. But I actually didn't drop by about the crystals, even though I'm happy you're working on that."

"What's up then?"

"Just wanted to check in and make sure you were coming to the charity gala."

"Yes, and I'm so excited because of that new gown we bought last month. I thought it would be perfect."

"Absolutely. It is the dressiest event of the year. I'll let you borrow some of my jewelry, too. Layton will want to show you off to everyone. The up-and-coming star of Optimism."

She felt her cheeks redden. "That might be a bit of an overstatement."

"Stace, I don't know how many more times we have to tell you how special you are before you start to realize it." Morena walked over and put her hand on her shoulder and squeezed. "You're the future of this organization."

Nina Marie's words of warning echoed in her head, and she couldn't help but ask. "You really think Layton wants me to become so powerful? It's not like he's on the way out anytime soon."

Morena quirked an eyebrow. "What in the world makes you say that? Your increase in power is never at Layton's expense. He understands that very well. You're his prodigy, Stace. Your success is a positive reflection on him. So don't even let negative thoughts like that creep in."

"I'm sorry."

"There is no reason to apologize. You're highly valued around here, and I never want you to question your place at Optimism."

"I don't want to let you or Layton down."

"Talk to me, Stace. Where is all of this coming from?"

She certainly couldn't tell her that Nina Marie had sewn seeds of doubt in her mind. But where was all of this coming from? Her own insecurities. "I think maybe sometimes I just wonder if I really fit in."

"Optimism is your home. You fit in here and you add to our organization. It wouldn't be the same if you weren't here. So don't ever doubt your importance, and if there's anything that I can be doing better to make you more comfortable, please let me know."

She felt tears fill her eyes. "Morena, you're so nice to me. I don't deserve your friendship."

"Come here." Morena pulled her up out of her seat and gave her a big hug. "No more doubts for you, and we're going to have a fabulous time tomorrow night. So make sure to bring your A game."

She felt much better after having that talk. Nina Marie was just jealous that she didn't have people in her life like Layton and

Morena. She wouldn't think any more about it. She had crystals to learn.

**

Nina Marie waited anxiously for Abe to arrive. She'd had a lot of second thoughts about inviting him to the Optimism charity gala, but there was also a part of her that wanted to see Layton's face when he saw who she had on her arm.

It had been over between her and Layton for a long time, but the wounds were still fresh, especially after he'd tried to take his ultimate revenge on her. She'd gotten the better of the breakup, though and she planned to keep it that way. Layton couldn't stand to have a strong woman take charge and dominate the relationship. It was one of the many reasons why they would've never worked out.

She'd gone all out this evening and was wearing a gold beaded floor-length gown that cost a fortune. When she answered her door and saw Abe on the other side in a signature black tux, the butterflies in her stomach took flight.

His eyes locked onto hers. "Wow, you are absolutely stunning."

"Thanks. This is a get-all-decked-out type of event. Sorry to have pushed you into wearing a tux, but that's the protocol, and you look so handsome that I'm glad I forced the issue."

He had asked her if he could wear a suit, but she'd insisted on a tux. And boy, was she glad that she had. He looked absolutely ravishing. Her goal of making Layton jealous was sure to be reached tonight.

"I feel a little bit out of my element, but I get that these charity things are all about rich people getting together, boozing it up, and making bids. The only problem with that, for me, is that I'm not rich and I don't drink." He laughed.

"Really?"

"Yeah. I'm a go-all-in type of guy, so I decided early in life that drinking probably wasn't going to go well with my personality."

"I can totally appreciate that." She liked that he had self-control. It was a rare quality these days. "Hopefully you won't be

109

completely miserable tonight. The upside is that they do have excellent food as well, not just the booze."

"I'm sure I'll have a great time since I'll be with you." He flashed her a dazzling smile.

"Then let's get out of here."

He drove them to the Hudson Art Gallery where the gala was being held. The gallery was one of the hot spots in town to hold events like this. If there's one thing she could say about Layton it's that he would not pinch pennies on something like this. Only the best for the Optimism charity event.

"How many people are going to be here?" Abe pulled his Jeep toward the front of the building while making subtle eye contact with the valet, who looked to be quite busy.

"A few hundred, but all the movers and shakers in town will be there. I'll be able to introduce you around. You never know what type of business contacts you could make."

"That'd be great, but I'm not trying to drum up business tonight. I'd just like to enjoy myself and spend some time with you."

"Well, that can definitely be arranged."

The valet opened the car door for her, and she waited for Abe to join. He linked his arm into hers and escorted her to the front entrance of the gallery.

"You seem taller tonight," he said.

"Very high heels. The length of this dress demands it."

They walked into the gallery, and she couldn't have been more proud to have Abe on her arm. The party was already in full swing, and she recognized many of the people in the room. She wasn't a natural socializer like Layton, but she'd taught herself how to play the game with the best of them. Pasting a smile on her face and grabbing solidly onto Abe, she walked further into the room.

"Let's start making the rounds," she said.

"And what does that exactly entail?"

"Just follow my lead."

Much to her surprise, Abe did just that and more. He was charming everyone they met. Telling jokes and stories all with an ease that took her off guard. This man continued to impress her with each additional moment they spent together.

After they'd talked to several groups of people, her eyes caught the big prize—Layton. He looked at her, his blue eyes questioning. Then his eyes focused on Abe. He started to walk toward them.

"Game time," she said softly. "That's Layton Alito."

Abe pulled her closer to him, wrapping his arm around her waist.

"Nina Marie." Layton leaned in and kissed her on each cheek. "Aren't you looking absolutely ravishing this evening?"

"Thank you, Layton. The event seems to be a hit, as always."

He nodded, and then turned his attention to Abe. "I'm Layton Alito, CEO of Optimism."

Abe reached out and shook his hand. "Abe Smith."

Layton raised an eyebrow as they broke their handshake. "Glad you could join us this evening. What type of work are you in?"

"Construction," Abe said.

Nina Marie got a strange vibe from Layton. Something felt off here, but she didn't know what it was.

"That's wonderful. I hope you'll look around, maybe bid on some items and, of course, have some of the food." Layton paused. "And it's nice to see that we're expanding our attendance to those who are believers. We're all here for a good cause at the end of the day regardless of your religious background."

Abe's dark eyes narrowed, but he didn't say a word.

"Layton, could I have a word please?" she said. She didn't know what Layton was trying to cook up, but she didn't like it one bit.

"Of course."

She and Layton walked a few steps away from Abe, giving them some privacy. "What in the world do you think you're doing here, Layton? I get that you may be insanely jealous because I have a man like Abe in my life. But it's really even beneath you to stoop to that level."

Layton tilted his head to the side. Then he chuckled loudly. "You're really so blinded by this man's looks and charm that you haven't picked up on it, have you?"

"Picked up on what?"

"That man is definitely a believer."

She crossed her arms in defiance. "That's totally crazy." Layton was just being his usual awful self. She refused to let him mess this up with Abe.

"Have you asked him? Have the two of you talked religion?" he asked, challenging her.

"Yes, in fact we have."

"And he told you what?"

"That he's actually not a Christian at all. He's skeptical."

"He's lying," Layton said flatly. "And he's brought in some unwelcome guests."

"What do you mean?"

"Angels," Layton seethed.

She let out a breath. "Layton, I can't deal with these games of yours. I don't know how we're ever going to work together successfully if you keep acting like this."

He pulled her closer to him and held onto both of her hands. "I wouldn't lie about something like this. That man has an angelic presence around him. They are here with him tonight, and if he lied to you about his true feelings, then he's even more of a threat."

A shiver shot down her back. Looking into Layton's eyes, and holding onto his hands, she felt like he was telling her the truth. Did that mean that that Abe was lying to her? "Why would he lie to me about this?"

"That's what you need to figure out. My advice is to act like you don't believe me. Keep him around and determine what he's up to. He has to have some sort of angle."

Her gut tightened as she started to play our various scenarios in her mind. "You're right."

He smiled. "I don't hear you utter those words often."

"I wish you weren't, but I guess he did seem too good to be true." She'd been a fool, but she refused to let Abe get the best of her.

"Buck up, my dear. Go get a drink and bid on some items. That man will be sorry he ever messed with you. I speak from experience." He patted her shoulder and then walked off.

The anger flooded through her as the sense of betrayal kicked in. She'd get her revenge, if that were the case. First, she'd have to figure out what Abe was doing. For now, she had to be convincing to him that she didn't believe Layton and that Abe was still good with her.

She turned around and saw he was standing by the bar with a glass of what was presumably soda. As she started to replay their entire set of interactions, many questions popped through her mind. She made her way back over to him.

"Are you okay?" he asked her.

"Yes. I am so sorry about that. Layton is crazy. He's letting his jealously cloud his judgment. I must apologize for his comments about your beliefs. That was completely weird and inappropriate."

"Yeah, I wasn't sure where he was going with that. So I thought it best to just stay quiet."

She held his hand in hers, but she still couldn't sense what Layton was saying about him.

"Are you sure you're all right? You look a little flushed. He didn't hurt you, did he?"

"No, no. Nothing like that. He has a way of getting under my skin." She needed to play cool.

He squeezed her hand. "Don't let him ruin our night."

"Definitely not." She forced a smile. But then she no longer had to force it as she saw Stacey walking toward the bar area. "You'll excuse me for a moment, Abe. I need to speak to someone."

"Of course. I'm going to browse the auction items."

She quickly walked over to Stacey. "Stacey, your dress is gorgeous."

Stacey made eye contact, but she could sense her hesitancy. "Thank you. Yours is fabulous, too."

"This is your first charity gala?"

"Yes. But definitely not my last."

"Have you given any more thought to my offer?"

"Actually, I have, and while I greatly appreciate it, I can't be disloyal to Layton and Morena. Not after all they've done for me. That just wouldn't be right."

113

This girl was so naïve. It was time to up the stakes. She reached out and grabbed onto her arm, holding on tightly.

Stacey's eyes widened. "What're you doing?"

"You feel that?"

Stacey jerked away from her. "What're you doing to me?"

"Trying to show you how powerful you could be." She'd pushed some of her spiritual energy onto Stacey and shown her what it was like to use that power to inflict pain. "You don't realize what you're missing out on. I could show you so much. Expose you to skills and practices that Layton is not equipped to provide you."

"I don't know how else to tell you no."

"You'll eventually come around. I just hope for your sake that it's not too late."

CHAPTER TEN

Stacey watched as Nina Marie walked away. What had this woman done to her? Her arm ached from Nina Marie's touch. Was this some type of witchcraft? She needed to find Morena and get her help—fast. Why wouldn't Nina Marie leave her alone?

Quickly, she made her way through the party looking for Morena. When she found her standing talking to Layton and a man she didn't recognize, she let out a sigh of relief. They'd protect her from Nina Marie.

"Hello," she said to the group.

They all greeted her warmly, including Layton who had a slew of compliments.

"Stacey, I'd like to introduce you to the newest member of the Optimism non-profit board. This is Deputy Assistant District Attorney Tony Sampson."

She shook his hand and smiled. He was probably around six feet tall with short blond hair and green eyes. Although most men seemed to look handsome in tuxes, she couldn't help but think he was good looking. That only distracted her for a brief moment from her immediate problem. But she didn't want to be rude. "It's wonderful to meet you, Tony. I think you'll love working with Optimism."

"Thank you, Stacey. It's already been a great experience, and I'm just getting started."

"I'm sorry to interrupt, but Layton, could I steal you for a brief word?"

"Of course. We'll be right back," he said to Tony and Morena. Layton took her by the arm and led her down a long hallway. "Tell me what's wrong."

"It's Nina Marie. She put her hands on me tonight, and it scared me to death. The pain I felt was indescribable."

"Are you all right?" He swept her up into his arms into a tight hug.

She couldn't help it as tears filled her eyes. "Layton, she wants me to work with her. She said that you couldn't teach me everything she can, and when I told her that I didn't want to be disloyal to you, she hurt me."

Layton sighed and then pulled back from the hug. "First, thank you for your loyalty. It will be rewarded—have no doubt about that."

"I wouldn't have it any other way."

"I'll speak to Nina Marie, but you should see this as a huge compliment. She recognizes how special you are, and she wants you for herself and Astral Tech."

"She has a strange way of showing it. My arm is still aching."

"She was trying to demonstrate her power. Trying to show you the things you could do if you let her be your teacher."

She shook her head. "Layton, I don't want to hurt people like that."

He ran his hand down her cheek. "You're so innocent, Stace, and I can appreciate that, but at some point you'll realize just how dangerous this fight is that we're in, and unfortunately, sometimes using force is necessary. As much as I hate to say this, maybe Nina Marie is right."

"What?"

"You could probably benefit greatly from her teaching."

"You want me to work with her?"

"Not work for Astral Tech, but accept her training. Because you want to know something?"

"Tell me."

"I think we can use this as an opportunity to take Nina Marie down once and for all."

"I'm so confused." She didn't understand how Layton's thought process worked.

"Because once she tutors you, then you will eventually become stronger than her. Then between you and me, we can vanquish her once and for all."

She sucked in a breath.

"Don't be afraid. This is all part of the plan."

"I am scared, but I've learned to trust you. You haven't led me astray yet, and you've always been there for me. So if you think I need to do this, then so be it."

"Go back to her. Tell her you've changed your mind. Let her think I'm not involved. It will be much better that way. You'll get the benefit of all she knows. Then you and I will bide our time until you're strong enough."

"Thank you, Layton. For everything."

"And one word of advice. I saw the way you were looking at Tony. He's not worthy of you, and he already has the hots for Morena. So best to stay away, okay?"

Was she that transparent? She had to work on that. "Thanks for letting me know. I have bigger issues to deal with than men at this point."

"Agreed. Now go and find Nina Marie and put our plan into motion."

Layton left her reeling from his comments, but she had to put on her big-girl heels and deal with this head-on. He'd never failed her before, and he had so much more experience in all of this than she did. And if he were right, then maybe she could become more powerful than she ever imagined. It could change her life forever. Wouldn't that be worth the risk?

Now she'd have to go seek out Nina Marie and tell her that she'd had a change of heart.

She winded her way through the large crowds. The atmosphere was festive, especially as the night wore on and the guests were having more than enough champagne to make their bidding process a success.

Finally, after searching for what seemed like forever, she spotted Nina Marie across the room locked into what appeared to be a deep conversation with a tall, dark, and handsome man.

She touched the crystal that hung around her neck, the lapis lazuli, and decided that now would be the time to start trying to test out its powers—and her powers with it. She grabbed onto the crystal and said a few incantations she had prepared. But instead of targeting Nina Marie, which would be an utterly useless endeavor at this point in her spiritual ability, she turned her attention to the mystery man with her.

She watched with glee and awe as he took a step back from Nina Marie, who then reached out. As she approached, she could start to hear their conversation.

"I don't know what happened. I just had a wave of dizziness hit me," he said.

She chanted a few more words before making her entrance. Nina Marie didn't even notice her because she was so focused on her male friend.

"Hi," Stacey said.

Nina Marie looked at her and then back at her guest. "Hi, Stacey. Just give me a second."

"Sure," she said.

"Abe, maybe you should go sit down on one of those couches. I'll get you some ginger ale and be over in a moment."

"That sounds like a good idea. Sorry to be rude." He tilted his head toward her and then walked away to the lounge area.

"Sorry about that. Walk with me, Stacey, while I get Abe something to drink."

"Ginger ale won't help him," she said. She'd decided she needed to let Nina Marie know that if she was going to do this, she was going to take it seriously. Nina Marie probably wasn't going to be happy with her tactics, but she had to prove a point, and he was just stuck in the crosshairs.

"What do you mean?"

"I did that to him."

"Whatever for?"

"I wanted to let you know that I changed my mind about working with you. You were right, and I was letting my emotions get in the way of my long-term goals."

"That's great news, but why attack my date?"

"I was actually just trying out a new spell and working with crystals. I'm sorry about that, but the good news is it seemed to really work."

Nina Marie ordered a ginger ale, and they started walking back to the lounge area. "I have a question for you."

"Sure," she said.

"We're going to go take him this drink. I'd like you to talk to him for a minute and let me know what your read is on him."

"In what sense?"

Nina Marie leaned down. "His religious inclinations," she said softly.

"I assumed if he was with you that he was an Astral Tech member."

"No. I've recently started seeing him, but I have some conflicting information about his true allegiance. This will be a perfect first test for you. On the spot, no preparation, just pure instinct. And obviously you can't come right out and ask him about it."

Her pulse thumped quickly as she prepared for the challenge. She could do this.

They found Abe sitting on one of the plush navy couches in the lounge area.

"Here you go. Drink this," Nina Marie said. "It should help settle you."

"Thanks." He took the drink from her hand. "I'm feeling much better now though."

"Then let me formally introduce you to my friend Stacey Malone, and Stacey this is Abe Smith."

She took the opportunity to really take a good look at him as she offered a friendly smile and gentle handshake. "So nice to meet you, Abe. Glad you're feeling better. There are a lot of people in there." She let her hand linger in his as long as she possibly could without it turning awkward. She'd learned a lot about reading people's energy. Now it was time to see if she could put that into practice.

"Yeah, very crowded," he said.

"This is really a big deal. Nina Marie told me there would be a lot of people, but this even exceeded my expectations."

"Layton goes all out for this event," Nina Marie said.

She studied him carefully. She estimated him to be in his thirties or forties. He wasn't the type of guy she would normally be attracted to, but she could see that he could have appeal to Nina Marie. But that was beyond the scope of her assignment. She needed to keep him talking because the more he talked, the better she could read him. "Do you work with Nina Marie?" she asked, already knowing the answer.

"No." He smiled over at Nina Marie. "I work in construction. I literally ran into Nina Marie at the mall the other day. We hit it off, and I was happy when she invited me tonight."

Something was off with him. It didn't take a clairvoyant to know that. "You don't exactly look like the shopping type."

He laughed loudly. "I'm not at all. I had to buy a gift for my niece's third birthday. Is it that apparent that I'd rather poke my eye out than go shopping?"

Everyone laughed at that statement. This guy was smooth. Too smooth. Too prepared with stories. At least in her opinion, but she'd been put on alert, so maybe she was just being paranoid.

"You guys chat for a moment. I have to say hello to someone that caught my eye before they leave," Nina Marie said.

Nina Marie was giving her a chance to evaluate him one on one, which was good.

"So what do you do?" Abe asked her.

"I'm currently in college and interning at Optimism."

"You work with Layton?"

"Yes, I do. Do you know him?"

"I just met him tonight for the first time. Although I must admit, I'm not sure I've sorted out all the differing players and politics. Two competitors that seem to be on friendly terms." He shrugged. "It's all beyond me. I'm not a CEO nor do I want to be one."

"I'd love to be CEO one day, but I know I have years ahead of me to get that experience. I have to ask you something, though, since you're new to all of this. Are you into the New Age way of life?" That was an innocent enough question given the context of their conversation.

"Honestly, I'm not familiar with it. Nina Marie has been giving me some information on it. At this point in life, I'm not the religious type."

"But you were at some point?"

He nodded. "I grew up in a religious family but once I became an adult, that all wore off. Too much hypocrisy."

"Just like Pastor Dan."

"You know him?"

"Yes. I used to go to Windy Ridge Community Church."

"Wow. Do you think he's guilty?"

"It's a hot topic amongst this crowd tonight, for sure. I have to say I was a bit surprised given what I knew about him, but I've come to realize that most people have secrets." As soon as she'd said the words, she hoped she hadn't pushed it too far.

But he seemed relaxed. "Exactly. The world only sees what we put out there, and there are plenty of people walking around this earth wearing masks."

"You're getting all philosophical on me." She smiled. Yeah, it seemed like he was hiding something, but she didn't get a strong believer vibe from him. Nina Marie would be happy with her findings.

"Ah, looks like you're saved by Nina Marie's return."

Nina Marie walked back over to them. "What did I miss?"

"We were just getting to know each other," Abe said. "On that note, you ladies please excuse me for a minute to get some more ginger ale. It seems to be helping me a lot."

"So what did you think?" Nina Marie asked.

"I think he's holding back. That he's hiding something. Some angle he's working, but I didn't get a Christian vibe from him at all—not in his words or his energy. Who is telling you otherwise?"

"I didn't want to taint your approach so I didn't tell you before, but it's Layton."

"What?" Her heart sank. "And he's sure?"

"Yes. But I wanted a second opinion."

"What do you think?"

"I think I'm too close to be objective, and for that matter, maybe he worked his gentlemanly charm on you, too."

She shook her head. "I really don't think so. I'm not saying he is embracing our beliefs either, but he wasn't exactly quoting the Bible at me."

"That's my concern. What if this is all a subterfuge of some sort."

"But to what end?" She couldn't figure out how to put this all together.

"Whatever he's doing, I intend to figure it out. If it turns out that he is up to something, he's going to regret the day he decided to take me on."

**

Grant awoke in the middle of the night gasping for air. Where was he? What was happening? He tried to take a few deep breaths, but he couldn't get enough air. It felt like there was a huge weight pushing down on his chest.

Fear struck him as he started to wonder whether he'd be able to catch his breath. Was he having a panic attack? He tried to move, to get up out of the bed, but he couldn't move. This had to be a nightmare. He'd wake up any minute and think how crazy this was.

After another minute of struggling to breathe, it hit him that this was no dream. This was real life. The room felt incredibly cool but his body was on fire. A trickle of sweat dripped down the side of his face.

Could he be facing a spiritual attack right now?

He'd heard Olivia tell stories of how she faced spiritual warfare as a child, that dark forces came at her during the night, but he never thought that something like that could happen to him. Unlike Olivia, he wasn't prepared. He didn't have the experience and foundation to fight like she did.

He'd become a Christian, but he'd wrongly assumed that the hardest part would be taking that first step in faith. No, now things were much more difficult for him. The questions, the doubts, the confusions surrounded him, especially with all that had happened with Pastor Dan.

He did the only thing he thought he could do. He started reciting scripture. First, barely anything came out of his mouth. But the more he spoke, the more air he was able to get.

The problem was that he had only memorized a few verses, but at least it was something. *"Greater is He that is within you than He who is in the world."*

Then he went onto the Lord's Prayer, and then Psalm 23. As he uttered the last line of the Psalm, he could feel the weight lifting off of him.

He was able to sit up and suddenly he didn't feel warm at all, but much cooler. *Dear Lord, what just happened to me? I'm so confused.*

He jumped up out of the bed and turned on the lights. He walked from his bedroom and into the kitchen, flipping on all the lights as he went. Taking a look at the clock, he saw that it was almost three in the morning. He couldn't call and wake Olivia up, but he really needed to talk to someone. It occurred to him at a time like this he would really want to talk to Pastor Dan, but that was impossible with him in prison.

He'd been warned that as he kept walking down the path of faith that he would be challenged, but it confounded him that any demonic force would take the time to bother him. He was a nobody, and certainly not a strong and powerful warrior of God like Olivia or Dan. He was a rookie, prone to make rookie mistakes. Did he have more of a role to play in this than he realized? And if so, how was he in any shape to handle that?

The questions and doubts that surrounded him only seemed to be getting more entrenched, but even with all of that, he had no intention of abandoning the journey that he had started.

Were the forces of darkness toying with him? It was strange to think that not many months ago he thought all of this spiritual realm stuff was complete fantasy. But now that he'd experience it multiple times firsthand, there was no way he could deny it. Tonight's event had been the scariest yet, even more so than when he was attacked last year in his house. This felt even more sinister.

If it had been a year ago, he wouldn't have believed in any of this. He would've credited the whole thing to a crazy nightmare. But it wasn't a year ago and his life had forever changed the moment he took that case representing Optimism, and even more than that, once he'd met Olivia Murray.

He was in this strange limbo where he knew in his gut what he wanted to believe, but he didn't understand why all the doubts and questions bombarded him.

"Why me?" he said out loud.

He fired up the coffee pot and then went to grab his laptop out of his bag. He might as well do some work to try to move on from what had just happened. But he feared that he might never be the same.

**

Tony had offered to meet Olivia at her office. He'd had some time to review all of his evidence and was ready to put a plea offer on the table. But it was one he knew she'd never go for. It was his duty, though, as an officer of the court to try. Because if he didn't at least put something out there, the judge would think that very odd.

Deep down, of course, he wanted this thing to go to trial because it would be good exposure for him on a high profile case. Hopefully, once she heard what he was offering, then they could just move this thing forward in the process.

The BCR offices were in a swanky office building north of the city. He often wondered how different his life would have been if he would've taken the offer to work in the big Chicago law firm when he finished law school at the University of Chicago. He'd graduated near the top of his class and had plenty of offers, but he'd always wanted to be a prosecutor.

So he'd taken the government salary versus the six figure private sector one, but he had a long term plan. One that involved running for office one day, and this case was exactly the type of thing he needed to build up his portfolio of work and raise his public profile in the community.

As he walked into Olivia's office building, he was reminded of what he'd given up and the sacrifices he'd made. He just kept telling himself that one day it would be worth it. He rode the elevator up to the main floor for BCR and waited while the receptionist alerted Olivia to his arrival.

He knew the BCR office had just recently opened, and they had clearly spent a big chunk of change on the décor, in addition to the office space.

Olivia walked out to greet him, and he provided an obligatory smile. "Nice to see you again," he said.

"Come on back to my office and we can talk. Just follow me."

He did as she directed. There was something different about this woman, but he couldn't quite put his finger on it.

"Here we are. Please have a seat."

As he stepped through her office door, he tried to keep his expression neutral, but it was difficult. The view of the Chicago skyline from her window was absolutely breathtaking. "If I had an office like this, I don't think I'd ever leave. Did you invite me over here to rub it in?" He laughed

"It is very nice. But believe it or not, fancy offices can only get you so far. You have to love what you're doing or it's not worth it. No matter how great the view is."

"And do you?" he asked.

"What?"

"Love what you do here at BCR?"

"I love being a lawyer."

"Ah, but that doesn't mean you love being a lawyer in a big international law firm."

"It has its ups and downs. I have law school loans that I'm paying off. So it was the best route for me." She paused. "Now I know you didn't just come over to have a friendly chat and check out the BCR offices, so what's on your mind?"

She was right about that, but it was good to talk to his opponent. She didn't realize it but everything he learned about her could be future ammunition to use against her. "I'm here to talk about the case. You know we have the preliminary hearing scheduled for next week."

"Yeah."

"So let's talk a plea deal before that hearing happens."

She raised an eyebrow. "I'm listening."

"Look, I've gone through all the physical evidence. The state has a very strong case against your client. Not to mention a highly credible witness that a jury is sure to believe."

"I hear what you're saying, but you still haven't presented your offer, Tony."

"Ten years."

Her brown eyes widened and then she laughed. "You've got to be kidding me."

"Hear me out."

"That's ludicrous."

"No. I don't think you get the full picture here. Because I can prove the amount is over a hundred thousand dollars and it involves a church, this makes it a Class X felony under Illinois law."

"I am well aware of the felony classification."

"Then you should know that carries up to a thirty year sentence."

"Up to."

"Right, but that's why the ten years is more than fair."

"You're missing the most important piece of information in all of this. My client is innocent."

Now it was his turn to laugh. "You've got to be kidding me. I know you don't normally practice criminal law and you're taking this on pro bono, so let me do you a professional courtesy and tell you that this is a rock-solid case. One of the most air-tight cases I've prosecuted in years. I've got both the tangible evidence of the electronic transfers from the church account to his private account plus the testimonial evidence, and no juror is going to be sympathetic toward a pastor who steals from his church. You're just going to have to face all the facts that the deck is completely stacked against you this time."

"And I want to be crystal clear to you so as to not waste your time. My client is innocent, and I plan to mount a vigorous defense on his behalf."

Either this woman was an amazing actress or she actually believed that her client didn't embezzle the money. Both prospects were disturbing. "I've prosecuted hundreds of cases in my career, and I've learned that almost all the defendants say that they didn't do it, but the simple truth is that they often did."

"There's nothing simple about this situation."

"Seems open and shut to me. Tell me what I'm missing."

"That's because you don't know about the background of the situation."

"Enlighten me then."

"There's more going on here than just an open-and-shut case as you call it. For one, I believe my client was framed. And for two, there are spiritual forces at work here."

Uh oh. Was she really going to try to go down that rabbit hole? The framing defense wasn't entirely unexpected, but spiritual forces? "What are you going to argue to the jury? That angels took the money?"

"You think I'm joking around here but I'm very serious. There are two New Age companies in town that have declared war against Windy Ridge Community Church and Pastor Dan. They will stop at nothing to destroy him and the church. What better way than to frame him for a crime like this that he didn't commit. They knew it would have a highly negative impact. All they have to do is sit back and watch it unfold. I can't allow that to happen."

This woman appeared to be on some sort of spiritual crusade which made no sense to a guy like him. "I think you're either completely grasping at straws to try to help your client, or worse, you're totally delusional."

She shook her head. "Do you believe in God, Tony?"

He hadn't been prepared for a religious discussion with her. He'd need to play it safe. "Yes, of course. Don't most people?"

She leaned forward in her chair, making direct eye contact with him. "Then you should realize that there is such a thing as spiritual warfare, and Windy Ridge happens to be a battleground right now."

He really wondered if she was on some sort of meds or something. "I know we don't know each other very well, but I have to ask you if you're sure you're feeling okay because you aren't making rational sense right now."

She smiled at him. "Believe me, you're not the first person to think I was delusional and you won't be the last. But as far as this case goes, right now you're on the wrong side as far as I'm concerned. You're a pawn in this game orchestrated, I'm sure, by Layton Alito at Optimism."

Oh, well, that got his attention. What did she know about Layton? "How in the world could Layton be involved with this?"

"I see that you know him. I guess that shouldn't surprise me."

"I'm a member of the Optimism non-profit board. Of course I know him."

She gasped. "But I thought you said you believed in God? Why would they let a Christian on a New Age board?"

"Beats me. The board is all about charitable events and community service. They haven't mentioned New Age anything." That wasn't entirely true, but he wanted to see how this was going to play out.

"This is all wrong," she said. "They're going to try to use you to make sure that they can get to Dan. Do they know you offered a plea deal?"

"Absolutely not. I don't discuss my legal strategy with anyone outside of the prosecutor's office." The more she spoke the more uncomfortable he became. It wasn't like he believed what she said about spiritual warfare, but he was concerned about being used for someone else's agenda. Her visceral reaction to him taking the Board position was troubling.

"You're in the middle of this now whether you want to be or not, and if you truly do have faith, you're going to need it because if Layton or Nina Marie sense that you're not on their team, then they'll come after you, too."

"Are you trying to threaten me?"

"No. Just the opposite. I'm trying to warn you."

A chill shot down his back at her words. As she spoke, she did so calmly but seriously. He didn't quite know how to handle all of this new information so he tried to shrug it off for now. "While I appreciate your concern, I will be just fine. I trust you will take the deal to your client and let me know what he says."

"Of course."

"Remember, it's a good deal." He stood up ready to get out of her office as quickly as possible. That is not how he expected the meeting to go. He needed to do some of his own digging to figure out if Olivia was crazy or if he was the one that was in trouble.

CHAPTER ELEVEN

Olivia had received a strange voicemail from Grant asking if she could come by, and she was anxious to get to his house and talk. It'd been a long day in the office, especially after the strange conversation with Tony. She'd visit Dan tomorrow and get his thoughts on the deal. She'd strongly push him to reject the plea. He was innocent and there was absolutely no reason for him to admit guilt to a crime he didn't commit and sit in prison for ten years.

She knocked on Grant's door and he opened it. He pulled her inside and wrapped his arms tightly around her.

"Grant, what's going on?" she looked up into concerned eyes.

"I'm glad to see you."

"You look tired." He had dark circles under his eyes.

"Come on in and I'll tell you all about my night."

He took her by the hand, and they sat down beside each other on the couch.

"I wanted to call you after it happened but it was in the middle of the night, and then I had a motions' hearing today for one of my cases. So that's why I thought it would be easier for us to talk tonight after we were both done at work."

"Something happened to you." She could tell just by looking into his eyes, and she had some ideas about what it could be.

He gripped tightly onto her hand. "I know I can tell you and you'll understand."

"You can tell me anything. I'm here for you, Grant." Her heart ached as she waited to hear what he had to say. Grant wasn't easily rattled, so she knew this was something big.

"I woke up in the middle of the night, and I literally couldn't breathe. There was this huge weight pushing down on me. I couldn't do anything. I couldn't move. As hard as I tried, I couldn't do anything but lie there, and I was deathly afraid. A type of fear that I don't think I've ever personally experienced before as it relates to my own safety."

"What did you do?"

"I didn't know what to do. So I just started quoting some Bible verses. I don't know a lot of them by heart, but I did what I could. By that point I was sweating and felt like I was burning up. I kept up with the verses and then after a few minutes everything stopped. I could breathe normally and move again. I got up out the bed and didn't go back to sleep."

It had been years, but Olivia was all too familiar with waking up in the middle of the night to face an unseen foe. "You did the exact right thing, Grant. You can't battle the forces of evil. You're just a man. The battle is the Lord's. The word of God is the most powerful weapon we have."

"So you don't think I've lost my mind?"

"Of course not."

"Okay, assuming that all of this happened, there's something that's bothering me a lot."

"What?"

"Why would they come after me? It's not like I'm the strong one here—at least not in a spiritual stance. I could run away from this whole thing, and it wouldn't impact things one way or another."

"That's where you're wrong, Grant. You're an integral part of this battle in Windy Ridge. If anything, what you experienced only further demonstrates that." She paused, making sure she chose her words carefully. "If the forces of darkness get you to give up on your faith journey, they'll have scored a major victory."

"And that's the last thing I want. I didn't know if I should bring this up to you because I didn't want you to think less of me."

"Don't say that, Grant. I want you to be able to talk to me about everything." She squeezed his hand tightly.

"I'm bombarded by doubts and thoughts and questions that are very dark and depressing. Mocking, even. It's hard to describe. I'll be going about my work and then all of a sudden a hateful thought about Christ will pop into my mind. Questions about why I believe. Judgments about my past. I could go on and on."

"This is what the enemy does. He puts those thoughts into your head to try to make you question your faith. You can combat those types of negative thoughts in the same way that you dealt with the actual physical assault last night."

"I need more verses," he chuckled. He let go of her hand and wrapped his arm around her shoulder. "I know it's not funny. I'm just not good at coping with stuff like this. You're much better with the unseen realm than I am. I was just thinking earlier that a year ago, all of this would've seemed totally impossible to me. The fact that there was an invisible war going on around us would've seemed like something out of a novel. Not something I was experiencing myself in real life."

"The important thing is you're in this place right now. The fact that you're a target shows you're stronger than you think and you're continuing your walk with God. I know it's scary, but you're more than capable of facing this down."

He placed his left hand on her cheek and tipped her head up to look at him. "I know one thing. I don't know what I'd do without you in my life, Olivia."

"Then don't think about it."

As his lips met hers, it was the most amazing feeling. A feeling she never wanted to end. Having him in her life made everything seem right. She leaned into the kiss and enjoyed the moment of respite from the rest of the world, allowing herself to get lost in him.

When the kiss ended, she considered kissing him again, but there were other pressing matters to attend to and she had promised herself that she wouldn't let her feelings for Grant take away from her work.

"I'm sorry," he said. "I launched into my whole thing without even asking how your day went."

She let out a sigh. "Well, Tony Sampson paid me a visit today. He's offering a deal. Ten years of prison time."

"What kind of deal is that?"

"One that according to him is fair given that it's a Class X felony with up to thirty years."

"Yeah, but maybe that's just his starting point for negotiations. Are you taking it to Dan?"

"Yes, I'm seeing him tomorrow and will strongly advise him against it."

"I don't think Dan would take a deal anyway. He's too honest. He wouldn't admit to something if he's innocent."

"I hope you're right. There's something else though that's even more interesting than the plea offer."

"With Tony?"

"Yeah. Get this. He's a member of the Optimism non-profit board."

"Seriously?"

"Yes. That can't be a coincidence, and I did some digging. He just so happens to be the newest member. He claims Layton hasn't pushed any of the New Age ideology on him and that he's actually a believer. But the whole thing seemed highly suspicious to me."

"What did you tell him?"

"I did what I thought was right and warned him about how dangerous Layton and both groups are."

"And how did he take that?"

"He seemed to brush it off, but I could also sense that the conversation had made him uncomfortable. Maybe he really doesn't know about everything Layton is involved in. Hopefully now he'll take a closer look. I don't like how this all seems to be fitting together though."

"Doesn't it just strengthen your position that Layton is behind this? Dan was setup."

"Yes. The preliminary hearing is next week. We'll get a sense then of how quickly we're going to move to trial. I'd like the sooner the better, but I'm not sure what Tony's strategy is. He wants to use this case to help his career. The longer he can keep it in the news and on the top of people's minds, the better for him."

"Another reason he came in with the plea deal at ten years, because he knew you'd probably be unlikely to take it, especially at this stage of the prosecution."

"But he also is seasoned and knows that a judge would want to know that he'd made an effort on that front."

"Exactly."

"I have a case update, too. I spoke to Abe. He attended the Optimism charity gala with Nina Marie. Said he got a little spooked because Layton called him out as a Christian. He thinks his cover is still intact with Nina Marie and that she shrugged off Layton's comments, but he has his guard up nonetheless. Since he feels a bit under pressure, he's going to try to make his move soon and attempt to get information from her that hopefully can help show Dan was framed. Or at least point us in the direction of how we might show it."

"I hope he's careful. If Nina Marie thinks that he is playing her, it could be bad. You know how she is."

"I do, and I warned him again to be careful. He mentioned that he also met Stacey Malone at the event."

She shook her head. "It tears me up that they've locked their evil tentacles into her."

"I agree, but she's still her own person. She has to take responsibility for her actions, as well."

"Doesn't mean I like it any better, though."

"I hear you."

She rested her head on his shoulder. This felt so natural to her. Being with him and talking about the day. If only they were talking about normal lawyer stuff and not this.

"What're you thinking?" he asked.

"How glad I am to be here with you, but wondering if there will ever be an end to all of this."

"There has to be," he said. "Once Dan is acquitted, that will be a huge blow to those who want to take down the church."

"I hope you're right, and let's not forget, I still have to win the trial first."

"You will. I have the utmost faith in your abilities, and Dan does, too. He couldn't have a more fierce advocate than you. The jury will sense that you believe in his innocence. I truly think that."

**

Nina Marie hadn't been able to stop thinking about Layton's warning concerning Abe ever since the charity gala, and now her natural sense of paranoia was really getting to her.

She'd invited Abe over to her place for dinner, and she planned to get down to the bottom of things once and for all. He'd be on her turf, so that would work to her advantage. Also, now that she was armed with this information, she would be alert.

In her heart, she longed for Layton to be wrong. She was enjoying spending time with Abe, and they seemed to have a legitimate connection. But there was a sinking feeling deep in the pit of her stomach that Layton could be right. That Abe could be playing her, and that thought not only hurt her, it made her furious.

Stacey hadn't gotten the same impression from Abe that Layton had. So maybe there was hope that Layton was just trying to once again mess with her happiness. She couldn't afford to take any chances, though, because if Layton was right, then she had to figure out what Abe was up to.

Her doorbell rang, and she smoothed down her black skirt and adjusted her pastel pink knit top. She opened the door and there stood Abe—again with flowers in his hands. But this time they were daisies.

"I know you told me not to bring anything, that you had it all under control, but I couldn't resist. I don't like showing up somewhere empty-handed." He gave her the flowers and then leaned in and kissed her cheek.

Already she felt off-kilter by his one simple gesture. She had to remind herself what tonight was about. It wasn't about being swept off her feet by this man, no matter how nice he appeared to be on the outside.

135

"Come on in. I hope you like Italian food. I've got my special sauce simmering."

He took in a deep breath. "It smells heavenly."

She flinched at the use of his word, but he didn't seem to even notice. He genuinely seemed to be excited about the food. She was an excellent cook, but rarely made big meals since it was just her. She'd almost forgotten how much she enjoyed it. If only it could have been under different circumstances. Like Abe being a totally genuine man who wanted to get to know her. It was time to find out.

"Have a seat. I thought we could maybe chat a bit and have some appetizers I fixed. I know you don't drink, but I have soft drinks and tea. Just let me know what you'd prefer."

"I'd love some tea."

"Perfect."

She got his drink and poured herself one as well. Better to not be clouded by any alcohol tonight because she needed to be on her game.

She placed the tomato and mozzarella salad she had prepared on the table and took a seat across from him. "So what did you think about the charity event?"

"It was good. It wasn't my normal scene, that's for sure, but everyone seemed very nice."

"I'm sorry that you didn't feel well."

"That was the strangest thing. By the time I got home, I felt completely fine, like nothing had ever even happened to me."

"Don't worry about it. I'm just glad that you feel okay now."

He smiled. "I'm better than fine now."

Why did this man make her feel so special? It bothered her even more that this could be an act. "I hope Layton didn't offend you too much with his comments about your faith."

"Now that was weird. I've never had anyone say anything like that to me before, and to think he did it in the middle of a party. Is he always like that?"

Wasn't that an interesting deflection. "Layton says what is on his mind in most situations."

"How in the world could he even think he'd know what someone's personal beliefs are? Is this all connected to the New Age stuff?"

Did he care about her business? Maybe he was some sort of corporate spy for another company. "Layton has a strong radar when it comes to various beliefs and faith. Which made me wonder if you were maybe saying that you were against Christianity because you knew that I was and you wanted to have a chance with me?"

He grinned. "You give me too much credit to think through all of that. Like I told you, I believe there's a lot of hypocrisy in the church."

"Saying that there is hypocrisy doesn't mean you reject the beliefs though. It just means that you criticize how some believers act."

"Aren't you a theologian tonight?"

"Am I getting too heavy over appetizers?"

"No. I'm just kidding. All of this religion stuff means a lot to you, so I'm happy to talk about it as much as you want."

"When's the last time you went to church?"

He paused and ran a hand through his hair. "It's been a few years. There was someone who hurt me badly, and I stopped going to church to avoid seeing her."

Could they really have that type of connection? She had told herself she was going to be patient tonight and take it step-by-step to conduct a thorough investigation, but she was having a hard time.

"What's wrong?" he asked, his brown eyes full of concern.

And for some infuriating reason, she still couldn't get a good read on him. All she could tell for sure was that this man sitting across from her genuinely seemed to care about her. She needed to give herself more time. "Nothing. I'm going to start the pasta. I know you must hungry for something more filling than cheese and tomatoes."

He laughed loudly. "I do love to eat."

They made small talk while she finished preparing the meal, and then she provided him a hefty portion of pasta and a large breadstick.

"I can't tell you how long it's been since I've had a home-cooked meal," he said.

Her heart warmed again at his words. "I hope you enjoy this then."

"Believe me, I have no doubts about that."

She watched as he devoured his pasta quickly and had no shame in asking for seconds. "You must have one amazing metabolism."

"Yeah. And I do a lot of physical activity for work. Maybe one day it will catch up to me, but it hasn't yet."

"I'm thrilled that you're enjoying it." And she meant it.

"So what's the story with Stacey? Something seemed a little off with her."

"In what way?"

"I don't know how to describe it, but I just got a strange vibe from her."

"If I tell you this, you'll probably question my sanity and hers, too."

"I doubt that."

"She's the reason you weren't feeling well." If this guy was legit, what better time than now to start letting him into her life and what being around her would entail.

"I don't understand."

"Stacey was experimenting with some crystals and you were her target."

"Whoa." He leaned back in his chair. "Are you talking about spells and witchcraft?"

"Yes. That's exactly what I'm talking about."

"You really believe that?"

"I do. Now don't get me wrong. There are a lot of scammers and fakes out there who have zero ability and try to prey on innocent people. But there are also people who are spiritually gifted, like Stacey."

"And what about you?"

"I am, as well. I figured it was better to start to show you the real me so you can understand what I'm all about."

"I like you a lot, Nina Marie, but you have to realize I'd be a little skeptical."

"I know. I'm not expecting you to fully jump on board, but I want to be honest with you. If we don't have honesty, then we have nothing."

"Why did you turn to this way of life?"

"Because like you, I was hurt, and I knew I needed to make sure that never happened again."

"So witchcraft makes you feel better?"

"It's a bit more complicated than that."

"Assuming these types of powers exist, do you use them for good?"

"I guess that depends on whose definition of good you're using."

"You obviously have issues with Windy Ridge Community Church. If you did something to hurt the church, would you consider that good?"

"I would. That church does nothing good, it's just a way to mislead people into believing things that will end up hurting them in the end."

"So if you had a way of hurting the pastor you would do that?"

"What are you insinuating?" Her guard was now fully up. She didn't like the direction the conversation had just taken.

"Using your powers to setup an innocent man to take the fall?"

She sucked in a breath. "Whoa, who are you? A cop?"

He shook his head. "Definitely not a cop."

"But you're not Abe Smith either, are you?"

He raised an eyebrow. "I'm worried if I tell you, then you may cast a spell on me."

His sarcasm was evident. It was time to end this once and for all. She reached over and grabbed onto both of his hands and squeezed tightly. And then for the first time she sensed it. What had been so blatantly obvious to Layton but she'd been blinded to. This man was a Christian. And a liar.

"You should get out of my house."

"It doesn't have to be this way, Nina Marie. There's another way."

"What, are you going to try to pull the evangelism thing on me now? You really have some nerve. Don't you realize that I could hurt you? I'm giving you a chance to just walk away, even though you don't deserve it."

He put his hands on her shoulders. "Listen to yourself, Nina Marie. The fact that you can show that type of compassion toward me does mean something. No, I'm not going to start preaching to you. I'm far from a perfect person, and my faith is not as strong as others I know. But I can tell you that God can work through anyone—and that includes you. He may have a bigger plan for you than you'll ever know. Just walk away from this madness. I will help you."

"You can't be serious."

"I am."

How had this discussion gotten so completely turned on its head? Once again this man was getting the best of her, and she couldn't figure out why. Why hadn't she inflicted pain on him? Was it because he was still standing there, holding onto her and showing some feelings amongst all the lies?

No, she had to end this. Now. "Let me make this easy for you, Abe, or whatever your name is. I am aligned with the evil one. He is my master. Not your God."

She expected to see shock in his eyes, but what she saw was much worse—disappointment.

"I know who you are and who you worship, and I'm still telling you that there's hope."

"You sound like Olivia."

A flash of recognition crossed his face, and it was at that point she knew.

"It's Olivia, isn't it? She sent you?"

"That isn't important now."

She shook her head. What a mess this had become. "What do you want from me? Why this charade? Was it to embarrass me? Take me down a notch?"

"Nothing like that at all. But there's an innocent man sitting in prison right now."

Then it hit her like a freight train. This was all about the pastor. They thought she was involved. They didn't even realize that this was Layton's plan, not hers. "You're barking up the wrong tree, and again, it's time for you to go."

He took her hands in his. "I never planned to actually develop feelings for you in all of this, Nina Marie. But I have, and the fact that I do care means you haven't seen the last of me. I'm not going to give up on you."

He stood up from the dining room table and walked out of the room.

Her hands were still burning from his touch, and her heart was breaking.

CHAPTER TWELVE

Olivia called a meeting to regroup post her discussion with Dan about the plea. She was relieved when Dan had said that he wanted to fight this. Which meant they were heading to the preliminary hearing and then would figure out how soon they'd be going to trial.

Abe sat across from her in the conference room, and they were waiting for Grant to arrive. Olivia looked down at her phone and saw a message from Grant. He was running late and wanted them to start without him.

"Looks like Grant is tied up for a bit. We should go ahead and get started."

Abe nodded. "A few things we need to discuss."

Immediately, she sensed something was wrong. "What is it?"

"The first thing is about some of my recent findings." He slid a manila folder in front of her. "I did a deep dive on all of Dan's financials. Yes, his wife's illness put a strain on their finances, but nothing so dire as to be a motive for him to steal from the church. Given their very frugal lifestyle, they had a chunk of money saved up. The medical bills did pretty much wipe that out, but he wasn't in a desperate situation. I also found out that he was able to work out a payment plan with the hospital to cover the expenses not covered by his medical insurance. All the documents are highlighted and tabbed to make the key connections you need. There's also absolutely nothing linking him to the offshore account, and all of his bills and expenses are accounted for. Which means for their offshore theory to work, he'd have to be doing something else with the money. That's not to say they won't make the argument."

"Like what?"

"Paying off gambling debts, paying for illegal activities that wouldn't have a paper trail. That type of thing. But at least this cuts against their act of desperation argument because of his wife's illness."

"That is the best news I've heard in a long time." She was relieved to have something of substance to help build her case. "What else?"

"The other thing is that Nina Marie and I had a pretty eventful night last night."

She could only imagine how that had ended up. "I want to hear all about it."

He leaned back in his chair crossing his arms in front of him. "Honestly, I don't even know where to begin, but there is definitely something going on with that woman."

"Yes, there's a lot more to her than first appears."

"Unfortunately, she figured out last night that I wasn't Abe Smith."

"It was only a matter of time. She has great instincts about these things."

"The strangest thing, though, is that I still felt compelled through all of it to try to speak to her about God."

"Really?"

"Yes. I had a strong feeling that I needed to."

"Do you believe there could be hope for someone like her?" she asked.

"I believe there's hope for everyone." He paused. "But since she now knows I am not who I said I was, I think she's also connected the dots back to you. I'm sorry about that because it was my fault. She said your name, and I had a reaction that I let show and she caught on."

"Were you able to figure out if she had something to do with the false allegations against Pastor Dan?"

"No, and I'm not so sure that she's directly involved."

"Layton is probably calling the shots as usual."

"I wanted to talk to you alone, though, because I wanted to know about how you would feel if I tried to reconnect with her?"

"To try to help her?"

"Yes. I haven't been able to stop thinking about the conversation I had with her. She told me point blank that she is on the devil's side, but there was something else there. The tiniest of openings. Yes, she was saying the words, but she wasn't all in. I could sense it. If she really had been totally committed, she would've thrown me out without another word, but she didn't. We still talked a bit after my cover was blown."

"She's a very complicated woman."

"She's been hurt badly before, and it's shaped her entire viewpoint. I don't know the details, but I think it has to do with a past relationship."

"I picked up on that before as well, and I've tried to reach her but she is pretty far down in a dark hole. I'm not saying we shouldn't try, but I wouldn't get your hopes up that she's going to be able to change. That she would want to change."

"Well, you won't believe what else she told me."

"Uh oh."

"She claimed Stacey Malone put some sort of spell on me at the charity event."

"What happened?"

"A sudden sickness hit me out of the blue. I was perfectly fine one minute, and then I felt like I was going to pass out. According to Nina Marie, Stacey was just experimenting with some New Age crystals, and I happened to be the one who was the target."

"Stacey is an entirely different problem, but she's entrenched right now with Layton. It's a very sad story." Her heart ached for Stacey, but she had chosen this path and there wasn't anything that could be done right now besides praying for her.

"Nina Marie also claimed that she has some spiritual powers, too. I have to tell you, all of this seems very foreign to me.

I do believe in God, but I haven't been to church in years. There's been something going on in my head since I started working this case. A desire to try to reconnect with the Lord. I haven't felt anything like it in a long time, so who am I to question it?"

Olivia continued to be amazed at how God was working through all of their lives. Even in this instance, drawing back someone who had distanced himself. "I know it's a strange set of circumstances, but I am happy that this experience is making you want to reconnect with your faith. If there's any way I can help with that process, I am more than willing. I know we all have a lot of on plates right now, but at the end of the day, these things are the most important."

"So can I ask you something else?"

"Sure."

"Do you believe in all of this stuff? The witchcraft and spells and all of that?"

"I believe that those who serve the devil can have spiritual powers and practice witchcraft. And, unfortunately, Nina Marie has demonstrated that she does practice the dark arts. Stacey abandoned the Christian faith to go become a member of Optimism. So she is also seeking out the powers of darkness. I personally have experienced things that, if I told you about them, would make you think I was crazy. But I just also go back to Ephesians 6:18. *We wrestle not against flesh and blood.*"

"Yes, I'm familiar with that verse. My grandmother cited it often. She was a big believer in angels and demons, but I never had given it that much thought before. I haven't wrapped my head around all of that yet, but I haven't felt the need to pray in a while, and I felt it very strongly last night."

"What caused you to distance yourself from God in the first place?"

He ran his hand through his hair. "Funny you ask that because it's actually a source of commonality for Nina Marie and me. There was a woman in my church. She broke my heart. I was going to ask her to marry me, and I found out she was cheating on me with one of my friends—also someone who went to that same church. I never wanted to go back there again. And instead of just finding a new church, I walked away completely. It was just easier to handle that way. That was a few years ago now."

As she listened to his story, she wondered if this man could get through to Nina Marie. The problem was that he'd already betrayed her trust from the get-go. "And now you're here. Working on this case."

"Yes. God seems to have led me back. Not through the most likely route, but back nonetheless."

"And maybe He's even given you a greater challenge with Nina Marie." She'd been praying every single day for Nina Marie that she could turn away from the darkness and see the light. Hearing all of this only made her want to redouble her prayer efforts.

"I'll do what I can. I know one thing. There's no way I can just walk away from this."

"God is going to work through this situation, Abe. I truly believe that." She looked over and Grant was walking into the room.

"Sorry I'm late." Grant took a seat beside Abe. "I got stuck in a client meeting and I couldn't leave."

"No problem," she said. It had actually worked out that she had gotten some time with Abe.

"Catch me up," Grant said.

"Dan is on board with fighting this thing and he rejected the plea," Olivia said. She also filled him in on Abe's research into Dan's financial background.

"Great." Grant turned and looked at Abe. "And how did it go with Nina Marie?"

"Long story short, my cover is blown, but I don't think she's the lynchpin to whatever happened with Dan. Olivia sent me the name of a forensics computer expert that I'm going to work with on examining the church's account. See if we can come up with anything on that end. We also have to discuss how far you're willing to go with regard to the electronic accounts we don't have authorized access to."

She knew exactly what he was talking about. "Dan wouldn't want to be freed by any illegal means, and you shouldn't take that risk either."

"Understood," Abe said. "I'm assuming you don't need anything from me for the preliminary hearing?"

"No. The state will put on evidence to show that the trial should move forward. Given all the facts we know, I expect the judge will find in the state's favor."

"All right. Well, I'll leave you two to discuss legal matters."

"Keep me updated, Abe," she said. "On everything."

**

As Layton had instructed, Stacey set up a meeting with Nina Marie. She still wasn't quite sure why Layton thought this whole mentoring thing was such a great idea, but she was loyal to his wishes. After all he had done for her, it was the least she could do.

But going down this road meant pretending like he had no idea that she was going to be tutored by Nina Marie. Hopefully she could pull it off. It made her a bit nervous because she wondered if Nina Marie would be able to sense her true plan.

Pushing those doubts out of her head, she walked into enemy territory—the Astral Tech office. Their office seemed much more New Age cliché than did Optimism's. Incense was burning in the reception area, and the motif was blue with plenty of moons and other similar decorations.

There was also an unmistakable tech company feel to the building. The lobby had a laptop and several tablets on display with the Astral Tech app. She knew they'd developed the app to try to reach a younger, more tech savvy audience. It was a brilliant marketing tool, but she wondered how effective it was in really spreading the true message.

"Stacey, so glad to see you." Nina Marie walked into the lobby area smiling widely.

"Thanks for having me here." She needed to remain calm and not let all of the subterfuge get to her.

"Of course. Meeting here makes the most sense. You won't have to worry about anyone else from Optimism ever seeing you. Follow me. I want you to make yourself completely at home while you're here."

"I still don't know how to thank you. I really don't think I'm that deserving of any type of special training." And that was true. She wasn't accustomed to the praise she'd been receiving lately.

"That's the first thing we're going to work on. You need more confidence. There's no need for you to be so humble. If a man had your level of skills, he surely wouldn't be. Now come on into this office and we'll get started."

She looked around at the room that had a small window, a desk, and a navy couch—to go along with all the other blue décor.

"Stacey, before we even get into any of the spiritual elements of things, I wanted to talk in general about you. What are your goals in life?"

"I want to graduate college and have a high-paying job so I'm able to be financially independent and buy nice things. My parents barely make ends meet. I want to do a lot better than them, and so far Layton has provided things that I've never had before. Like nice clothes." She looked at Nina Marie. "I'd love to be stylish and put together like you. It's like you never have a hair out of place."

"I think you and I aren't all that different. I also didn't grow up with much. I was smart enough to figure out I needed an education and a good job, but I still made a slew of bad decisions along the way. And that's one of the reasons I wanted to mentor you, because I see so much of myself in you."

"What would you have done differently?" Yes, Stacey was playing both sides here, but if she was going to learn from Nina Marie about the spiritual realm, why not seek out other advice about life from her?

"I've alluded to this before when warning you about Layton, but I've actually made much worse mistakes than Layton. When I was in my late twenties, I fell in love with a man who I thought at the time was perfect for me. Little did I know he was cheating on me from the moment I started seeing him. To make matters worse, I never saw it coming because he had such a veneer about him. He talked the talk. Believe it or not, I met him in church. To everyone else he was a complete gentleman, but I learned differently."

"What happened?"

Nina Marie looked at her, and a chill shot down her back. She feared what Nina Marie was about to tell her.

"It wasn't just the cheating. He became crazy possessive and jealous, and then one day, he saw me talking to another man after a church social event. It was a completely harmless conversation. I had no romantic interest in the guy at all, but my boyfriend came into my apartment after he drove me home from the event and that's when it happened."

Fear streaked through Stacey, fearing the worst. "What did he do to you?"

"He hit me that night. Ultimately, I ended up being hurt badly."

Stacey sucked in a breath. "I am so sorry. What did you do?"

"At the time, nothing. Then when it happened again, I confided in a friend at church."

"Did he get arrested?"

Nina Marie laughed. "No. My friend accused me of making it up. I was ostracized from my social circle, and I actually feared for my life because I thought my boyfriend was going to retaliate against me for talking about what happened. I left town and never went back."

"I can't even begin to imagine."

"It messed me up, no doubt about it, but at the end of the day, I took that awful experience and realized that Christianity was a farce. That I couldn't ever trust any man, and the only one looking out for me was me. With that newfound freedom and knowledge I sought out other spiritual avenues."

"And how did you find out about New Age?"

"I moved to Santa Cruz, California. They had a thriving group of people there I met through frequenting a New Age bookstore. I started talking to them about their beliefs, and I was instantly intrigued by the idea that I could be powerful myself. That I didn't need to rely on anyone or anything else for that, but that was just the tip of the iceberg. I met people involved in all different aspects of occult practice, including those who were active in the darker arts. Looking back, I understand now that I was proactively seeking the darkness because I was hurting so badly, and I desperately wanted something different than the Christian faith. So I thought, what better way to make a clean break than to use the powers of darkness and the evil one to my advantage."

"Were you actually a Christian before that or was it just the jerk you were dating?"

"That's a good question. He's the one that introduced me to that church. I never felt like I completely fit in, and I never fully committed to Christ, but I had started down that road until I saw my boyfriend's true colors and felt firsthand how it was to be betrayed by those people at church who were supposedly there for me."

Stacey's head felt like it was about to explode from hearing Nina Marie's story. As she looked at this woman, she suddenly saw her in a different light. No wonder she was the person she is today. Being treated like that would make anyone have issues, and it sickened her to think those people weren't there for her in her time of need. "I guess I can't be too surprised about the response you had from your church friends. It's all about appearances and protecting their own."

"It took me some time—years really— but I vowed I would never be a victim like that again. If that meant making some deals with the devil, then so be it. It's a bargain I was more than willing to make for my own personal safety and independence."

"And what exactly did you bargain away?" Stacey almost didn't want to know the answer.

Nina Marie took hold of her hand. "I made the strategic decision that I cared more about what happened while I was alive on this earth as opposed to what happens after."

"So you do believe in God and the devil, angels and demons?"

She nodded. "Yes. But I don't think the lines between good and evil are as clear as people want to make them. My ex-boyfriend claimed to be a godly man, and he was pure evil."

"Do you actively go to the devil and ask for things like Christians do with God?"

Nina Marie sighed. "Not in the exact way you're thinking. It's not like I'm making sacrifices. It's more that he's the source of my power. Which leads us to you."

She nodded. "Have you grown stronger over time with what powers you have?"

"Most certainly. At first, I was just dabbling in this and that. Some witchcraft and spells, some divination, some meditation. Once I did more research and exploring, connecting to the right people, I learned to hone my skills. But I'm under no illusion that it's all me. I rely on the evil one to be the source of my power. That's what I want to make sure you understand."

"You may need to explain that more."

"It's all well and good to have your spells and practice witchcraft and mediumship, but to really tap into true power, you need to actively go to him and ask for certain abilities."

"And he'll just give them to me?"

"Ah, well, in my experience, he seems to pick and choose who he wants to work through. But you, my dear, have that special something I think he will find most appealing."

Thoughts swirled around in her mind. Was she ready to go all in and ask the devil for things? For power?

Yes, she'd participated in some of Layton's rituals before, but this seemed to be on a different level.

"I can sense your hesitation, and I must say, this isn't something you should go into lightly. If you're not ready for that next step, then I don't want to force you to take it. We can work on the other skills I mentioned, all things that matter and are important. If you'd like to think about the other."

She greatly appreciated Nina Marie's offer. "It's not that I don't want to do it, but I have to admit I'm a bit scared."

"Then I'll make it easy for you. Let's focus on some other things for a bit, and we can revisit this at a later time."

"Thank you. That sounds good." Relief flooded through her. In her gut, she knew she wasn't quite ready to make that leap because when she did, it really would be something she didn't think she could change her mind about later.

"Let's talk about what you have been doing. You've mentioned crystals. What other things are you working on?"

Stacey went on to explain what she'd experimented with so far, including her special interest in casting spells. "Morena has been a big help to me in all of this."

"There's no doubt Morena's an accomplished witch, but I want you to be able to go beyond that."

"I appreciate the fact that you think I have something special. I don't want to let you down." She paused. "Have you heard any more about what is going to happen to Pastor Dan?"

Nina Marie raised an eyebrow. "Are you worried about him?"

"I know this isn't a popular thing to say, but I've given it a ton of thought, and I can't see him stealing money from the church."

"Can you keep a secret?"

"Of course."

"Layton is behind all of this. If you want more information, you should go to him directly. Given how much he cares for you, I think he'll explain everything."

"So you're saying that Dan is innocent?" She didn't like how this was unfolding. Her pulse thumped wildly.

"I don't think he stole that money, but that doesn't mean he's innocent. I have no idea what other things he's done in his life."

"But why? Why set him up?"

"Because bringing down Windy Ridge Community Church is a goal of both of our organizations. Layton had someone on the inside that could make it happen. I've already said too much. You should go to him on this."

Stacey frowned. "All right."

"You have compassion for the preacher?"

"He was always nice to me. I didn't agree with some of his ideas, but I don't think he's a criminal."

"In this business you're going to have to be willing to get your hands dirty. It's another thing you need to think about. Do you understand?"

"Yes. I do." Stacey had a lot she needed to figure out.

**

Olivia walked into the courtroom eager to start the preliminary hearing. She spotted Tony right away and walked over to him.

He offered his hand and a smile. "Not too late to reconsider the plea deal."

She'd called him after she had met with Dan and told him they'd be rejecting the plea. "The answer hasn't changed."

"That's a shame. I guess you do realize that the judge is going to let this go to trial—no doubt about it."

"I agree with you on that, but there's a big difference in the judge finding probable cause to proceed to trial and a jury convicting my client."

"Fair enough. Well, my door is open if you change your mind about anything."

"Tony, have you thought any more about the other topic we talked about in my office?" She's been praying that Tony would figure out he was being played and drop the case, but that didn't seem likely at this point.

"I did and I think you're grasping at straws." He took a step closer to her and leaned down toward her ear. "There's absolutely no evidence tying Layton to this case. I did my due diligence. So I think it would be best if you didn't try to go down that road."

Maybe there was some hope after all. If he'd at least tried to vet her theory, then that was positive, even if he hadn't found anything. "I appreciate you looking into it. Don't give up so easily." She didn't want to push it, so she walked away to the defense table and waited for Dan to be brought into the courtroom. A courtroom that was filled with media.

According to Tony's email, he wasn't planning on calling any live witnesses at the preliminary hearing. He'd only be introducing documents to make his case. He thought that they would be enough to show probable cause, and he probably made the strategic decision to keep Beverly off the stand until trial.

Dan was escorted in by officers and led to the defense table.

"How're you doing?" she asked him.

"Good. Looking forward to this being over. You said there's no chance in stopping the trial, so I'm just ready to get it done. Prison makes me less nervous than this courtroom." He glanced over his shoulder at the media. "I don't like all this attention."

"Dan, you know I'm going to do all I can to prove your innocence."

"I do, Olivia, and I appreciate everything you've done. I just hope it's not the end to my ministry."

"Don't talk like that."

"I want to be able to go back to preaching and even if I'm acquitted, I fear the church won't take me back."

"Let's take it one step at a time. First, focus on getting an acquittal. Then worry about repairing the church and the trust relationship."

"All rise," the bailiff said.

They stood as Judge Matthews entered the courtroom. She watched as his dark eyes surveyed the courtroom. He knew this wasn't the run-of-the-mill criminal case. Not with all these eyes on them.

"All right," Judge Matthews said. "Today we have the preliminary hearing in the case of the State versus Dan Light. Mr. Sampson, I assume you're ready to go?"

"Yes, Your Honor." Tony stood up. "I hope to not take too much of the court's time today because as you will see that there is no doubt that this case should move forward to a speedy trial."

"Go on with your argument then," the judge said.

"The main basis for my argument to proceed to trial is the physical evidence in this case. I'd like to introduce as the state's exhibit one, banking records that show electronic transfers were made over a sixteen month time period. Transfers from the church account to the defendant's account. An account I believe he set up years ago to facilitate this type of embezzlement scheme, which also goes to show this act being carefully planned and thought out over time. The additional records then show transfers from the defendant's account to an offshore account."

"Any objection to authenticity, Ms. Murray?" the judge asked.

"No, Your Honor." The records were legit. The bigger issue was who actually moved the money and what did they do with it. She wanted to save her objections for things that really mattered.

"Let me direct your attention to page three, for example. There is a transfer of five thousand dollars on March third. The money is moved from the church account to the defendant's account."

"How did no one notice this at the church?" Judge Matthews asked.

"That leads me to state's exhibit two. A set of falsified records that show no transfers of cash. Someone doctored the paper records, and the church still uses paper statements to conduct its business."

The judge curiously quirked an eyebrow, then he took a minute to review the exhibits that Tony had presented him. "Do you have anything else?"

"No, Your Honor. I believe those exhibits are more than sufficient to get over the probable cause bar."

"Ms. Murray, the floor is yours. What do you have to say about these documents?"

"Thank you." She stood up. "My client was framed, Your Honor."

"Do you have any proof of that claim?"

"Not that I'm prepared to present today, but that will be our defense if this moves to trial."

He nodded, looked at Dan, and then back at Olivia. "Then I guess it won't come to a surprise to anyone, given the evidence I've been presented, that my ruling is in favor of the State. Let's talk about a trial date. Mr. Sampson?"

"Yes, Your Honor. The State is prepared to move quickly and would be eager to get this on your trial calendar."

"Ms. Murray?"

"The defense agrees with the State on the need for a speedy trial."

"Well, counselors, this may be an instance of be careful what you ask for. My docket cleared up because of a string of plea deals. So I will set this case to begin trial two weeks from today. Do either of you anticipate any pre-trial motions at this point?"

"No, Your Honor," Tony said. "We'll be in the position to proceed directly to trial."

"I can't rule out any pre-trial motions at this time, Your Honor."

"No problem. Just let my clerk know if we need to set a pre-trial hearing. If not, I'll see you both back here in two weeks' time, nine a.m., to pick a jury."

"Thank you," they both said in unison.

She turned to Dan. "It won't be long now. This will all come to an end."

"I'm fine, really, Olivia. Don't worry about me. Just focus on clearing my name so I can continue in the ministry in whatever capacity God chooses for me."

She felt tears well up in her eyes listening to Dan's plea. She grabbed onto his arm. "I'm praying for you. For all of us."

"That's the most important thing you can do."

As he was led away by the officers, she took a deep breath and started to pray.

CHAPTER THIRTEEN

Nina Marie sat on her couch with her feet up reading a new book that Stacey had recommended. Mainly Nina Marie wanted to make sure that Stacey wasn't clouding her brain with misinformation or fads.

When her doorbell rang, she set the book down and got up off the couch. She wasn't expecting any company tonight. As she looked through the peephole, she let out a groan. The very last person she wanted to see was standing there. Abe—or whatever his name really was.

She opened the door. "You really have some nerve showing back up here at my home."

"May I come in?" Abe asked.

She wanted to slam the door in his face, but as she looked up into his eyes, she realized she couldn't say no to this man. As angry as she was at him, there was still something so strong pulling her toward him. "You have five minutes."

He smiled and walked by her and into the living room.

"So, what do you want, Abe? Or should I call you something else?"

"My first name is Abe."

"And your last name?"

"Perez."

"Ah, much more fitting than Smith." She fiddled with her sleeves, realizing that this man put her on edge. She needed to regain control. "What do you want?"

"I haven't been able to stop thinking about you."

She laughed. "Are you kidding me? You played me for a fool. You were using me for whatever it is Olivia hired you to do. So spare me your lines."

"I'm a private investigator. I was just doing my job. What's happening between us is a totally different thing."

"Let's get this straight, Abe. There *is* no us."

"I see it differently."

"Of course you do. I still don't know why you're here in my living room right now."

"Because somewhere along the way, I developed feelings for you, and I don't want you to keep going down such a destructive path."

"What, you think you can just waltz in here and all of a sudden I'm going to fall at your feet, confess my sins, and ride off with you into the sunset?"

He took a step toward her and instinctively she took one back. He reached toward her and she flinched.

"Whoa, I'm not going to hurt you," he said. "You have nothing to fear from me." He lifted his hands in the air.

Looking at Abe now, though, she realized she did have something to fear—but it wasn't physical violence. It was her heart being broken. "I don't know what you want from me."

"I want to be able to spend more time with you."

"First, how could I ever trust you after you came to me under false pretenses? And second, you and I have major differences of opinion. We're not compatible. I'd never date a Christian." *Not ever again.*

"Well, first, you're right. I did come to you as a PI, but now I'm coming to you as a man who wants to know more about you. And as far as me being a Christian and you being … whatever it is you identify with, I believe we can work through that."

She had to give it to him. He was persistent. "There are some things you just can't work through. I made a decision years ago to take a different path. There's no turning back from that." It was just like she told Stacey, and that's another reason she wanted Stacey to be sure about her decisions.

"That's the thing, Nina Marie. It doesn't have to be that way. There's always another option as long as you have breath in your body, and I'm here offering to walk that journey with you if you'll let me."

"Did Olivia put you up to this?"

He shook his head. "Not at all. This was my idea. I did have to ask her if it was all right if I approached you in my personal capacity."

"Did she tell you I was a lost cause?"

"Just the opposite. She believes you can change, too."

Her anger started to come to the surface. "Why does everyone believe I want to change? Do I seem unhappy to you? I have everything I could want. Just look around this place."

He gently took her hand in his, sending a shockwave through her.

"You don't really believe that. Being fulfilled in life isn't about having material things. You want more out of life than that. We all do."

"Once again, why should I believe a word that comes out of your mouth after all the lies you told me?"

"The only lies I told you were my name and profession."

"What about all the talk about you negative feelings toward Christianity? The hypocrisy. The whole nine yards?" Did he really think she was that stupid?

"At the time I made those comments, I meant them." He ran his hand through his hair. "Can I have a seat and try to explain?"

Well, she'd come this far, might as well hear how he was going to try to get himself out of the hole he'd dug. "Yes." She motioned toward the couch. She sat down beside him but left enough space to make her comfortable.

"Someone I loved hurt me badly. She was a churchgoer, as was a close friend who she was cheating on me with."

She sucked in a breath. This was hitting far too close to home for her. She needed to deflect a bit. "A lot of people are cheated on."

"But after that happened, I couldn't go back to that church anymore. I was humiliated, angry, and hurt. Instead of trying to seek out another church, I just walked away and left it all behind. I figured that God didn't really care about me all that much and wouldn't miss me."

"Let me guess. After a little time passed, you found your faith again and lived happily ever after."

"Far from it. Like I said, I've harbored a lot of pain and resentment the past few years. So when you asked me about my feelings when we first met, yes, I needed to play a role, but I was telling you how I really felt."

"Then what changed between then and now? It hasn't exactly been a long time."

He took her hand again and as much as she wanted to pull away, she didn't.

"Ever since the first time we met, something has started to change in me. I've felt a longing to reconnect with God, and at the same time, a fierce longing to connect with you."

She took another deep breath. "Are you trying to say that I'm the reason you've gone back to your faith?"

"I know it seems crazy, but God can use people and circumstances to work His will. And if I can come back to the Lord, I think you can, too."

A single tear slid down her cheek. What was wrong with her? She never cried, but for some reason an immense sadness washed over her. "You just don't understand, Abe. I've crossed a line. Even if I wanted to come back from that, which I don't, it wouldn't be possible. There are some things you can't just turn around."

"I think you've told yourself that as a defense mechanism. You've been hurt, too. I know you aren't going to change your beliefs in the blink of an eye. All I'm asking is that you give me a chance. Give us a chance."

How could she have even let this conversation get this far? She served the evil one. She practiced witchcraft and all sorts of dark arts. And now this man sitting next to her was asking her to turn away from all of that and take another path. A path with him! Why wasn't she just saying no and throwing him out? "I don't know how to respond to all of this."

160

"I know you've been hurt just like I was hurt. By someone who claimed to be a believer but didn't act like one."

She shook her head. "You don't understand. In my case it was much more than being cheated on."

"Your reaction earlier. This man was abusive toward you?"

She nodded. "Yes." She'd told Stacey about the physical violence, but it went even deeper than that.

"I would never hurt you like that, Nina Marie. You have to know that. I've never raised a hand to a woman."

Could she really trust this man? "I think I need some time alone. You've laid a lot on me."

"I totally understand, but please don't think that you're too far gone. God can always bring you back, no matter what you have done. Even if you've aligned yourself with evil, it's not too late to change." He stood up from the couch. "I'll let you think about what I said, but I hope to see you again soon."

She walked with him toward the door. He leaned in and kissed her gently on the cheek before leaving her house. She reached up and touched her cheek. What in the world had just happened?

**

Micah and Ben looked down on Nina Marie. It had been a risk to even come into her house, but they decided to go into the danger zone because Abe had taken such a huge step of faith. Olivia and Abe's prayers were having a huge impact.

"I have to admit, I never thought we'd be in this position with Nina Marie," Ben said.

"After Olivia saved her life, Olivia said that she wasn't going to give up on her, and it looks like all the effort and prayer is making a difference," Micah said. "Sometimes even we have to remind ourselves just how powerful prayer is and how those prayers can change people's lives."

"This just shows that Nina Marie does have the desire to change, even if she's not fully ready to admit it to herself."

"Not so fast," a booming voice said.

Micah turned and saw Othan and his sidekick Kobal.

"What do you think you're doing here?" Othan asked. "She is one of ours. She has come to us freely. This is our house, not yours."

"People can change," Ben replied.

Othan laughed. "Are you kidding me? Nina Marie is one of the evil one's favorites. There is no way he would ever let her go without a huge fight. She's not strong enough to defy him. It won't ever happen, no matter who you send here."

Micah watched as Kobal made his way to the couch to get near Nina Marie. Ben instantly swept down and inserted himself between Kobal and Nina Marie.

"Since when did God's angels protect one of the devil's own?" Othan asked.

"She has shown a willingness to change, and we're going to do everything in our power to help her. She doesn't even want you here now. You're the unwelcome ones," Ben said.

"We'll see about that," Othan said. "She'll stay loyal to us. You just watch."

"If you're so certain, then you should have no problem leaving and going about your other business."

"Fine. I am certain. Kobal, let's go to some place where we're actually needed."

Othan and Kobal vanished as quickly as they had arrived.

"Nicely played," Ben said to Micah.

"I didn't know they'd go for that, but their egos are so large, I thought it may work. We don't need them hanging around here and putting negative thoughts and doubts in her mind. We need to do as much as we can to help her. If there's any chance to save her soul, we can't give up. Especially with the strength of prayers that are being lifted up for her."

"Abe is praying now. He hasn't prayed like this in years," Ben said.

"Praise the Lord."

**

Olivia sat behind her desk across from Associate Pastor Chris Tanner. He'd agreed to come by her office and talk to her as part of trial preparation.

"I received the subpoena to testify from the State," Chris said. "I guess I shouldn't be surprised that they'd want to call me as a witness, but I still don't like it."

"All you have to do is tell the truth. Your testimony will hold a lot of weight with the jury."

He raised an eyebrow. "And you want to make sure that I'm not going to throw Dan under the bus."

"That's one way to put it. I'd like to think you'd be happy if I could prove that Dan was innocent."

"Of course I would, but I've also told you all along that my first and primary duty is to the church body, not to Dan."

"Are you sure there's not something else? Something else you aren't telling me?"

"Like what?"

"I don't know, but I feel like you're keeping something from me, and I'd hate to hear about any surprises for the first time when you're on the witness stand."

"I've looked at the documents, Olivia. I don't see how there is any other explanation for what happened."

"What if I told you that I could prove that Dan was set up?" She couldn't prove that as of today, but she wanted to see his reaction.

His eyes widened. "That's not possible. How? Who?"

"Why is it not possible?"

"Because the only people with access to the accounts were me, Beverly, and Dan. I know I'm not guilty, and Beverly certainly didn't do this. So I don't see how it could be a setup. The electronic transfers into his account are crystal clear."

For the first time, a nagging feeling deep in the pit of her stomach made her question Chris's innocence. She'd been so focused on Beverly. What if it was Chris all along? "I've seen falsified records which show that no money was taken out. Someone had to create those records. And we still don't know who controlled the offshore account. The bank is fighting the subpoena, and I don't expect the bank will comply given the loopholes in international law."

"But the first level shifting of funds is clear."

"So give me your theory then. Why would Dan do this?"

163

"I mentioned it before that ever since his wife got sick, he'd been so stressed and worried. I honestly think it got to be too much for him. The medical bills piled up, and even with insurance, I'm guessing that he was drowning. He never said anything, but it's a pretty reasonable thing to assume. So he set up a scheme to take money from the church account and put it into one of his. All the while keeping a totally different set of paper records that didn't show anything being removed. I personally think he planned to only do it a couple of times. But after his wife's death, he spiraled into darkness and kept on going with his plan. It wasn't until Beverly started digging around into the online system that she found all the discrepancies."

"And I'm assuming when you're put on the stand, this is going to be your testimony?"

He nodded. "Yes. I'm sorry, Olivia, but I'm going to tell the truth as I know it."

"I wouldn't want you to do anything but that. I'm just trying to figure out why you believe all of that to be the truth. It seems a whole lot more like speculation to me."

"Do you have a better explanation?"

"Well, I actually do have evidence showing Dan might have been struggling, but nothing to justify him taking such radical action as stealing. He was still able to cover all of his bills on his salary and the savings that he and his wife had accumulated over the years."

"I didn't know that."

"Now you do, and I will be introducing that evidence at trial. I believe Dan was framed." She leaned forward. "And I'm going to be able to show it with or without your help." She hoped her message was loud and clear. If Chris was somehow involved in this mess, she'd have no problem taking him down.

"Olivia, I get that you're in a tough spot. I appreciate the fact that Dan has someone like you in his corner. You're a fierce and loyal advocate."

"But?"

"We both have to do what we have to do. I can't compromise my position just like you can't yours. I'm relieved to hear you have some evidence to support Dan's story. I just hope it will be enough. There are still a lot of questions in my mind."

"Thanks for taking the time to talk with me. This will all be over soon."

Grant walked into her office. "Hey, Chris. Sorry, am I interrupting?"

"No," she said. "We're finished up."

Chris stood and shook Grant's hand. "Hope to see you two in church on Sunday."

"Of course," Olivia said.

Chris walked out of her office, leaving her alone with Grant.

"How did that go?" he asked.

"Do you think there's any way that he could be involved in this?"

"I don't think so, but at this point, I'm not sure what or who to believe."

"His testimony is going to be highly damaging to us." She rubbed her temples as a headache started to come on.

He walked around to where she sat and pulled her up out of her chair and into a tight hug. "Don't start doubting your case now, Olivia. God will come through. Just keep looking for the answers."

"Oh, believe me, I'm not giving up. I just want to plan the strategy and be able to put that reasonable doubt into the jury's mind. Between the physical evidence and the testimony of Beverly and Chris, though, it's going to be an uphill battle. I presented the information to him about Dan's financials, and while he said he was glad I found it, I'm not so certain. It's like he doesn't want to believe that Dan is innocent."

"You'll figure out a strategy. I know it."

"Thanks for having faith in me. I need to meet with Nina Marie. I feel like she's at a crossroads right now. She might know something."

"Why would she help prove Dan's innocence though?"

"I'm at the point where I have to try everything."

**

Nina Mariè felt like she might be losing it. Her whole world seemed to be turned on its head. For the life of her, she couldn't figure out why she had felt compelled to listen to Abe—

and even more, to consider what he was saying to her. To actually contemplate that she could live her life differently? There was no rational explanation for any of it.

Her choices to follow the New Age ways and occult practices had been her own. She enjoyed the life she had created for herself. She was happy—wasn't she? Yeah, sometimes she got lonely, but she was independent by her own choosing. Everything was about what she decided for herself.

Abe's words kept replaying in her ears because deep down she knew he was at least partially right. All of her material things were nice, but ultimately she was lonely and felt lacking.

But when she practiced the dark arts and wielded her powers, she became strong. Why would she give that up and risk the ire of the evil one?

Because there's a different way, a tiny voice whispered in her head.

Looking around she saw no one. "I really am losing it," she said out loud.

I am the way, the truth, and the life, the voice said.

"Who's there?" she asked. Then it occurred to her. Could there be angels in her house? Would they dare to come into her home?

She couldn't recall a time in her life where she was more conflicted. The fact that she was even having these thoughts made her think that something was wrong with her.

To make matters worse, she was waiting on another visitor she didn't want to deal with. Olivia had called and asked to meet her at her place. She said it was important, so she decided to take the meeting even though she knew that might not be the best decision given her current state of weakness.

A light knock at the door let her know Olivia had arrived. She welcomed Olivia into her home and invited her into the kitchen.

"Would you like some coffee or tea?"

"Coffee would be great," Olivia said.

So, the acceptance of a drink meant that she planned to stay a bit. She was interested to know what Olivia had up her sleeve. She put the coffee on and sat down at the table across from Olivia.

"You said it was important. What do you want to talk about?"

"I need your help."

"With what?"

"This trial. I know you have information that could help me defend Dan."

Nina Marie rolled her eyes. "You've seriously lost your mind if you think I'm going to help out the pastor. Have you forgotten who I am?"

"No, it's because I know who you are that I'm asking you. Because deep down I think there is good in you, Nina Marie. No, I know there is good in you, and that even though your judgment has been clouded by darkness for years, that you wouldn't want to see an innocent man go to prison for a crime he didn't commit." She paused. "And I also know that you can't stand Layton, and this would give you an opportunity to foil his plot. Assuming you were truthful to me at the beginning in saying that this was all Layton and not you."

She admired Olivia's tenacity, coming at her from all angles. Olivia knew her well—well enough to know that playing the Layton card was smart and strategic. Before she could say anything, Olivia kept talking.

"You won't get anything out of this. If Dan goes to prison, Layton will claim victory. He'll toss you to the side and consolidate power around his big win. You don't want that to happen, do you?"

Olivia raised an interesting point, and one she foolishly hadn't even been thinking about. There had been too many others things on her mind. She stood up and poured them each a cup of coffee. Placing Olivia's in front of her, she had to confront the situation directly. "What are you doing to me, Olivia?"

Olivia picked up her purple coffee mug. "What do you mean?"

"Something very strange is happening to me. I'm not myself, and I have the sinking suspicion that you're the cause of it."

"I haven't done anything *to* you, Nina Marie, but I have been praying *for* you. Very hard and consistently."

"I told you not to even try that with me."

"I know what you said, but I also believe prayer is more powerful than you can imagine. The Holy Spirit can intercede and change your heart."

"You have no right to do that to me. I make my own decisions." She had the mind to try to hurt Olivia right then and there. She had the power to do it—or at least she thought she did.

Undaunted, Olivia reached over and grabbed onto her hand. "You do have the right. You have free will and choice. It's completely up to you whether you heed the call of the Lord and reject the devil and his dark ways."

"If this is completely my decision, then why am I affected by your prayers?"

"I believe deep down you do want to go another way, and that is enough to allow your heart to open. Whether you want to believe it or not, you and I are connected. I saved your life for a reason, and I don't want that risk to have been taken in vein."

"And what about Abe?"

"I did hire him as a PI, but whatever he is pursuing with you right now is all him. I had nothing to do with that. I believe God is working in his life right now, too, and in yours, whether you want to embrace it or not. Abe's a good man."

She huffed. "Are there really any good men?"

"I know that someone you loved hurt you. You've never told me any details, but I've read between the lines enough to know that it was a huge betrayal of trust. I get that, but not every man or every Christian is corrupt just because some people made mistakes."

"I'd say being beaten and raped by someone who you thought you could trust is a lot more than a mistake."

Olivia's eyes widened as she squeezed her hand. "Nina Marie, I had no idea."

"It's not something I ever speak about. At least not … the physical violence is about all anyone ever gets out of me. I'm telling you the other to let you know just how far gone I am. How damaged I am, and my reasons for not trusting *anyone*. The path that I'm on may not bring me complete fulfillment, but it brings me safety and the power of my own life. My own body."

Olivia closed her eyes for a moment and then looked back at her. "You may not know this about me, but one of my passions is assisting victims of domestic violence. I did a lot of work at clinics in law school and have volunteered my time on a pro bono basis while at the firm. I can't pretend to know exactly the pain you've gone through, but I can say that keeping it all bottled up inside is not the way to heal."

She couldn't say that Olivia's revelation surprised her. It was just the type of thing that Olivia would do because that was the type of person she was. A good person with a moral compass unlike anything she'd ever known. "There's no such thing as healing, Olivia. I died a long time ago. I'm just doing the best I can." As the words came out of her mouth, she couldn't believe she'd shared this most private aspect, the darkest secret of her life, with her enemy.

But could it be that Olivia was no longer an enemy? Maybe she hadn't been for quite awhile.

"With God, there is hope, but with the powers of darkness, there is only pain. No matter how strong you may think you feel, it's just temporary. What God offers is something different. Yes, there are trials and tribulations in this world, but then there is eternal peace with Jesus."

Nina Marie couldn't help but roll her eyes. "How did this go from a conversation about giving you information to trying to convert me?"

"It's all tied together, isn't it?"

"I need to think this all through. If I cross Layton on this, he will try to destroy me."

"Do I need to remind you that he's already tried to kill you once? He'd have no hesitation doing it again, regardless of whether you choose to help me."

"I hear you, but I still need time to think."

"And while you're thinking about helping me, why don't you think about all of this other stuff, too."

She blew out a breath. "Given how much you and Abe are hassling me, I don't really have much of a choice."

Olivia smiled warmly.

She saw everything in Olivia that she wasn't. "I'll never be like you, Olivia."

"You don't have to be like me. You just have to be you, and I'm just hoping it's a better version of you that sees the light and turns away from the evil one."

A piercing pain shot through her head, forcing her to shut her eyes.

"Nina Marie, are you okay?"

"I don't know. My head." A wave of nausea rushed through her as the pain only amplified. A throbbing sensation at her temples. She was gripped by pain and couldn't move.

"You're under attack," Olivia said.

Nina Marie tried to speak but no words could be formed.

Then Olivia started praying out loud, telling the demons to leave the house. Calling out the name of Jesus.

After a few minutes the pain left her as quickly as it had hit her. She opened her eyes looked up at Olivia.

"They know," Olivia said. "And they're not going to lose you without a fight."

Nina Marie feared that, one way or another, she wasn't going to make it out of all of this alive.

CHAPTER FOURTEEN

As the day came to start the trial, Olivia sent up a prayer. Nina Marie hadn't provided any information up to this point that could help her prove Dan's innocence. She'd just have to do the best with what she had and pray that God took care of the rest.

She planned to rely heavily on all the facts and history of Dan's financial situation. Abe had come through along with her forensics expert on one other piece of the puzzle. While they couldn't say for certain where the person was located who made the transfers, they weren't at the church or at Dan's house. She was going to use that to her best advantage.

Her last meeting before the trial with Dan had gone much smoother than expected. Dan had told her he was at peace with whatever happened, but she was going to fight as hard as she could for an acquittal.

Standing outside the courtroom in one of the hallways away from the media, Grant pulled her close to him. "You can do this, Olivia. This is much bigger than this case. The battle is so much larger."

"Thanks for the reminder, Grant." She smiled up at him. Through all of this, he'd been her rock. Even with his own questions and concerns, he never let her falter.

He leaned down and kissed her forehead and took her arm in his, escorting her into the courtroom.

A couple of hours later, they had picked the jury, broken for lunch, and were ready for opening statements. The jury composition wasn't perfect for her, but it wasn't atrocious either. Evenly divided, six men and six women. Eight of the twelve self-identified as Christians. The State had wanted a mix because they weren't sure how this was all going to play out. She feared the four non-Christians would automatically be skeptical of Dan and probably would not be in their corner. She could only pray that the eight Christians on the jury would be open to hearing his defense. A defense that she was still refining, given the damaging evidence against him.

"Mr. Sampson, please proceed with your opening statement," Judge Matthews said.

"Thank you, Your Honor." Tony walked up to the podium with his eyes fixed on the members of the jury. "Ladies and gentleman of the jury, thank you for taking the time out of your busy schedules to do your civic duty as jurors for this trial. This is a sad story that unfortunately doesn't have a happy ending. But it's my job as the prosecutor for the state of Illinois to lay out this case. It's your job as the jury to listen to the evidence presented to you and deliberate upon it."

She carefully studied the jury to see how they were responding to Tony. So far, they all seemed engaged. Tony was a gifted speaker with a strong presence. She had her work cut out for her.

"The defendant, Pastor Dan Light, has had a rough go of it. His wife was diagnosed with an aggressive cancer two years ago. The strain that put on him and his wife was too much. The evidence will show that in a state of desperation, Pastor Light made the decision to withdraw money from Windy Ridge Community Church's bank account. An account to which he was one of only three individuals who had access. To cover up his actions, he then falsified the paper records so that Beverly Jenkins, the church's financial administrator, wouldn't notice the withdrawal."

Olivia noticed that he chose to call Dan by the name of Pastor Light. That was to solidify in the jury's mind that he was a pastor and therefore had a fiduciary duty to his congregation—one of the elements he would have to show to prove embezzlement with special circumstances.

"You will see many documents like the one I'm displaying up on the screen right now. A bank statement showing a withdrawal from the church account." He flipped to the next document. "And that exact amount being deposited into an account owned by Pastor Dan Light. What's more, ladies and gentlemen, is this was not a one-time transgression. This was not a monetary lapse of judgment that was later remedied. No, having been pushed to the brink because of his mental distress caused by his wife's illness and death, Pastor Dan continued down this criminal path."

"Objection, Your Honor. Argumentative and misleading." She had to stand up and stop Tony's flow even if her objection would likely be overruled.

"Overruled," the judge said.

But at least that provided a moment of interruption to Tony's opening argument.

"The defense attorney doesn't want you to hear about her client's struggles because those tragedies provide the motive for him to act. It is true that, as the State, I have the burden of proof—to prove beyond a reasonable doubt Pastor Light's guilt. Let me direct your attention back to the screen. The elements I must prove on the embezzlement claim are as follows."

Her eyes went up to the screen. As was customary, they'd exchanged opening statement slides to ensure that they had time to object to any of the contents before the trial. This slide simply stated the elements so there was nothing she could object to.

"First, the State must show that there is a fiduciary relationship between Pastor Light and the victims—here, his church congregation. As the senior pastor of Windy Ridge Community Church, there is no doubt that there is a fiduciary relationship. Second, Pastor Light acquired the money through that relationship. The fact that he was one of only three people who had access to church funds satisfies this element. Third, I must prove to you that Pastor Light took the money from the church account for his own personal gain. Here, he transferred it to his own personal account, and then he transferred it into an offshore bank account for his own use. And finally, I must prove to you that Pastor Light's actions were intentional. As I said before, the pattern of behavior and the documents you will be presented will show that he indeed acted intentionally. As dismaying as this case may seem to you, the evidence that you will be shown cannot be explained away—no matter how savvy of a defense lawyer Pastor Light has."

She shot to her feet. "Objection, argumentative and inflammatory, Your Honor."

"Sustained."

"Understood. In conclusion, let me simply say that this is not a close case. You'll hear live testimony from reliable witnesses and be presented with uncontested documents to prove the facts. Thank you for your time and attention."

Dear Lord, please give me the words to say here. She'd practiced her opening countless times, but all of a sudden it didn't seem adequate enough. The jury appeared to be buying into Tony's theory of the case. She needed something, anything, to put that reasonable doubt in their minds from the get-go. She knew what she was going to have to do, but Dan wasn't going to like it. In this instance, though, she had to be his advocate, not his friend.

Taking a deep breath, she stood up and walked to the podium. Her approach was going to be a bit different since she was on the defense side. But her goal was to draw in the jurors and plant as many questions in their mind as possible.

"Ladies and gentlemen of the jury, I, too, greatly appreciate your time and attention here today and throughout the trial. My client, Dan Light, is the senior pastor at Windy Ridge Community Church where he has served in that capacity for almost a decade. The prosecution would have you believe that Mr. Light suffered some traumatic times and went off the deep end, resorting to illegal activities. Nothing could be further from the truth. Let's take a step back and look at what Mr. Sampson did not tell you this morning. He didn't tell you that the account the money was allegedly being siphoned off into hadn't been touched by Mr. Light in years. In fact, it was an account set up for his first child with his wife—a child that sadly died through a miscarriage four years ago. After that tragedy, Mr. Light had no need to ever use it again."

She surveyed the jury as she spoke. They still seemed interested in what she had to say. "Mr. Sampson also didn't tell you anything about the two quote reliable witnesses that he plans to call. The first is the church's financial administrator, Beverly Jenkins. Ms. Jenkins had the same level of access to all accounts that Mr. Light did, and in fact, she was in charge of the day-to-day financial operations of the church. Has the prosecution even considered her as a suspect for this crime? No, they haven't."

"Objection," Tony said.

"Your objection is what, Mr. Sampson?" the judge asked.

"That's speculative," Tony said.

A weak objection. She didn't even know why he made it. Maybe the same reason she had made hers. Just to break up the flow.

"Overruled. Please continue Ms. Murray."

"Thank you. As I was saying, no effort has been made to determine what Ms. Jenkins' involvement could be in this crime. Mr. Sampson also failed to tell you that the other person he will call to the stand is Associate Pastor Chris Tanner. A man who also had the same level of access to the church funds." She paused. It was now or never. "A man who stood to gain from any criminal allegations against my client since Mr. Tanner is next in line to be the senior pastor of a large, well-respected church."

She stepped out from behind the podium and took a step closer toward the jury. "And Mr. Sampson didn't let you know that the Windy Ridge Community Church has been under direct attack by New Age groups within this community. Groups that have vowed to bring down the church in any way possible. You will hear from witnesses who will explain this all to you, and then you can judge for yourself whether my client has been framed for these illegal acts." There, she'd put it all out there. Now she'd just have to deliver on all of it.

"The evidence I'll present will paint a much different picture than the prosecution would have you believe. Of course,

Mr. Light was highly distraught over his wife's illness and subsequent passing. But the financial documents you'll see here show that Mr. Light had worked out a payment plan for his medical bills. That he wasn't in a situation where he would've taken such drastic and illegal actions. Actions that would be against his moral beliefs. You'll also hear from a forensics expert who will testify with certainty that the person who made the wrongful transfers never did so from Mr. Light's house or the church."

She took a breath and kept talking. "And I will remind you throughout that the prosecution is the one with the burden of proof, and the prosecution must carry that burden of proof beyond a reasonable doubt. That is a very high standard. In criminal cases, it's what our society demands because the result of a criminal conviction is the deprivation of a person's liberty. Once you hear all the evidence, I believe that you will have a lot more than a reasonable doubt about what happened here in this case and will enter a verdict of not guilty. Thank you."

She returned to her seat and saw that Dan didn't appear too happy with her, but she knew that was going to happen. He'd thank her later if her strategy worked.

"Your Honor," Tony said. "My first witness won't be available until tomorrow morning due to a medical appointment that couldn't be avoided. I'd ask permission for us to recess and pick up first thing tomorrow."

"That's fine. We start promptly at nine a.m. tomorrow." The judge went on to remind the jury about the instructions regarding not speaking to each other about the case and the juror social media policy.

Dan leaned in toward her and whispered. "You shouldn't have thrown the two of them under the bus."

"I knew you wouldn't want me to, but I prayed long and hard about it and felt it was my only option. I'm sorry, but I told you that I'd do absolutely everything in my power to clear your name, and I meant it."

He nodded. "I know, Olivia. I'm fortunate to have you in my corner, but this thing is going to get ugly."

"It's already ugly, Dan. You've been sitting in prison."

"I trust you. I do."

She only hoped that she wouldn't let him down.

Grant had to make sure Olivia ate. This trial was going to be a lot on her. Yes, he was there as co-counsel, but pretty much in name only. She was doing all the heavy lifting. He was really there for moral support, and if anything came up, he could run it down.

So as she sat at his kitchen table, he spooned a large helping of spaghetti onto her plate.

"Okay, you told me we had to wait until dinner to discuss what happened. I've decompressed enough, now I want to talk," she said.

"Sure." He helped himself and put two large rolls on his plate and one on hers. "I think Tony's opening was convincing."

"I did, too."

"It was simple, easy for the jury to follow, and his confidence was striking. You can tell that he believes Dan is guilty. I'm afraid that goes a long way in the jury's mind."

She took a bite of spaghetti and nodded. "Yeah, that's why I had to go for the nuclear option. I figured if I didn't start planting seeds of doubt from the beginning, I'd never be able to dig myself out of that hole."

"And how did Dan take it?"

"He wasn't happy. But at the end of the day, he knows I have his best interest in mind and I'd never want to hurt him or those he cares about. I had no choice. And the reality of the situation is that I don't know for sure that Chris and Beverly are innocent in all of this."

He placed his hand on her knee and squeezed. "You did well, Olivia. Most defense attorneys wouldn't have been able to come out of the gate swinging like that after the prosecution's opening, but you showed no fear. And how you presented it was half the battle."

"Thanks for saying that, but you can critique me as well. I can take it. Whatever you think I can do to improve."

He shook his head. "You were wonderful. This is going to be tough regardless, given the options and the electronic paper trail. But you have strong points to make that I think the jury will be open-minded about."

"I should warn you that I'm not going to hold back on Beverly and Chris. The cross-examination of those two is absolutely critical to the case."

"Have you given any thought to calling Layton?"

"I don't think he'd help our case, and he's such a smooth operator, he might only increase the likelihood that the jury would buy their version of the facts. I'm still holding out hope that Nina Marie will come through with something I can use."

"I wouldn't hold your breath. I know it seems like you and Abe have made tremendous strides with her, but at the end of the day, until she renounces her association with evil, we can't trust her."

"I know that. I'm praying that's going to happen. There isn't anything too big or difficult for God to handle. I'm in the pray without ceasing mode for real right now."

He smiled and his heart warmed as he looked at her. Her strong faith was one of her most engaging qualities. He had no doubts they were meant to be together. "Whatever happens, just know I'm here for you, no matter what the result is or how tough times get."

"You haven't had any more attacks against you have you? I've been so caught up in the trial I haven't even asked, and knowing you, you may have decided to keep it quiet."

"Actually, no. Just that one crazy night. I'm not sure what that was all about."

"I think you're stronger than you realize, and the forces of darkness know it, too. They didn't want to mess with you again right now."

"I'm not as strong as you are."

"We're very different people. You've taken a huge leap of faith in a short time and thrived in hard situations. I'd say that's something that scares Satan's demons away."

"Eat the rest of your food. You need all the energy you can get for a full day tomorrow. He'll be putting on Beverly and Chris right out of the gate."

"Don't worry. I'm going to eat all of it."

"Then I'll drive you home and you can get a good night's sleep."

"I doubt I'll get any sleep tonight."

178

Olivia walked into the courtroom the next morning prepared for the worst. The direct examinations of Beverly and Chris were sure to be fodder for the jury. Something tangible that they could hold onto, and she was even more nervous about what she might have to do to try to discredit them.

But at the end of the day, one of the three people was most likely guilty, and she knew it wasn't Dan. Her best guess was Beverly, but she hadn't been able to completely rule out Chris either.

She squeezed Dan's hand as he took a seat beside her.

"How did you sleep?" he asked.

"Prayer was more important than sleep."

Dan smiled. "We had very similar nights. Olivia, listen to me. I really need you to understand that I will be fine regardless of the outcome. I feel like you're shouldering this huge burden, and it's not fair. My fate is not tied to this trial. There is nothing that can happen to me on this earth that will change my eternal situation with God."

"I know that, Dan, but I also don't want you smeared through the mud for something you didn't do. You deserve so much better than that."

"I thank God every day for bringing you into my life." He looked back to the bench directly behind them where Grant sat. "How is he doing?"

"Rock solid. He's had some rough patches over the past month, but he's come through it stronger and ready for the fight. He's been a source of real comfort for me."

"So you've finally taken the plunge with him, huh?"

"Is it that obvious?"

"The bond the two of you have is apparent to anyone who can see. I can only pray that this is the beginning of a long and wonderful journey for the two of you. I hope that you can have what I had with my wife."

She sensed he was getting emotional and so was she, but they couldn't afford to have the jury see them look upset because they'd have no idea the cause. "Okay, let's focus on the task at hand. The judge and jury should be coming in any minute."

"Got it." He seemed a bit relieved to have shifted topics anyway.

"And Dan, prepare yourself. This is going to be tough today to listen to what Beverly and Chris have to say. Take some deep breaths, keep praying, and remember that I'm going to stand up for you."

"I never doubted that."

Judge Matthews came into the courtroom followed by the twelve jurors. She hoped they had a restful night and were ready to pay attention because she was going to be throwing down the gauntlet.

Once everyone got settled and the judge dealt with some administrative items, he looked over at Tony. "Mr. Sampson, are you ready?"

"Yes, Your Honor. I'd like to call Beverly Jenkins to the stand."

Beverly walked up from the audience and into the witness box. She wore a floral blouse and black pants. Her salt-and-pepper hair was pulled back in a simple, loose bun, and she wore simple wire-framed glasses. She looked like she could've been anyone's grandmother. Olivia knew this exam was going to be rough. There was no way around it. She'd already heard what Beverly had to say before, and it was going to be very damaging to Dan.

She watched as Beverly was sworn in—placing her hand on the Holy Bible. *Dear Lord, here we go.*

Tony stood at the podium, choosing to start his questioning from there. "Please state your full name for the record."

"Yes, I'm Beverly Lee Jenkins."

"Thank you, Ms. Jenkins. Can you tell everyone a little bit about your background?"

"Sure. I was born and raised in Windy Ridge. I started going to Windy Ridge Community Church as child."

"What about your professional background?"

"I'm trained as a CPA—that's a certified public accountant." She smiled. "But I stopped my tax practice years ago to work at the church as the financial administrator."

The jury was already in love with Beverly. Her mannerisms, her tone, her smile. This was going to be even worse than Olivia had expected.

Tony moved from behind the podium and walked up toward the witness stand. "So in your role as financial administrator at the church, you have access to the church financial records?"

"Objection, leading on direct, Your Honor. He's getting into substance now. It shouldn't be allowed."

"You're right, counselor. Sustained. Please refrain from leading your witness on direct, Mr. Sampson."

"Of course. Ms. Jenkins, why don't you tell the court what your responsibilities are as the church's financial administrator?"

Olivia had made the decision to object to try to keep some control over the situation—albeit a small measure.

Beverly looked over at the jurors as she was certainly told by Tony to do. "I'm responsible for the day-to-day financial operations of the church. I balance the books, take in and process all money that comes in and goes out, and, of course, I'm also responsible for paying all the bills, too."

"Do you have full access to the church's bank account?"

"I certainly do."

"And who else has that type of access?"

"Pastor Dan and Pastor Chris."

"And by Pastor Dan you mean the defendant Dan Light?"

"Yes."

"And Associate Pastor Chris Tanner?"

"Yes."

Now would come the really bad part where she would accuse Dan.

"So at some point did you notice something strange going on with the church finances?"

"I did. I'm what they call old school. I prefer to do all my accounting activities on paper. I knew I could access the account electronically, but I never did after I initially setup my passcode. I just relied on the paper. It's a system that's worked for me, and I never had any issues or reasons to make a change."

"Your statement makes it seem like you then encountered an issue of some sort?"

"Yes, I did. The paper statements were sent directly to Pastor Dan, and then he would put them in my church mailbox. But that month, our church secretary said something about not receiving the normal statement. So I went into the online system, and that's when I saw it."

"Saw what?"

"There was a discrepancy in that month's accounting. I was expecting to see about five thousand more dollars in the account at that time. I thought there had to be some mistake with the bank, but just to be thorough I started scrolling through the past months and tried to reconcile with the paper copies I had in my files."

"And were you able to reconcile the paper statements with the online statements?"

Beverly shook her head.

"I'm sorry, Ms. Jenkins, but you'll need to give a verbal response for our court reporter."

"I'm sorry." She took a breath. "No, I wasn't able to reconcile the accounts. In fact, I found that for a period of sixteen months there had been monthly transfers to an account—all the same account, but one I wasn't familiar with."

"And what did you do at that time?"

"My first instinct of course was to take it to Pastor Dan. But…"

"Please continue, Ms. Jenkins."

"But then I looked at the timing and started to think about Dan and all he had gone through with his wife's illness and death. I knew that had to take a financial toll on him. So the thought, however awful it was, did cross my mind that he was somehow involved. I prayed hard that wasn't the case, but after much prayer, I took everything I had and turned it over to the police." Beverly's eyes filled with tears.

It took every bit of strength Olivia had not to have a physical reaction. She didn't believe this woman. Yeah, she said everything that sounded right, but she trusted her gut. And her gut was telling her that this woman was lying. Could she have been connected to Layton somehow? It seemed unlikely, but she knew better than to underestimate Layton's reach and influence.

"I know this ordeal has been extremely difficult on you, Ms. Jenkins. I appreciate your time today." Tony looked at her. "Your witness."

She had to tread carefully but tactically. "Ms. Jenkins, why is it that your first thought or instinct when you saw the discrepancy was to think of Pastor Dan?"

"I'm sorry. I don't think I understand your question."

"Why assume that Pastor Dan, the man you've known for a decade and that you trusted as the senior pastor of the church you've attended since you were a child, why assume that it was him? Wouldn't the natural thing be to assume there was some type of hack or theft by an outside party? Some security breach of the account?"

"Well, I'm not quite sure. I think in my mind I was just thinking that there were only three people who had access. Guess that's my old-school way of thinking again. You know I'm not a young tech-savvy person like yourself."

Ugh. Beverly was totally winning this line of questioning. "Well, what about Associate Pastor Chris Tanner. Did his involvement not seem plausible to you?"

"It really didn't. The only one of us who I knew could possibly have financial troubles was Pastor Dan, and that was just because of the tragedy with his dear, late wife."

Things were not going well. So she made the strategic decision to make a big move.

"Ms. Jenkins, do you know Layton Alito?"

Beverly's eyes widened for a moment before she quickly neutralized her expression. Hopefully her tell was long enough for the jury to see it. She looked over at the jury, and they were all focused on Beverly.

"No, I don't think I do."

"Ms. Jenkins, do I need to remind you that you are under oath."

"I'm sorry, dear. Of course I know *of* Layton Alito because of his work in the community that sometimes is at odds with the church—as you very well know. But I don't personally know Layton Alito."

"I'll remind you again that you're under oath."

"I'm sorry. I don't know him."

At least she'd have this for impeachment purposes if she could find some evidence tying the two of them together.

"Do you consider Pastor Dan to be a trustworthy man?"

"I certainly did before all of this. Now I'm not sure what to believe."

"You don't have any direct, personal knowledge that my client, Dan Light, made any of these bank transfers, do you?"

"Well, no, I don't have personal knowledge about it. Just what we've previously discussed."

"Thank you, Ms. Jenkins. That's all I have for now."

She turned and walked back toward her seat, and that's when she saw her. Nina Marie was sitting in the courtroom.

CHAPTER FIFTEEN

N ina Marie watched as Associate Pastor Chris Tanner testified, and his testimony was eerily similar to Beverly's. Then for a few long hours after lunch there was testimony from the officers involved in the investigation and employees from the bank where Dan and the church had their accounts.

Olivia was able to establish from testimony of the bank employees that Dan's finances were stable. Bank statement after bank statement was flashed up on the screen while Olivia had the banker go through and account for all of Dan's money over the past eighteen months. While it wasn't proof that he didn't embezzle, it did paint a picture for the jury that was helpful to Dan. He wasn't on the brink of losing everything. Yes, things were tight, but probably not different than most of the finances of all of the people on the jury.

She watched with keen interest as Olivia called her forensics expert, Blake Sanchez. Nina Marie remembered Blake from the litigation with Optimism. Olivia had hired him to try to unravel Layton's electronic web of lies. From what Nina Marie understood, he was one of the best. Olivia asked him a bunch of questions to establish that he knew what he was doing before getting to questions about the actual case.

"Mr. Sanchez, turning to this matter, please explain to the jury what forensic analysis you conducted."

"Of course. I examined all electronic metadata and performed a forensic analysis on each of the transfers from the church account to the account of Mr. Light."

"And what did that tell you?"

"I was able to determine with certainty that none of the transfers took place within a five mile radius of Mr. Light's home or the church."

"Were you able to tell the location where they did happen?"

Blake shook his head. "Unfortunately, no. Whoever did this was able to cover that electronic trail."

"And what does that tell you?"

"That they were highly skilled in computer forensics and they didn't want to be caught."

"Objection, speculation," Tony said loudly.

"It's his expert opinion," Olivia answered.

"Overruled," the judge responded.

Nina Marie looked at the jury. She couldn't get a good read as to how this testimony was going with them. She feared they'd think that you could hire a computer guy to argue anything.

"Your witness," Olivia told Tony.

Tony walked toward the witness stand. "Mr. Sanchez, isn't it possible that Mr. Light could still have taken these actions and completed them outside of his home or the church?"

"Yes. That's possible."

"So, really, all your testimony boils down to is the fact of two areas you can pinpoint where the transactions didn't occur."

"Yes, but I think those facts are instructive."

"That will be for the jury to decide. That's all I have for this witness."

Nina Marie held back a yawn. It had been a restless night thinking about everything that had gone on in her life recently. To say she was torn would be an understatement. In a way, she wanted to give Abe a chance. Wanted to step out of the darkness, but she'd lived this life so long this way that she wasn't even sure if she could leave behind her current life, and would the evil one even let her? He'd probably try to kill her first. That would be a risk in and of itself.

But the last thing she wanted was for Layton to take over the entire city, and this whole plot he had cooked up against Dan was the first big step to doing just that.

She was at a crossroads. A decision now would make the difference in the rest of her life—no matter how long or short it ended up being. Her decision also had eternal implications. Yes, she'd made the strategic decision once to go to the dark side, but if it were possible to change, would she want to?

If you'd asked her that question a couple of months ago, it would've been a no-brainer. What she was trying to figure out was what was so different now. Deep down, she knew that a critical turning point had come in her life when Olivia had risked her own self to save her. To see Olivia's complete act of selflessness was a wakeup call. But that still wasn't enough. The introduction of Abe into her life had started to change how she was thinking. But what if it was all an illusion?

She realized that she'd zoned out during the last set of testimony as the judge started to speak.

"It's about four thirty," the judge said. "There's been a lot we've packed in today. I'd like to let the jury go and reconvene at nine sharp in the morning."

The jury filed out followed by the judge.

Nina Marie stood and waited to get a moment with Olivia. When someone grabbed onto her arm, she startled, turning to see Layton, his blue eyes flaring with anger. What was he doing there?

"Hello, Nina Marie. Wanted to get a front row seat?"

"I have to admit I was curious."

He tightened his grip on his arm. "Don't lie to me. Something is going on with you. I can sense it, and beyond that I had a visit from Othan last night who told me some very interesting things about what you've been doing."

"Let go of me, or I'm going to let out a scream that will have those officers over here in no time flat."

Reluctantly he dropped her arm. "You need to tell me what's going on. Are you in some type of trouble? If so, I can help you. You have to know that."

Her behavior was so uncharacteristic that Layton must have thought she was under some type of duress. She wasn't ready to have any sort of conversation with Layton about this. "Layton, why do you all of a sudden care for my well-being? It's a little late for that. Remember you tried to kill me only months ago?"

He sighed loudly. "Will you never let that go? I thought we were well beyond that. I heard very troubling news from Othan about you questioning your spiritual position. You bring a Christian to my charity gala, feigning ignorance." He threw his hands up. "I honestly have no idea what has happened to you, but I do want to help. I know you might find it hard to believe, but I want you on my side."

"Is that what this is all about? Not my well-being but fearing that I'll turn and fight against you?"

"Of course that's a consideration, but given the fact you're even considering such a ludicrous idea makes me think that something has happened to you that you're not wanting to talk about." He paused and reached for her again, but she took a step back. "Just don't do anything stupid that you'll regret. Take some time, go on a trip. You can use my condo on the beach in the Caymans."

"I don't need a vacation. What I need is for everyone to stop trying to control my life."

"Layton, Nina Marie." Olivia walked right up to the both of them. "I imagine this is a spectator sport for the two of you."

Why was Olivia acting so hostile? She made eye contact with her, and then it hit her. Olivia was trying to help her out.

"Didn't appear to be going too well for you, huh?" Layton asked Olivia.

"I only came over here to tell you that you may have won the day, but you haven't defeated us."

"It's only a matter of time," Layton said. "There's no amount of lawyering skills that can win this one for you, Olivia."

"Then it's fortunate for me that I'm depending on a higher power than my own skills."

"I've heard enough. I'm off to celebrate," Layton said. He turned to Nina Marie. "Call me when you're ready to talk." He walked away, leaving her standing there with Olivia.

"Are you okay?" Olivia asked. "I saw him grab onto you."

Nina Marie touched her arm, still tender from the contact. "Yes, I'll be fine, but we need to talk. Can you come over to my place so we can talk privately?"

"Sure. Give me a few minutes to gather up my stuff and I'll head on over."

Nina Marie rushed home and tidied up a bit. Although it wasn't like much was out of place. It was more out of nerves of what was to come.

Olivia wasn't far behind, and she ushered her into the kitchen and offered her tea. "Okay, I'm glad you're here. I have to tell you some things."

**

"What is it you want to talk about?" Olivia asked. There was a lot going on with Nina Marie right now. She wanted to be supportive, but she also really needed her assistance with this trial.

"I've given a lot of thought to our conversation about this trial."

"And?"

"I want to help."

Olivia let out a breath. Thank the Lord. "That's wonderful. Does that mean you're ready to choose a different path?"

Nina Marie held up her hand. "Let's not get ahead of ourselves. All I'm committing to at this juncture is helping you in the trial."

"I'll take that for now."

"What do you need from me?"

"What do you know about Pastor Dan being framed?"

"Beverly Jenkins is your inside woman."

Olivia nodded. It was just like she thought. There was something off with Beverly's story from the beginning. "I figured as much, but to hear it confirmed is still troubling. What could possibly be her motivation? Money?"

"From what I understand, Beverly and Judge Louise Martinique met at a hair salon a while back and became fast friends. I think Louise is actually responsible for turning her."

Wow. Louise was bad news and very powerful. "Where does Layton come into all of this?"

"This scheme was his idea, and let me tell you he was very proud about it. He bided his time. Had Beverly conduct business as usual at the church. He couldn't have any suspicion about her. She needed to be above reproach."

"And you saw from the testimony today that's exactly how she came off." It was some of the worst testimony she'd ever had against her in a case.

"Layton played it close to the vest right up until he was ready to spark the plan into action. When I found out Beverly was working for Optimism, I was shocked. Then when I heard what Layton had cooked up, I had to admit I was excited. It's no secret I've despised Dan and the church."

"But now you want to help him?"

Nina Marie rubbed her temples. "I have no idea what is happening to me, Olivia. All I know is that I want to help. Maybe it's because I know how much this means to Layton, and anytime I can get back at Layton, I try."

Olivia could tell Nina Marie was trying to justify this in her mind, but Olivia could see the changes happening in Nina Marie. All of the prayer was having an impact on this woman, and for the first time, Olivia really could tell that change was possible. *Thank you, Lord, for what you are doing in Nina Marie's life. Continue to soften her heart and open up her mind to the power of the Holy Spirit.*

"Olivia, are you still with me?"

"Yes, sorry." Olivia needed to focus and lock in Nina Marie's help. This was literally the answer to her prayers, both for Dan and for Nina Marie. "What are you prepared to do to assist? Will you take the stand and testify?" It was a big thing to ask, but that's really what she needed.

Nina Marie didn't immediately respond.

Olivia placed her hand on top of Nina Marie's. "You've come this far. You can do this. All you have to do is to tell the truth. Tell what you know."

"You know the prosecution will try to discredit me."

"Let him try. I can clean up anything in re-direct."

"I believe you."

Olivia sat in awe as she looked into Nina Marie's eyes. The eyes that had once held pure evil—a servant of the devil, a practitioner of the dark arts. And now this woman was coming to the aid of the man who she once wanted to destroy. God was truly all-powerful. "I'm not going to abandon you, but I need you to consider doing something else for me, too."

"What?"

"Your association with the devil. I need you to renounce it."

"You're worried that I may change my mind?"

"No, it's not that at all. I'm worried for your safety. As long as you align yourself with him, there's only so much I can do. But if you open your heart to Christ, you'll have more protection."

"Do you really think anything or anyone can protect me from the evil one's wrath?"

"The grace and power of the Almighty can, but only if you accept His help."

"I thought we were going to table this part of the discussion for another day."

"I'm afraid we can't afford to wait. Not with your safety on the line. Your testimony is going to set off a chain of events, and we have to be ready for that."

"I'm afraid that no matter what I do, I won't make it. Why would God want to protect someone like me? Someone who has worked against Him for years. A blasphemer, a witch—and all the time being proud about it?"

"Because that's what God's grace is all about. Jesus died on the cross for the sins of all humankind. All you have to do is repent for your sins. Turn from the ways of darkness. Ask for forgiveness, and accept Christ into your heart."

Nina Marie jolted as a loud booming thunder sounded outside and the lights started to flicker.

"It's just a storm," Olivia said. But she wondered if something more sinister was happening. It wasn't every day that the evil one was losing one of his favorites.

"Is it?"

Olivia took both of Nina Marie's hands in hers. "Pray with me, Nina Marie. Can you do that?"

The room turned much cooler, and a shiver went down her spine. *Dear Lord, please send your angels to protect us. We need the spirit of the Living God in this room right now.*

"Yes. I'm ready," Nina Marie said. "But do you think this is safe? For either of us?"

She started with the word of God. "In Second Kings when Elisha is surrounded by the enemy, his servant is distraught because he sees that they are totally surrounded by an army of horses and chariots. But Elisha told his servant, don't be afraid. 'For they that *be* with us *are* more than they that *be* with them'. Elisha then prayed that his servant's eyes would be opened, and they were. And then his servant saw that the mountain was actually full of horses and chariots of fire protecting Elisha."

"Do you really think that God would send that type of protection for me? For you, that's a different story. But me? Just look at me. At what I've done."

"Yes. But first you have to turn away from the darkness."

Another huge flash of lighting and booming thunder hit. The lights flickered again before going out. The room was dark except for the flashes of lightning illuminating the kitchen.

A heavy presence of darkness settled in the room, but Olivia refused to let that deter her. She knew this wasn't going to be a simple task. They were going to have to fight for it. Fight through it.

"They're not going to let this happen," Nina Marie said softly. "I can't have you risk yourself again for me, Olivia. I can't guarantee your safety here. I'd understand if you got up and walked away right now. I'll still testify for you."

"Absolutely not. I'm not going to leave you."

"I've never had a friend like you before, Olivia."

"We're going to get through this, Nina Marie, but I need to know that you're ready."

"I'm as ready as I'll ever be."

"Expect opposition."

"I don't want them to harm you."

"Don't worry about me. I need you all in, though."

"I'm all in."

192

A heavy weight rested on her shoulders. Whispers of darkness pricked her ears. But she couldn't let the foe stop her now. Not when Nina Marie was so close to rejecting the ways of the devil. This moment was more important than anything that could happen in a courtroom. A person's soul was literally at stake.

"Now repeat after me." Olivia hadn't ever done anything quite like this before, but with God's help she wasn't going to stop, no matter what Satan sent their way. "Lord, I am a sinner. I have turned from your ways. I have actively sought out the devil. I have sought the forces of darkness. I have practiced witchcraft and all manner of dark arts." With each word of her mouth the weight on her shoulders got heavier and heavier. Like someone was pressing her down into the seat, but she listened as Nina Marie repeated it all aloud. Her words were steady and sure.

"And now, Lord, I ask for forgiveness. I want to turn away and repent for those sins. I ask that you wash away my sins with your blood, the blood of our Lord and Savior Christ Jesus." As she said the words a force took ahold of her neck, squeezing. She knew it wasn't Nina Marie because their hands were still locked together tightly.

Nina Marie repeated the words, but now Olivia couldn't speak. Another crash of lightning and thunder filled the air. She prayed silently in her mind for help.

"Olivia, are you okay?" she asked.

Finally, the evil force broke his hold. "Yes, but they are coming. Something was squeezing my neck. We need to continue. Don't let go of my hands. We'll get through this together."

Nina Marie repeated the words Olivia said next. "I ask that you come into my heart, Jesus. I believe that you died on the cross for my sins, that you were buried, and that you rose from the dead on the third day. Now I want you in my life and in my heart, Jesus. I renounce the ways of the evil one and all of his demons, of all of the dark arts and occult practices I have sought out and participated in. Wash me clean with the blood of the lamb."

Olivia could feel the evil presences filling the room. It wasn't just one, but many demons. She remembered the words about Elisha she had just spoken a few moments ago, and she also believed that the angels were there as well. The battle raging around them. Most of it in the invisible realm that she couldn't even see or know. "The angel of the Lord encamps around those who fear him, and he delivers them."

Nina Marie started to repeat the words, but then stopped midstream. Olivia felt Nina Marie's hands slip out of her own.

"Nina Marie, are you okay?"

As the lightning and thunder cracked, she could see that Nina Marie was slumped over in her seat. *Dear God, don't let them have killed her.*

**

Nina Marie awoke in a daze. She was in her own bed, and it was still dark out. What had happened?

She looked over to see Abe sitting in the chair in the corner of her bedroom.

"You're awake," he said. He walked over to the bed and knelt down. "How're you feeling?"

"What happened? Where's Olivia? Is she all right?"

"Yes, Olivia is just fine. She called me over last night. It appears the two of you were on the receiving end of a vicious spiritual attack."

"Where is she now?"

"She went home to try to get a couple of hours of sleep. The trial resumes this morning."

She sat up in the bed. "I have to be there. I have to testify." Her mind was jumbled with thoughts. "And you're sure that Olivia is safe?"

"Yes. I saw her with my own eyes. She was a bit shaken up, but not seriously harmed."

"And you stayed here all night?" She looked over at the clock and saw it was five thirty in the morning.

He smiled. "I did. I wasn't going to leave you alone. I told Olivia to go get some rest and I would make sure nothing happened to you."

"Did she tell you what I did last night?"

"Yes. How're you feeling about that this morning?"

Tears filled her eyes. "I feel a little shaky. It was scary, and believe me, I'm used to dealing with stuff like that. But being on the receiving end of the forces of darkness is something else."

He held her hand in his. "But the most important thing is that you opened up your heart to the Lord. Your life will never be the same again. The battle has already been won in Christ."

She truly didn't deserve to have a man like Abe in her life. It gave her hope that there was something different than what she had known. "I know you've already done so much, but could I ask one more thing?"

"Sure."

"Would you make sure I get to the courthouse safely this morning?"

"Of course, but Nina Marie, you shouldn't live in fear. You now have the Lord on your side."

She pulled him up off the floor so he sat on the edge of her bed. Wrapping her arms around his neck, she felt safe for the first time in years. "Thank you, Abe."

"You're welcome, but Olivia did the heavy lifting, and you had the willingness to change."

"But only because you showed me another way. That there was something beyond what I had resigned myself to." A wave of peace flooded through her, but she was under no illusion that the battle was over. No, Layton and his evil forces would come after her, especially after what she planned to do in the courtroom today.

"Why don't I go make some coffee while you get ready?"

"That sounds perfect."

Abe gently kissed her on the forehead and stood up from the bed. Once he'd left her bedroom, she threw back the covers. She was still wearing her outfit from yesterday. A hot shower would work wonders for her.

As she headed toward the bathroom, she wondered what her new life was really going to be like.

Then it hit her. She'd be resigning as CEO of Astral Tech. Not only would Layton come after her, but disgruntled Astral Tech members would as well. But in the end, it would be worth it. She'd have to find a new career, a new purpose, a new everything.

After a long, hot shower, she stepped out into a steamy room and wrapped a towel around her, and that's when she saw him. "You're not welcome in my home anymore."

Othan stood looming large in front of her, towering over her, his dark hair sleeked back with his bright blue eyes locked onto her. She'd only seen him once before, but she knew from Layton that he hung around often.

"You can't get rid of me that easily. You have a lot of debts to pay. Do you really think we're just going to let you go? You're evil, Nina Marie. You can't just change that with one flimsy prayer."

Her heartbeat sped up. What if he was right? But Olivia had said she could repent and everything would change. Olivia had told her she needed to stand firm—or at least that's how Olivia had described it. "Get out of my home."

He didn't budge.

"In the name of Jesus Christ, get out of my home."

He still didn't budge. What was the problem? *God, I know I'm new at this, and I'm a total mess. But I believe that I can change and that you will be there for me. Please help me get rid of this demon, Jesus.*

A loud shriek came out of Othan's mouth before he disappeared.

Then there was a banging on the bathroom door. "Nina Marie, are you okay."

"Yes. One second." She grabbed her bathrobe from the hook and tied it tightly around her before opening the door.

"What happened? I heard a loud noise," Abe asked.

"This is going to be a fight." A chill ran down her back.

"I've got your back, Nina Marie." He pulled her into his arms, and there was no other place she would've rather been. *Thank you, God, for sending me this man.*

CHAPTER SIXTEEN

Layton Alito had called an early morning breakfast meeting with Morena and Stacey. Something was terribly off with Nina Marie, and he feared that she might try to sabotage everything he'd been working on.

Could she have really fallen for this Abe guy so hard that it made her change her ways? That wasn't like Nina Marie at all. If anything, Nina Marie never let a man get close to her. He knew all too well. She had used him in their relationship. He'd been the one who was scarred from it, not her.

At the end of the day, there was one person whom he could place the blame on for all of this, and it wasn't the man. No, it was that continuous thorn in his side, Olivia Murray.

If only he'd been able to destroy her when he had tried to take out Nina Marie. But Olivia had proven to be so much stronger than he could've ever imagined, and she was protected by a vast force of angels. She was unlike any person he'd ever dealt with, but that didn't mean he was going to run away. He was a fighter.

"What's going on?" Morena asked. "It's early for a meeting."

It was seven in the morning, and they gathered around his large kitchen table while his personal chef prepared breakfast.

"We've got a problem," he said. "Nina Marie has completely gone mad."

"I just met with her not too long ago," Stacey said. "Just like you asked me to."

"And how did she seem then?" he asked.

"Like she was still wrestling with her past. She said she didn't want me to end up a victim."

"I knew some stuff happened to her years ago that set her on her path to darkness, but we never spoke in detail."

"She seemed protective of me, if anything," Stacey said. "So are you saying that she's leaving the New Age way of life?"

"I think it's a distinct possibility," he said. "Even more of an issue for me currently is her trying to mess up this trial. We are so close to getting a conviction here. Having Pastor Dan thrown in prison and convicted of embezzlement would be the death knell to Windy Ridge Community Church. It would probably shut its doors. Its congregation would scatter, and we already know we have some potential recruits lined up who have expressed interest."

"So what do you want us to do to help?" Morena asked.

"We have to stop Nina Marie from doing whatever is it she's planning on doing."

"How much does she know about the details of what happened?" Morena asked.

"She knows enough to destroy this whole thing. If she confides in Olivia, then Olivia can use that knowledge to try to get an acquittal."

"Would Nina Marie testify?" Stacey asked.

"I highly doubt it, but at this time, I think she'd tell Olivia all that she knows, and that would be bad enough."

"We'll do whatever you need," Morena said.

"Come to court with me. That way we'll be there to try to manage whatever goes down today."

"Don't worry, Layton. One way or another, we'll make sure Dan is taken out," Morena said.

"I knew I could count on the two of you."

**

Olivia steadied herself at counsel's table as Dan was brought in by the officers and took his seat beside her.

"You won't believe what happened last night," she said in a soft voice.

He leaned closer to her. "What?"

"Nina Marie gave her life to Christ. She's coming today to testify."

Dan's jaw dropped. "Praise be to God. I never in a million years would've thought that to be possible. How did you do it?"

"It wasn't me. It was all the Lord, but the night wasn't without incident. We had some company join us that wasn't in favor of her changing."

"I guess that's not surprising. Were either of you hurt?"

"Nothing major." She rubbed her neck remembering the vice grip of the last night. "So I'm telling you all of this because today could get crazy."

"I'm ready for whatever happens. The Lord is with us, Olivia."

Olivia could only pray she'd be ready for it. She turned around, surveying the courtroom, and let out a breath as Nina Marie and Abe walked in together, hand in hand. There had been a piece of her that worried Nina Marie might back out. That this would all be too much for her to handle. And could she really blame her?

But just as she was letting out a sigh of relief, Layton, Morena, and Stacey also walked in and sat on the side behind the prosecution. This was a recipe for disaster. Layton would stop at nothing and she knew that. *Dear Lord, protect us here today. Let Nina Marie testify about the truth, Lord, so that your servant Dan may be cleared of all of these charges.*

With the judge and jury in place, it was now time. "I'd like to call to the stand Nina Marie Crane."

"Your Honor, I object." Tony stood up. "This is a late addition to the defense's witness list."

"It is late, Your Honor, but the defense just discovered that this witness had relevant testimony yesterday, so I would argue that we should be able to put on our witness. We won't be springing any new documents on the State. This is just testimony and this is a criminal trial, after all, where I think this sort of testimony should be allowed and not suppressed." She purposely used that word to put the bug into the judge's ear that if he wouldn't allow the testimony, it would be one of her grounds for appeal.

"I agree with you. You'll get your opportunity for cross-examination, Mr. Sampson. I have no doubt you can think on your feet."

Thank you, Lord. First hurdle overcome. Nina Marie walked up to the witness stand. She wore a tailored black pantsuit and pink pearls around her neck. As the Bible was presented for her to be sworn in, Olivia could sense the brief moment of hesitation. But then Nina Marie made eye contact and placed her hand on the Bible.

Olivia glanced over her shoulder. Layton's eyes were locked onto Nina Marie. She could only imagine what kind of evil he was plotting, along with his cohorts beside him. *Lord, protect Nina Marie.*

"Please state your name for the record."

"I'm Nina Marie Crane."

"And what is your current job?"

"I'm CEO of Astral Tech."

"And what is Astral Tech."

"It's a New Age company focusing on technical applications like the Astral Tech app."

"And can you tell the jury what you mean by New Age?"

"New Age has a lot of meanings, but Astral Tech focuses on an individual spiritual journey."

"And are New Age beliefs consistent with Christianity?"

"No, at least not the way they are practiced at Astral Tech."

"And are you the only New Age company in town?"

"No. Our competitor is Optimism."

"And who is the CEO of Optimism."

"Layton Alito. He's actually in the courtroom today."

That got the jury's attention.

"Objection, Your Honor. I have no idea how this has any relevance to what is going on in this trial."

"Your Honor, if I might, I'm just laying the foundation. It will all become very apparent soon."

"I'll give you a few more questions, Ms. Murray, but that's it."

"Thank you, Your Honor." She turned her attention back to Nina Marie. "Are you familiar with Optimism's position with regard to Windy Ridge Community Church?"

"Yes."

"And how so?"

"Because both of our groups are often aligned directly against the church." Nina Marie kept her eyes on Olivia and didn't look to the audience.

It was time to put it all out here. "What do you know about Beverly Jenkins and her connection to this case?"

"Objection, speculation," Tony said.

"Overruled."

"Beverly Jenkins is working with Layton Alito and Optimism to set up the pastor."

Noise broke out in the courtroom. The judge banged his gavel. "No more outbursts, or I will clear the courtroom."

"How do you know that?"

"Layton told me that he had someone on the inside of Windy Ridge Community Church. That it was Beverly Jenkins."

"Objection, hearsay."

"It's not hearsay, Your Honor. She's providing her account. She has personal knowledge as a participant in the conversation."

"Overruled."

"And what did Layton Alito tell you about Beverly Jenkins and the financial operations of the church?"

"That Beverly had setup Pastor Dan Light to take the fall for embezzlement."

Once again the courtroom erupted in chaos.

"Enough," the judge said, banging his gavel. The courtroom quieted at his stern rebuke.

"And why would Ms. Jenkins do that?"

"It was all part of Layton's grand scheme to take down the church. He knew that if the pastor was convicted of embezzlement, the church would..." Nina Marie's words trailed off and her skin paled. Then her body went limp as she sunk down in the witness seat.

Fear shot through her.

An officer rushed toward Nina Marie. "Call for the paramedics!"

**

The judge called for a recess while the paramedics worked on Nina Marie. Tony had just gotten a report on her condition. Thankfully, she came to after a few minutes. Her blood pressure was up to normal levels. He'd seen a lot in his time as a prosecutor, but nothing so dramatic as a witness passing out on the witness stand.

The paramedics had taken her into one of the conference rooms for privacy, and he saw that his opposing counsel was seated on the bench outside the room. He needed to confront her and figure out what in the world was happening. He'd seen lawyers take desperate measures before, but this was taking things to a new level.

"Talk to me. What's going on here, Olivia?" He took a seat beside her.

Her eyes were a little red from crying. "I told you that there was evil operating in this case. You didn't want to believe me."

"Why should anyone believe Nina Marie's testimony? Especially since it appears she is not well."

"She is well. Layton is responsible for what happened to her."

"Do you realize how insane that sounds? I can't tell whether you're crazy or just unethical and pushing the envelope."

"I'm neither. I'm telling you the truth, and so was Nina Marie. This whole thing has been a setup from the start. Beverly Jenkins is working with Layton and Optimism. Their mission is to spread their occult beliefs in this community and take out the church."

He fiddled with his cufflinks as he sat there. He wasn't sure how to handle all of this. It seemed like a stretch. And he totally didn't believe any spiritual force was responsible for Nina Marie's medical condition. But what if there was a kernel of truth to this Beverly angle? He had a duty to address it.

"I can tell that you're trying to process this, but remember, you represent the people of this state. The last thing you want on your record is the conviction of an innocent man, and even if I can't prove it today, I will prove it."

That argument hit him squarely in the gut. His future could be destroyed if it turned out that Dan was innocent post a conviction. He couldn't allow that. But he also needed to make sure he wasn't made a fool. "Can we talk a deal again?"

"No. He's innocent. Nothing less than an acquittal will suffice. For a man of God, this is a fatal accusation. He needs to be completely exonerated."

"We'll see how her story holds up under cross. Assuming she's well enough to testify."

"She will be."

But he heard the doubt in Olivia's voice.

When one of the paramedics walked over, Olivia shot out of her seat.

"She's asking to see you, ma'am, but I don't want her standing up just quite yet."

"I'm going to go check on her," she told Tony.

As he sat there, he wondered what kind of case he had gotten himself into. Could there be any measure of truth to all of this spiritual stuff? He had no clue, but he had to do whatever was necessary to protect his career.

**

A couple of hours later, Nina Marie was back on the stand. She refused to let Layton get the best of her. She was more prepared now for his frontal attacks. She should've known better than to underestimate an enemy like him. There was nothing off the table as far as that man was concerned.

"Ms. Crane, thank you for coming back. I trust you are feeling better?" Tony Sampson asked.

"Yes, thank you." She didn't know what his endgame was. He wasn't evil like Layton, but he definitely had ambition, and she knew all too well how dangerous that could be.

"Now isn't it true that you and Mr. Alito were involved in a lawsuit last year? That Optimism actually sued your company, Astral Tech?"

"That is true." She knew exactly where he was headed on this one.

"And isn't it also true that you and Mr. Alito had a romantic relationship?"

"Yes."

"And it didn't end well?"

"Well, I broke up with him."

A few members of the courtroom audience laughed.

"I see. But given your complicated history with Layton, why should the jury believe you?"

"First, because I'm telling the truth. Second, Layton and I made up—or at least had a truce. Once he concocted this plan, he wanted both of our companies to come together and mount an offensive against the church because he thought we'd be stronger if we stood together."

"And did you?"

"We've been working together until just recently when I had a change of heart. But I can assure you that Layton is behind this. Dan Light is innocent." Her words flustered the prosecutor who just stood there looking at her dumfounded.

"Do you have any proof to substantiate these claims?"

"I thought that was the purpose of my testimony today. To tell the truth about what I know."

"Let me rephrase. Do you have any tangible evidence to substantiate your testimony?"

"All I can tell you is what I saw and heard firsthand. This is a larger strategy to take down the church, and it was formulated by Layton and executed by Beverly."

Tony sighed. She was getting to him. "No further questions."

"Any redirect, Ms. Murray?" the judge asked.

"Yes, just briefly." Olivia walked up to the witness stand.

"Just so we're all perfectly clear, you were sworn in this morning, correct?"

"Yes."

"And you understand that lying under oath is committing perjury that can carry with it a criminal penalty?"

"I do."

"But you told the truth here today, Ms. Crane?"

"Absolutely. Why would I risk my reputation over this trial if I were just trying to bother Layton? I know for a fact that Beverly Jenkins is the one who moved that money."

"One other question. Do you know what actually happened to the money once it was taken out of my client's account?"

"I bet if you looked into it, you would find that it went from the offshore account and into Optimism's account."

"Move to strike, Your Honor," Tony said. "Pure speculation."

"Sustained. Jurors you will disregard the last answer of the witness."

She knew enough about how the human mind worked that her having said the words could have an impact on the jury, even when they were directed to disregard.

"Thank you, Ms. Crane. I'm done."

"You may step down," the judge said.

It was over. She'd done it.

CHAPTER SEVENTEEN

The jury was brought back into the courtroom after their deliberation—a short two hours. She looked over at Dan. "It's all going to be all right. If there's a conviction, we'll appeal." She wasn't sure on what basis yet, but she would find something.

He nodded. "I can't thank you enough for everything you've done for me. You've gone above and beyond in every respect. I'll never be able to repay you for all the hard work you've put in and all the kindness you have extended to me each and every day."

"Ladies and gentlemen of the jury," the judge said. "I understand that you've reached a verdict?"

"Yes, Your Honor," the foreperson said. The woman was one of the eight Christians on the jury, but Olivia couldn't read too much into that—because it could cut either way.

The foreperson passed the verdict sheet to the bailiff, who handed it to the judge. He opened it and took a moment to read before handing it back.

Olivia held her breath as the verdict was going to be read.

"On the first count of embezzlement, a class X felony, the jury finds the defendant, not guilty."

Relief flooded through her body, and her eyes filled with tears as the foreperson continued reading. A full acquittal on each and every count.

When the foreperson was finished and sat down, Olivia leaned over and hugged Dan.

"Thank you for your service," the judge told jury. "And Mr. Light, you're free to go."

The courtroom was all abuzz. Grant walked up to her and gave her a huge hug and then turned to give one to Dan. "I think I'm still in shock," Dan said. "I will forever be grateful to you, Olivia."

"I wouldn't have had it any other way," she said. "It was an honor to defend the honorable."

She watched as Dan's eyes also filled with tears. "God is good. Even through the dark of night, He never left me. He's been by my side the entire time."

"Let's get out of here and celebrate," Grant said. "Everyone can come over to my place."

"Great idea," she said. She also wanted to find Nina Marie. Not just to invite her to Grant's but to check on her. Thankfully, she saw Abe was standing beside her. She didn't need to be alone. One thing she was sure of: Layton would be angry and looking for payback.

A couple of hours later, the mood at Grant's was festive. It had taken some convincing to get Nina Marie to come over, but she now sat beside Abe and laughed.

Olivia stood truly amazed at the work God had done. Not only in the lawsuit, but also in ultimately bringing a lost soul to Christ. The weight of it all was almost too much for her to take.

She walked over to Nina Marie. "Hey, can we talk for a second?"

"Sure." Nina Marie smiled and stood up from the couch.

The two of them went into the kitchen. "I have to thank you again for what you did, Nina Marie. Because of your bravery, an innocent man's name has been cleared of this awful crime. And I also got a call from Tony. He's going to open up an investigation into Beverly and Layton."

Nina Marie nodded. "I must say, it's been a whirlwind, but after I testified, I felt much more at peace. I still can't believe that I found the Lord through all of this. I never thought anything like that would ever happen to me."

"The Lord loves you. I don't want you to focus on what you've done in your past. You can move on and focus on how you now want to live your life. A life that is full of love, compassion, forgiveness, and grace."

Nina Marie's eyes filled with tears. "Olivia, I owe you thanks. I knew from the moment we first met that you were special. At that time, I viewed you as a potential enemy. But then you put your life on the line for me, and showed me through the way you live your life that there is a different path for me. I'm not going to say this transition is going to be easy. I've got a lot of darkness that needs to be dealt with in my life, but now I have that chance."

Olivia wrapped her arms around Nina Marie in a tight hug. "I'll be here for you, and you have a whole new group of friends now that will love and support you."

"I'll never be the same again."

Praise the Lord. What an amazing work He had done.

Grant walked into the kitchen. "Ladies, the food should get here in about half an hour."

"Thanks for hosting us," Nina Marie said.

"Of course. You're welcome here anytime," Grant said.

"I never thought you'd say that." She smiled. "I'm going to go back and find out what Abe is up to." Nina Marie left the kitchen to head back to the living room.

Grant wrapped his arm around Olivia's shoulder. "How're you feeling now?"

"So thankful for what God has done here—and what I believe He will continue to do in Windy Ridge. I knew this battle would be harder than anything we've ever fought, but the Lord held the victory. We just had to stand firm in knowing that He was and is in control."

He squeezed her shoulder. "You're an amazing woman, Olivia."

"You've been there for me."

"No other place I'd rather be."

She looked up at him but then was distracted by Chris walking into the kitchen. This wasn't going to be a pleasant discussion.

"Hi," Chris said.

"I'm sorry about what I did in the courtroom."

"No. I'm the one that should apologize. I already talked to Dan, but I needed to see you next, Olivia. You tried to tell me Dan was innocent—something that I should've believed myself. But instead, I only caused more problems for him and the church. I hurt the people I most wanted to protect."

"Don't give it a second thought. I know Dan respects that you were trying to look out for the best interest of the church, and we all need to stick together if we're going to face the next battle that is brought to this town."

"I know you're right. I can't imagine Layton is just going to go quietly into the night and leave us all alone."

Grant shook his head. "No way. He may nurse his wounds and regroup, but he'll never give up on his quest to destroy the believers in Windy Ridge."

"But tonight is not about Layton or the forces of evil," Olivia said. "So let's not give them time right now."

"I'm going to go say hello to Nina Marie and thank her for what she did," Chris said.

Olivia nodded and turned her attention back to Grant, who was looking at her intently.

"What's on your mind?"

"Come with me for a second." He took her hand and led her down the hall to one of the guest rooms and shut the door. "I know this probably isn't the best time, but it never seems to be the right time."

"What?" her pulse kicked up, fearing more bad news.

"Olivia, I want us to really give this a shot. I know that we haven't been able to focus that much on our relationship, and that is totally understandable. But I hope we can make some time for us now."

"Absolutely."

He smiled widely before he pulled her close to him and kissed her. A kiss that held the promise of a future together.

**

"Thanks for driving me home, Abe," Nina Marie said.

"No problem. I'll be back for dinner if you're still up for it."

"That's great. See you then." She got out of his car and headed toward her front door.

It had been a week since the trial had ended, and she had spending a lot of time getting to know Abe better. And today had been a huge step for her. It was her first time attending Windy Ridge Community Church. People welcomed her with open arms, even those that knew about her prior association with Astral Tech.

She'd resigned her position and left it up to them to figure out who would succeed her. She knew that if she was really going to be able to get through all of this, she had to make a completely clean break with everything New Age related.

While she realized that she had a ways to go on her faith journey, she was floored at the changes she'd already felt within her heart and her actions. She no longer had a yearning to seek out the darkness—just the opposite. *Lord, thank you for saving me.*

When she walked into her living room, she stopped short and her pulse quickened.

"Layton, how did you get into my house?"

He sat on the couch smiling, having a glass of wine, like he owned the place.

"Why is it that you don't seem happy to see me?" He stood up from the couch.

She took a step back. "You have no right to be in my home."

"That's where you're wrong, Nina Marie. I have every right. I gave you a little space after the trial to try to regain your senses. You were obviously not thinking clearly."

"Believe me, I'm thinking more clearly now than I have in years."

"So that's it? Just like that, you're switching your allegiance?"

"Why does it matter to you? If I'm no longer in the picture, that benefits you."

He nodded. "You'd think so, but this isn't just about our two rival companies. This is so much larger than that." He took a few steps closer to her.

She wanted to stand her ground, but fear also started to grip her heart. What was his plan here? "Why don't you explain it to me?" She took a large step back. She contemplated turning and trying to run.

But the next thing she knew, he grabbed onto her arms and backed her up against the living room wall. It was at that moment she realized he was really going to hurt her.

"I'm not leaving this up to the forces of darkness or chance. You took that witness stand and betrayed me."

"I have never had any loyalty to you—nor you to me. You've tried to kill me."

He nodded and his grip tightened on her. "But this is personal, and now I've heard that you're calling yourself a Christian, which means that the evil one will no longer protect you."

"I don't need or want anything from the evil one. I have changed, Layton, and you'll just have to accept that. I'm a follower of Jesus now."

Layton's blue eyes widened. "Then you leave me with no choice."

She saw him pull the blade out of his jacket and then the pain shot through her body as he slammed the knife into her gut.

"You'll die slowly. Very slowly over the next few hours. Bleed out."

She struggled to take a breath, and she knew she was dying. "At least I know I have an eternal home," she whispered.

Enraged at her words he pulled the knife out and slammed it into her body again and again.

Then there was no longer any pain.

EPILOGUE

Olivia felt the fresh tears flow down her face. She'd shed many tears over the past three days, but listening to Pastor Dan pray by Nina Marie's hospital bedside was proving to be too much for her.

Nina Marie was still in critical condition, but it was nothing short of a miracle that she was even still alive. Abe had decided to go over to Nina Marie's house much sooner than he had planned. And that's when he had found her unconscious and bleeding badly from stab wounds.

She'd suffered an enormous amount of blood loss and internal organ trauma. But the doctors said that she still had a fighting chance.

Grant's strong arms were wrapped around Olivia, propping her up, just like he always had—being her rock when she was weak.

The nurse entered the room and asked that they exit for a bit while she tended to Nina Marie.

Dan guided Abe out and she followed, walking hand in hand with Grant.

"Let's give Dan and Abe a few minutes alone," she told Grant.

"Another coffee run for the group?" he asked.

"That's a good idea." She tried to pull herself together as they started to make their way down to the hotel cafeteria food court.

"I know you're hurting. But because of everything you did for her, you literally changed her life."

"I didn't do it. God did. But I just pray she has a chance to live out that life. And I have no doubt Layton is behind this."

"The police are investigating. He won't be able to hide forever. It will all catch up to him one day," Grant said.

"I know. We can't always understand the Lord's plans. All we can do is trust in Him."

Grant squeezed her hand. "They tried to take down the church and failed. Maybe they'll leave us alone now."

"I'm praying for that, too," she said. "I'm also praying for a revival in our community." The church pulled together and rallied behind Dan after the trial, and that had warmed her heart.

"The outpouring of support that has come in after the trial has given me renewed hope."

"I know. But until Layton faces justice for what he did, it won't seem right."

"We have to be patient and vigilant."

"Where do we go from here?" she asked.

He looked into her eyes. "I'm not sure. But wherever we go, Olivia, we go together."

Excerpt from Trial & Tribulations: A Windy Ridge Legal Thriller

Do you want to read more books in the Windy Ridge series? If so, I'd love to hear from you. Please email me at racheldylanauthor@gmail.com or contact me at www.racheldylan.com. I'd love to hear from you!

Windy Ridge Legal Thriller Series
Book 1: Trial & Tribulations
Book 2: Fatal Accusation

When managing partner Chet Carter called, you answered—and you answered promptly. Just yesterday Olivia Murray had been summoned to Chet's corner office and told to pack her bags for a new case that would take her from Washington, DC to the Windy Ridge suburb of Chicago.

But this wasn't just any case. She would be defending a New Age tech company called Astral Tech in a lawsuit filed by its biggest competitor.

As she stepped out of her red Jeep rental, the summer breeze blew gently against her face. She stared up at the mid- sized office building with a prominent sparkling blue moon on the outside, and she had to admit she was a bit intimidated. It wasn't the litigation aspect that bothered her, though. It was the subject matter.

She threw her laptop bag over her shoulder, adjusted her black suit jacket, and walked toward the door. Ready for anything. Or at least she hoped she was.

The strong smell of incense hit her as her first heeled foot stepped through the door. She thought it was a bit cliché for a New Age company to be burning incense in the reception area, but maybe it was to be expected. It reinforced her thoughts that this was all a money making operation—not a group of actual believers in this stuff.

The perky young blonde behind the minimalist glass desk looked up at her. "How can I help you?"

"Hi, I'm Olivia Murray from the law firm of Brown, Carter, and Reed."

The young woman's brown eyes widened. "Oh, yes, Ms. Murray. I'm Melanie." She stood and shook Olivia's hand. "Let me know if you need anything while you're here. The team is expecting you. I'll take you to the main conference room now."

"Thank you." Everything was already proceeding as normal. She couldn't let this whole New Age thing mess with her head. And besides that, she had her faith to get her through this.

Melanie led her down the hall to a conference room and knocked loudly before opening the large door. "Ms. Murray, please go on in."

Olivia didn't really know what she expected, but what she saw was a table full of suits arguing. She let out a breath. Regular litigation. Just like she had thought.

A man stood up from the table. "You must be our lawyer from BCR?" He wore an impeccably tailored navy suit with a red tie. He had short dark hair with a little gray at the temples and piercing green eyes.

"Yes, I'm Olivia Murray."

"Great. This is the Astral Tech leadership team. Don't let our yelling worry you. That's how we best communicate." He laughed. "I'm Clive Township, the CEO of Astral Tech, and this is my trusted inner circle."

A striking woman rose and offered her hand. "I'm Nina Marie Crane, our Chief Operating Officer."

"Wonderful to meet you," Olivia said.

Clive nodded toward a tall thin man with black hair who stood and shook her hand. "And this is our financial voice of reason, Matt Tinley."

"I serve as our Chief Financial Officer," Matt said.

Everyone greeted her warmly, but she felt an undercurrent of tension in the room. It was now her job as their attorney to get this litigation under control and that also meant getting them under control. Half the battle of litigation was controlling your own client before you could even begin to take on the adversary.

"Have a seat and we'll get you up to speed," Clive said.

She sat down in a comfortable dark blue chair at the oblong oak table and pulled out her laptop to take any relevant notes. She opened up her computer, but mainly she wanted to get the lay of the land.

"So the more I can learn about your company and the complaint that Optimism has filed against you the better. One of the first things I'll have to work on is the document collection and fact discovery effort. To be able to do that, I need the necessary background. I'll be happy to go over the discovery process with you, too, at some point so we're all on the same page."

"Where do you want to start?" Nina Marie asked.

"It would be helpful if you gave me a more detailed explanation of your company. I did my own research, but I'd love to hear it from you. Then we can move onto the legal claims brought against you by Optimism."

"Nina Marie is the driving force behind Astral Tech. So I'll let her explain our business," Clive said. "I'm more of the big picture guy and Matt is our number cruncher."

"Sounds good," Olivia said.

Nina Marie smiled. The thin auburn haired woman wore tortoiseshell glasses. Her hair was swept up into a loose bun, and she wore a black blazer with a rose colored blouse. "Astral Tech was my baby, but Clive has the financial backing and business acumen to make it happen."

"I'd like to hear all about it," Olivia said.

"We're a company specializing in bringing New Age theories and ideas into the tech space. We felt like we filled a void in that area. Yes, New Age has been quite popular for years now, but no company has really brought New Age into the current technology arena and made it work for the next generation. Through the Astral Tech app and other electronic means, we're making New Age relevant again. Our target audience is youth and young professionals. We don't even try to reach the baby boomers and beyond because it's a losing battle. They're too traditional, and they're not as tech savvy. We have to target our energy on the demographic that makes the most sense for our product."

"Excuse my ignorance, but you use New Age as a blanket term. I need a bit of education on what exactly you mean in the context of your business."

Nina Marie clasped her hands together in front of her. "Of course. I think a woman like you is in our key demographic. I would love to hear your thoughts on all of this. But to answer your question, New Age is a lot more than incense and meditation, although that is definitely a part of it. New Age is a way of life. A way of spiritually connecting. We care about the whole body—the environment, mysticism, spirituality. And we do that in an innovative way through the Astral Tech app that starts you on your path of self exploration from day one. You have to download it and try it for yourself. It will definitely help you understand our issues in the litigation better."

"Yes, the litigation. I read the complaint on the plane. Optimism's central claim is that Astral Tech actually stole the app from them."

Clive jumped in and leaned forward resting his arms on the table. "It's a totally bogus lawsuit. That's why we're hiring a firm like yours to nip this in the bud. We don't want any copycat litigation. This app was developed totally in house by Astral Tech employees. To say that there is any theft is absolutely false. We certainly didn't steal it. It's just a trumped up charge."

"What about the other claim regarding defamation?"

Clive nodded. "The defamation claim is actually a bit more concerning to me because it's subjective. We won't have a technical expert that can testify about that like we have on the actual theft claim."

She sat up in her seat. "What was said by Astral Tech that they are claiming is defamatory?"

218

"A few off handed comments about Optimism and their lack of integrity. They claim they're part of the New Age movement, but some of their actions indicate otherwise."

"Could you be more specific?"

"I can elaborate," Nina Marie said. "Optimism isn't really centered on New Age techniques in the same way we are. Their original founder, Earl Ward, was a connoisseur of many New Age techniques, but when he passed away Optimism's purpose shifted a bit under Layton Alito's rule, solidifying their allegiance to the dark arts. Layton is a ruthless leader who doesn't tolerate any type of dissent amongst his ranks."

Olivia felt her eyes widen, but she tried to hide her surprise. "Are you serious?"

"Yes, very," Nina Marie said.

"And Astral Tech isn't like that?" She couldn't help herself. She had to ask. It was better to know.

"We're a big tent. We don't want to alienate anyone who is seeking a spiritual journey," Clive said.

Well, that wasn't exactly a denial. What had she stepped into here? "And why New Age?"

Clive smiled. "Think about this as a lawyer. A businessperson. The world is becoming more and more open minded about spirituality. Which is obviously a good thing. Let everyone do what they want. We're moving away from strict codes of morality to something that fits with the modern person in this country. It's in. It's now. That's why we do it. We're using principles that have been popular for the past few decades and bringing them into the tech arena."

"For some of us, it's more than just about what makes money and make sense," Nina Marie said. "I'm proud to say that I'm a believer. A strong spiritual being. Those things have value. What we're doing matters. We have the ability to revolutionize the way people think about New Age principles."

Olivia could feel Nina Marie's dark eyes on her trying to evaluate whether she was truly friend or foe. A strange uneasiness settled over her. There was more to all of this than Nina Marie was saying. This was much larger than a lawsuit. Spiritual forces were at work here.

Focusing on the task at hand, she stared at her laptop and the page of notes she'd typed while hearing her clients talk. "I'll need to make sure you have a proper litigation hold in place to collect all relevant documents. I'll also want to talk to your IT person on staff right away about preserving all documents. The last thing we want to do is play cute and get sanctioned by the court. If Astral Tech has nothing to hide, then there's no reason to be evasive."

"But that's the thing," Matt said. "We believe we haven't broken any laws, but we also believe in our privacy and that of our customers."

Olivia nodded. "We should be able to petition the court for a protective order for any sensitive information that is turned over in the litigation, including customer lists. That's something we can handle."

Nina Marie stood up from her chair. "Let me take you to the office space we have set up for you while you're working here on this case."

"Thank you." While she was eager to get to work, she wasn't so excited about being alone with Nina Marie. But she followed the woman out of the conference room and down the hall, reminding herself that Nina Marie was still the client.

Nina Marie stopped abruptly about half way down the corridor. "I know this will sound a bit strange, but I'm getting a really interesting vibe from you."

"Vibe?"

"Yes. Do you have any interest in learning more about New Age spirituality? Anything like that?"

"No. That's not really my thing." She held back her direct answer which would've been totally unprofessional. She didn't feel comfortable in this environment, but she was also torn between her job and her faith. Could she really do both? Would defending a company like Astral Tech really be possible?

Conflicted feelings shot through her. No, she didn't believe in aliens or monsters, but she definitely believed in good and evil. Angels and demons. And this entire situation seemed like a recipe for disaster.

"I'm not giving up on you." Nina Marie reached out and patted her shoulder.

Nina Marie was quite a few inches taller than her, but that wasn't saying much considering she was only five foot three in heels.

"Once you learn more about our product offerings, I think you'll be excited to hear more about what we can do for a strong and smart professional woman like you."

"I appreciate your interest, Nina Marie, but my chief concern and responsibility is the lawsuit. So I think it'd be best if we could concentrate on that."

Nina Marie quirked an eyebrow but didn't immediately respond. Olivia followed her into another conference room, but this one was set up with multiple computer workstations around the large table. The rest of the décor matched the previous room they were in.

"This will be the legal work room for you. You should have plenty of space for everything you need in here."

"This is a great workspace." She looked around the room and was pleased by the size and technical accommodations. "I'm sure I'm going to run into a lot of factual questions as we start preparing for this first phase of litigation. Who is the person at Astral Tech I should go to with questions?"

"That would be me for pretty much anything that is detail oriented about the company or the app. Clive is good on the general business and philosophy but not so much on details. He's also not in the office everyday like I am. Matt can also serve as a resource both on the financial aspects and the spiritual ones."

"Got it." She'd never worked on such a strange case in her seven plus years of practicing law. Thankfully, she was steadfast in her beliefs. She just hoped that nothing in this litigation would require her to do things that went against her faith. Because she'd have to draw that line somewhere. And if it was a choice between her career or her faith, she'd always choose her faith.

**

Grant Baxter reviewed the document requests he had drafted one last time. He enjoyed being on the plaintiff's side of the table—even if it was for an odd client. Some wacky New Age group had retained his small but reputable law firm to sue Astral Tech—an equally wacky company in his opinion.

221

He didn't have any time for religion whether it be traditional or New Age or whatever. To him it was all just a convenient fiction made up to help people deal with their fears and insecurities. But if this case would help his firm take the next steps to success and keep paying the bills, then he was all for it.

He'd built his law firm, The Baxter Group, from the ground up—something he was very proud of, given all his long hours and sacrifices. Not a thing in his life had been given to him. He'd earned it all the hard way.

He couldn't help but chuckle as he read over the document requests that he had prepared. All the talk of witches and spirituality and the Astral Tech app. He'd never drafted anything like that before. His law school classes and nine years of practice had equipped him with many skills, but working on a case like this was totally foreign to him.

It wasn't like there were witches in a coven out to get him. People were entirely irrational when it came to religion. Luckily for him, he wasn't one of those people. He might be the only sane person in the entire litigation, and he planned to stay that way. One thing he was certain about. A jury was going to eat this stuff up.

"Hey, boss man." Ryan Wilde stood at Grant's door.

"What's going on?" Grant asked.

"I asked around town trying to find info on Astral Tech, but most of my contacts had never heard of them, and the few that had didn't really have anything useful to say except that they're trying to become players in the tech space."

Ryan was only about two years younger than Grant. They'd both worked in a law firm together for years, and Grant was glad that Ryan had joined him at the firm. If all progressed as planned, Grant was going to add Ryan as his partner in the firm.

"If you do hear anything, just let me know."

"Anything else you need from me?"

"Not on this. How are your other cases going?"

"I'm meeting with potential clients this afternoon on a products liability class action. It would be a good case to have."

"Keep me posted."

Ryan nodded. "You got it." Ryan walked out the door and then turned around and laughed. "I have to say, I'm glad that you're working this case and not me. I don't think I'd know how to approach it."

"Just like anything else. It'll be fine."

"If you say so. I hope you don't end up with a hex put on you or something like that."

Grant laughed. "Don't even tell me that you would consider believing in any of this."

Ryan shook his head. "Nah. I'm just messing with you."

Ryan walked out and Grant was anxious to start the discovery process and put pressure on the other side. It was one of those things he loved about being a plaintiff's lawyer. He was in the driver's seat and planned to take an aggressive stance in this case to really turn the heat up on the other side. Going through these steps reminded him how glad he was that he went out and started his own firm. He truly loved his work.

His office phone rang, jerking him back to reality.

"This is Grant Baxter," he said.

"Hello. My name is Olivia Murray from the law firm of Brown, Carter, and Reed. I just wanted to call to introduce myself. We're representing Astral Tech in the suit filed by your client. So I'll be your point of contact for anything related to the case."

Well, well he thought. Astral Tech had gone and hired a high powered law firm based in Washington, DC to defend them. "Perfect timing. I was just getting ready to send out discovery requests for documents. BCR doesn't have a Chicago office, right?"

"No, but I'm actually in town. I'm working at the client's office in Windy Ridge. So you can send any hard copies of anything to the Astral Tech office, and I would appreciate getting everything by email also." She rattled off her email address.

"Of course. And I have the feeling we'll be talking a lot. This litigation is going to be fast tracked if my client has anything to say about it. We're not going to just wait around for years letting things pass us by."

She laughed. "Yes, I know how it is. I'll look forward to your email."

He hung up and leaned back in his chair. Know thy enemy, right? He immediately looked her up on the Internet finding her

BCR firm profile. A brunette with big brown eyes smiled back at him. He read her bio. Impressive, double Georgetown girl. Seventh year associate at BCR where she'd spent her entire legal career. That would make her about two years younger than him— but definitely still a seasoned attorney and worthy opponent.

Astral Tech wasn't messing around. That let him know that they took this litigation seriously. They didn't see this as a nuisance suit. Game on.

**

"Do you think Olivia's ready for this fight?" Micah asked Ben looking directly into his dark eyes.

"It doesn't matter if she's really ready, Micah. It's a battle she has to fight and the time is now. We have no one else. She's the one God has chosen who has to stand up and take this on. She has some idea that she's meant to be here. But it might take her a little time to figure out exactly what she's going to be involved with."

The angels stood behind Olivia watching over her in the conference room. But she hadn't sensed their presence as she continued to type away on her laptop and hum a tune.

"She isn't fully appreciative of how strong she is, but she'll get there," Micah said. He stood tall, his blond hair barely touching his shoulders. The angel warrior was strong but kind—and fiercely protective of Olivia.

Ben nodded. "At least she has the foundation to build upon. A strong faith that has been growing ever since she was a little girl." Ben paused. "Unlike our friend Grant."

"I'm much more worried about him. He has no idea what he's going to be facing, and he doesn't have the skills to defend himself. Nina Marie and her followers are building up strength by the day, and she'll surely want to go after him. We can only do so much to protect Olivia and Grant against the forces of evil running rampant on this earth."

"But we'll do everything we can."

Micah looked at him. "You and me—quite an angel army."

"The best kind."

"Let's pray for her now."

The two laid their hands on her shoulders to help prepare her for the fight to come. A fight unlike anything they'd ever known before.

Excerpt from Lethal Action: Danger in the Deep South (Book 1)

Danger in the Deep South Series
Book 1: Lethal Action (Hope & Gabe)
Book 2: Devoted Defender (Annie & Caleb)
Book 3: (Jen & Mac)

Five years. Hope Finch was celebrating her fifth anniversary as an attorney at the prestigious New York law firm of Rice and Taylor by chugging down another cup of lukewarm coffee. She'd lost count at mug number six. As a fifth-year associate, she still had a lot to prove. Not only to the firm, but to herself as well.

She glanced at the clock on her computer screen and saw that she'd worked late into the night and skipped dinner again. Nothing unusual for her. The Wakefield trial was taking up all of her time—and then some. But there was no way she was going to say she couldn't handle the workload. As a midlevel associate, she should be able to run with the big boys. Or at least pretend like she could. If that meant coffee would be her only source of sustenance, then so be it. If she wanted to make partner within three years, then she had to stick to the game plan.

Hope shut down her computer and grabbed her laptop bag embroidered with the bright red R&T logo. It was very possible she'd still put in a little bit more time working tonight at home. Also part of her normal routine.

The big New York City law firm was relatively quiet for a weeknight. Only a couple of other associates were working away in their offices. She felt a tiny shred of guilt for leaving, but then quickly dismissed it. She was still on track for getting all of her work done in time for trial and sleep was necessary. She couldn't afford to make any mistakes right now. There was too much on the line. Both for her client and for her.

When the cold winter New York air blew against her face, she was glad to head home to her cozy apartment. It cost her a good chunk of her lawyer salary to live in a five hundred foot box close to her office, but it was worth it.

Cinching her pink pea coat tightly around her waist, she walked quickly down the dark street. Even at this hour, there were still plenty of people walking around. She loved the anonymity and hustle and bustle of the city. It gave her the freedom she felt she'd earned. She never understood how people could live in small towns where everyone knew every detail about your life. If she had it her way, no one would know anything about her. Except what she chose to share with them.

When she arrived at her high-rise apartment door, she turned the key in the lock, and dropped her bag on the floor. Immediately, she kicked off her tall heels, took off her coat, and unbuttoned her grey suit jacket. Home sweet home. It wasn't much, but it was hers, and for that she was proud.

She started to reach for the light switch but a strong hand grabbed her wrist throwing her off balance. She screamed as her pulse thumped wildly. The hand moved to her mouth and the other wrapped securely around her waist pulling her into him. The intruder stood behind her, and she couldn't see him.

This was it. This man was going to kill her. He was strong. She was no match for him. In that moment, she found herself clicking back through the events of her life like a movie reel. Her horrible childhood front and center. Not enough time to make all of her dreams come true and to fully recover from her past. Wondering how much time she still had left and filled with regret. She fought harder.

"Stop struggling. I'm not here to hurt you," he said. "I'm Special Agent Gabe Marino. I'm a federal agent. I work for the FBI."

The FBI? What was an FBI agent doing in her apartment? She didn't believe him, so she kept fighting. She bit down hard on his hand, and he let out a groan. Unfortunately, he didn't let go. Not willing to give up, she gathered up her strength and stomped on his foot.

Nothing was working though.

"Listen to me, Ms. Finch. I am going to drop my arms and step away from you. Don't scream." He slowly pulled his hand away from her mouth and loosened his grip. Then he turned on the lights, and she got her first look at her assailant. He was tall with short dark hair and chocolate-colored eyes. He wore a dark suit and a striped navy tie. He looked the part of an FBI agent, but he could be anyone.

"Here, let me show you." He slowly reached into his suit jacket and pulled out his credentials. He showed her his FBI badge and identification.

His identification looked legitimate, but she also knew it was easy to forge credentials if you had the right resources. She didn't believe him yet. "Why would an FBI agent resort to breaking and entering?" she asked.

"I didn't break into your apartment. Actually, I have a warrant." He reached into his pocket and handed it to her. "Go ahead, take a look."

She didn't want to take her eyes off of him, but she glanced down quickly and read the warrant. This guy might actually be legitimate. The fact that he hadn't hurt her yet added to his credibility. But what if he was trying to gain her trust only to hurt her? Hadn't she had enough struggles in her life?

"What do you want with me?"

He stood with his hands in his pockets. "Information. I need to know what your involvement is with Carlos Nola."

She took a step back providing her a little distance. "Mr. Nola is a board member of Wakefield Corporation. My biggest client at Rice and Taylor. Or I guess I should say that Wakefield Corporation is technically a client of my firm. Not me specifically. I work on their cases. Have since I started working there."

"I know that."

"If you know so much about me, then why did you have to break into my apartment? Why not set up a meeting with me at the firm?"

"Because I needed to be discreet. I'm working on a very sensitive case."

"I don't understand what you're after here." She looked up into his dark eyes and wondered what was really going on. If he was really FBI and asking questions about her client, that couldn't be good. He definitely had her attention.

"We can do this the easy way or the hard way, Ms. Finch."

She crossed her arms, not appreciative of his bossy tone. "I'm not saying another word, Mr. Marino, until you explain why you're really here. If you really are a federal agent then you know that I can't reveal privileged information about my firm's client, Wakefield Corporation."

"It's not Wakefield I'm that interested in. At least not directly. It's Carlos Nola. Like I said, I have a reasonable suspicion that you're involved with him and his questionable business practices. You'll get much more leniency if you work with us rather than if you try to protect him. So let me help you."

Could this really be happening? What was Nola involved in that was getting this scrutiny from the FBI? "Mr. Nola lives in Georgia. I've worked with him, and met him about five or so times in person, and every single time he was entirely professional. I would like to help you, but I really have no idea what you're talking about. He's a legitimate businessman. Respected in his community."

"This is about what is going on in his community— Maxwell, Georgia. That's where Wakefield's home office is."

"I'm well aware of that," she shot back. She wasn't telling this suit anything. She wasn't guilty, so that led her to believe that he was purely on a fishing expedition. She'd worked enough government investigations of big corporations to sense when there was actual evidence. If he had solid evidence he certainly wouldn't be hounding her.

"And you're sure there's nothing you want to tell me?" He took a step toward her.

"How do I even know you're from the FBI? For all I know you work for Cyber Future."

"Ah." He smiled. "No, I'm definitely a federal agent. How is the litigation between Wakefield and Cyber Future going?"

"That is not your concern, Mr. Marino. Now I'm going to have to ask you to leave my apartment."

"Are you sure you want to do that?"

"Yes. Please leave."

He cocked his head to the side. "If you are innocent, it's in your best interest not to say we had this conversation with anyone at your law firm. And if you're working with Nola, you're in danger. So don't say that you haven't been officially warned. This conversation isn't over, though. We'll be speaking again soon."

Before she could say anything he turned and walked out her door.

"No, we won't," she said out loud to herself.

What should she do? Should she tell the partners at the firm? No. First, she needed to figure out what was really going on. And that's exactly what she planned to do. If she went to her supervising partner at the firm right now he might pull her off the case. So she'd have to get to the bottom of this on her own. A constant theme of her life.

The litigation between Wakefield and Cyber Future had turned ugly. The breach of contract case should have been all business and routine, but it had gotten personal between both the executives and the lawyers representing the two companies. Cyber Future wanted to take down her client. Cyber Future was quickly becoming a competitor of Wakefield. Was Cyber Future behind this FBI inquiry? She certainly wouldn't put it past them. Cyber Future was out for blood.

**

Gabe Marino wrapped his navy scarf tightly around his neck and let out a deep breath. Hope Finch knew that he didn't have a solid case against her. Even getting the warrant was difficult. She put on a good show, that was for sure. When she looked at him with her big brown eyes and played dumb, he almost believed her. She would have most people fully believing her innocence, but she'd been working with Nola for five years. She admitted that much herself.

He'd been watching her for the past few days. All she did was go back and forth from the office keeping very long hours. It didn't appear that she even took a lunch break. He pictured her eating some microwavable meal at her desk and drinking coffee made in a fancy espresso machine supplied by the law firm.

He hadn't really known what to expect. Her file had made clear that she was a rising star at Rice and Taylor. She'd graduated top of her law school class. Obviously smart. She was also an attractive woman. Not that he was taking particular note of that. Every time he'd seen her over the past few days she'd worn her long blonde hair pulled back in a low ponytail. Her suits looked expensive. Maybe even designer. But he wasn't surprised given that she worked at one of the most prestigious law firms in the city and had the stellar salary to match. She would need to look the part. Her salary made his look laughable. It irked him that big firm lawyers were so grossly overpaid as they defended massive corporations. Meanwhile, federal agents who routinely put their lives on the line were often barely making ends meet.

He had a job to do, and he couldn't help the feeling that Hope was right in the middle of it all. He didn't believe in coincidences. Too many unanswered questions made him uneasy. Was she part of the plot that Nola was cooking up, or was she in potential danger? Gabe believed that Nola was running several illegal businesses in Maxwell using Wakefield resources to help him. Those businesses included drug trafficking and money laundering. All things that had no place in Maxwell.

As he walked to his hotel, he tried to focus. The cold New York City weather was messing with his brain. He could never live up here; he couldn't get back to Georgia soon enough.

This case was personal for him. He worked in the Atlanta field office of the FBI, but he was born and raised in Maxwell, Georgia, and he planned to always live there. The commute to Atlanta was forty five minutes, but it was well worth the drive and extra gas to live in Maxwell and maintain his quiet lifestyle. A lifestyle that was threatened by people like Carlos Nola.

There was something sinister going on in his town—the town he loved. And he intended to stop it. Hope Finch might be the key to unraveling the entire mystery. She knew more than she was letting on. She had to.

Carlos Nola was up to no good. Gabe knew that Nola was using Wakefield Corporation to help further his criminal enterprise that was infecting Maxwell. What he didn't know was if only Nola was involved. How far did Nola's influence reach?

Hope had been telling the truth about her meetings with Nola. His research indicated that they'd met recently in New York and periodically at her firm before that. Even if she wasn't working for him as part of his criminal ventures, she could still be useful in his investigation. As one of the Wakefield lawyers, she'd have unprecedented access to Nola. He wasn't giving up on her. There was still a lot of work to do, and Hope Finch was the center of it all.

**

Hope didn't know what to think when she'd gotten the email from her boss, Sam Upton, telling her that they needed to meet first thing in the morning. Sam was the partner in charge of the litigation between Wakefield and Cyber Future. Hope worried that she'd done something wrong. She recounted the work she'd completed over the past week. Nothing stood out in her mind that she could've messed up, but Sam was such an important partner at the firm she couldn't afford to make any mistakes. Not even a small one. If he removed her from the case, she'd be devastated.

She took a deep breath and smoothed down her suit jacket before walking to his office. His door was open, but she still knocked. Sam was nice enough to work for, but there was still a gulf between him being a partner and her being a mid-level associate. A pretty gigantic gulf—he held all the power, and she held none.

"Come in, Hope," he said. Sam wore a custom-made navy suit and blue striped tie. He'd been working at the firm for decades, and his personal tailor often visited him at the office.

She started trying to figure out how to explain away whatever it was that she must have messed up.

"So," he said, "I've actually got some exciting news. Or at least I hope you'll think so because I do."

"Okay," she replied. Now he really had her attention.

"First, let me say that you've been doing great work on the Wakefield case. Really performing above your level and everyone has noticed including the client. They've been highly impressed with your dedication to this case. You've really been keeping this train on the tracks."

"Thank you, sir." She clasped her hands with nervous excitement.

"How many times have I told you not to sir me, Hope?"

"I'm sorry."

He smiled. "And stop apologizing. Just listen up for a

232

minute. You know I was supposed to try this case with Harry, but there's been an emergency international arbitration for one of our biggest clients. Harry's on a plane to Brussels right now and won't be back for a couple of months. I decided to send him because they needed a partner over there with his international experience."

She started to try to process what all of this would mean. If Harry wasn't going to try the case with Sam, then who was?

He leaned forward in his chair. "Since you know the case so well, I want you to go to Maxwell, Georgia, and get us set up for trial next week. And then at trial you'll be second chair. My number two. Also means a literal seat at counsel's table and you examining and crossing select witnesses."

"Second chair?" She heard herself say the words out loud but couldn't fathom it.

"Yes, you've earned it. I know associates don't get much trial experience around here since our cases have such a high dollar value. So you need to take this one head on. You'll be working with our local counsel in Maxwell to prepare for trial. I'll be coming down there in a few days, but I want you on the ground now. You up for this?"

She didn't even know how to respond. "Of course I am." This is exactly what she wanted. What she'd been working so hard at the firm for five years to show that she had what it takes to make it in Big Law. This was her time to shine.

"Great. Now have your secretary book you a flight for this afternoon. Get out of here and pack. I want you on a plane and in Maxwell by this evening."

She nodded, realizing it was probably better not to start gushing to her boss. "Thank you, I won't let you down."

She remained calm until she got back to her office and shut the door. Then she let out a squeal as she hopped around her small office. Second chair! And going to Maxwell ahead of Sam to work with the client and the local law firm. This was a once in a career opportunity for someone like her. She hadn't felt this happy in years. If ever.

She couldn't let this chance slip away. She'd have to be on the top of her game the entire time. While Sam cared about all of his clients, he'd been college roommates with Lee Wakefield, the CEO of Wakefield Corporation. So Sam took this case personally. He wouldn't accept anything but her best—and then some. She'd proven herself to be a hard worker, and it was nice to see that it was actually paying off. But her work was far from done.

Hope gave her secretary instructions on booking the flight to leave New York around lunchtime and then went home to pack. She'd never been to Georgia. Much less the small town of Maxwell. This would be an experience she'd never forget, and there was also an added bonus. Now she could ensure she wouldn't run into agent whatever his name was again. Their altercation last night was strange, and it bothered her that he was making allegations against Carlos Nola.

A tiny shred of doubt crept into her thoughts. What if the FBI agent was right and Nola was involved in some illegal activity? Could her work actually be protecting and aiding a criminal? No. She refused to believe that.

She'd had a few meetings with Nola in New York, and he always seemed entirely professional. Friendly, a gentleman, and with a shrewd business acumen. There had never been any hint of impropriety in any of their discussions. She'd spoken to him on the phone quite a bit lately because of trial preparation, and she'd experienced no red flags of any kind. Wakefield Corporation was also a very well-thought-of business with board members who were highly respected in the community. No, there simply had to be some mistake on the FBI's part.

The FBI was mistaken, and it was her job to protect her client, Wakefield Corporation. Nola wouldn't do anything to jeopardize the business, because as a board member, he had a vested interest to stay above board with all of his business dealings.

She wasn't one to just sit back, though. She planned to find out what the FBI was really after before it was too late.

ABOUT RACHEL DYLAN

Rachel Dylan writes Christian fiction including the Danger in the Deep South and the Windy Ridge Legal Thriller series. Rachel has practiced law for a decade and enjoys weaving together legal and suspenseful stories. She lives in Michigan with her husband and five furkids—two dogs and three cats. Rachel loves to connect with readers.

Connect with Rachel:

www.racheldylan.com

Join Rachel's newsletter

@dylan_rachel

www.facebook.com/RachelDylanAuthor